DARK DAY OF THE SOUL

By

FRANCIS IKEH

Pen Press Publishers Ltd
London

ISBN 1 900796 14 7

First published in Great Britain by
Pen Press Publishers Ltd
39-41, North Road
Islington
London N7 9DP

A catalogue record for this book is available from
the British Library

Dedication

To my mother Lolo Nwannediya Eni - Ikeh
and my son Chuka Eni.

Introduction

Egator is a small town. It is only about one hundred kilometres from the capital. The capital was being rapidly developed, but the town of Egator had not benefited from the development until its youth started to migrate to the capital and other cities.

Modernization and development had been widening the gap between life in the cities and the countryside. Egator is one of such villages that was most hit by this gap. Its nearness to the capital did not help matters. The educated youth of Egator had been migrating to the cities in search of the good life. Most of them make so much money that they come back to the countryside to build magnificent houses, the type they thought were only meant for the cities. Egator was thus developing and nobody wants to be left out. The success of the few who had the courage to go to the cities to work, encouraged more to go to the cities. Even those who could not obtain university education migrated to the cities to work because everybody wanted to be part of the new life. They were employed in the factories and were sending money home. Some even had sufficient to erect bungalows for their people. They were thus regarded as successful. The general standard of living was improving as a result. However, with the migration, the population was becoming depleted.

There were no more young people to take over from the elderly people. Their farms and crops which formed the mainstay of their existence were being abandoned. Hunger was biting and poverty had taken a new turn. The people of Egator used to regard the possession of farms and large crops as wealth. It was easy in those days for a man to show off his farms and boast to his friends about his wealth. This wealth was not in cash or assets but farms. He can no longer do that. He does not even have the farms and the new form of wealth is the possession of other things other than farmland. The farms which used to be maintained with the strength of the young under the direction of the elderly have been deserted. There were no young people left to tend to the farms. The youngsters had taken to education and from there migrated to the cities. There was not even the young to take over from the ageing population. Since it was not everybody who had children who could migrate to the cities to work and bring home money, people were dying in large numbers. It was not only in farms that the people were feeling concerned, some aspects of their cherished cultures were being abandoned as well. The young people who went to the cities to live were getting used to their new way of life and consequently ignoring the cultures of their people. Some do not even come home at all. This means that they have been lost to the city, forever. This attitude of the young had started to worry the elders, who felt that their cultures and ways of life must be preserved and maintained.

They had made several attempts to attract the young back home to no avail. They enacted laws that would make it compulsory for the young to come home en mass at least once a year. But some young people had been carried away by the city life to the extent that they despised their villages.

Joda was a product of the countryside. He was born there and had all his education up to secondary school there before migrating to the city to look for work. He was the first-born of his father and his father would have liked him to stay in the countryside to take over from him. But things are different these days. Men no longer have absolute control over their children; everybody is becoming independent. Once a family member gets to the city, he draws his younger ones along. Some of these younger ones even go there to finish their education. Since Joda was one of the few who grew up in the villages, he made up his mind quite early that he would never be carried away by the city life. He promised himself that he would use all the money he would make in the city to help his siblings. He also promised to take over from his father and further the custom of his people.

After his marriage in accordance with the custom of his people, he migrated to the city where he started work. He soon realized that things were indeed different in the city. Very often, the desire to do is not matched with action. There are always forlorn hopes and unfulfilled promises. Most of the younger people who migrate to the cities do not even meet up with their personal needs and therefore are not bothered about the people back home. It is not that they do not care but they are entrapped. There are others who make it especially those with higher education. These groups send money back home and build houses. They however do not care much about customs and tradition.

They are the groups who are in the forefront to overthrow some aspects of the culture of their people.

Joda was affected by city life in a different type of way. It did not only pollute his ideas, beliefs and the way of life, it destroyed those beliefs. His enthusiasm to remain rooted to his village was destroyed. When he first came to the city, he was going home regularly and got attached to his father from whom he hoped to take over when the old man was gone. However, with time, he stopped going home as he used to do. When eventually his wife insisted on his taking total control of the family he stopped altogether. He subsequently abandoned his own people and left them to their fate. He believed that he had his own life to live.

In the town of Egator, a man's life is measured by his

achievements. These achievements are judged by three things. The first is that he must be married and have an acceptable family life. The second is that he must build a house. A man may build so many houses in the city but he is expected to also come home and build a house in the village. If he fails to build a house in the countryside, he is as good as not having any house. This is why most young men who have made it normally go home to build houses first before doing so in the city. Thirdly the man must have children. The people of Egator, like all other people in the world know that children are a gift of God. But they see it differently. They believe that "He who has children is greater than he who has money." They therefore expect a man who had married a barren wife to marry another wife or, alternatively get a concubine to give him children. Any man who fails to fulfil the above conditions is treated as a destitute and if he dies he will not be mourned.

There was a man who went to the city. He lived there for many years without going home. Nobody knew where he was. He was not married nor did he care about anybody. When somebody dies, he was not informed. He did not build any house either in the city or in the village. He eventually died. He had one good friend in the city where he lived. His friend just managed to learn that he hailed from Egator. He arranged with other friends and took back his friend's corpse to his people. This was at his personal expense. He was shocked and embarrassed by the type of reception he received with the corpse. He had thought he was doing something good for his friend and his people who did not know that he died. But that was not to be. His kindness was not recognized by the people. In fact, he was still discussing with the people, asking about further help he could render towards the burial of his friend when two young men took the corpse. They rushed it to the burial ground and got it buried. They came back to inform the people. The good samaritan was told about the burial. He was not happy. He did not understand why the rush and why no dignity was accorded his friend even in death. He thought it unusual and concluded that "this type of thing would never happen in his area." He thought that the people treated his friend that way because he had no money. He was partly right in his thoughts. Most of the problems of young men who go to the cities had to do with money. It is only those who have an abundance of money that could combine their new life with the old. They can afford to use their money to purchase cars that would bridge the distances from their abode to their homes. Those who cannot afford the high cost of fares tend to ignore their homes. They may wish to combine the two lives but the means may be too meagre. They consequently ignore the home people altogether.

The man rose up and left with his friends. His friend's death was forgotten while he was still there and the people had gone about their normal businesses. This type of story was not new to Joda. In fact he knew this particular culture of his people. He however turned his back on his people. His earlier beliefs had been completely overturned by the new life in the city. He has been cut off entirely from his roots. He was only going home when it was absolutely necessary, and would do those things which he thought absolutely necessary. Even though he got married in accordance with the custom of his people, he did not consider it necessary that his children should follow his footsteps and marry the same way. His first child was not betrothed at an early age as he himself was. This contradicted the culture of his people. He knew it, but did not care. His children were not brought up to know their roots. They never interacted with the people from the village except if that person had made it to the city. His first wife followed the same footsteps. She had never at any time believed in the strict adherence to culture. She had been blaming culture for marrying Joda who came from a poor home. She lived out her life in the city as she saw it and only went home when it was absolutely necessary. The city life was therefore what ostracized them from their people. Their common child did not fare better. She had lived from one home to another without any stable home. They all died the same way. When they died, their people did not care about them as they did not care about their people when they were alive. Their corpses were not taken to the countryside for burial. They were all buried in the city. Their lineage was broken and forgotten in the village where they were regarded as strangers.

Chapter One

Eka was a beautiful girl. She was a product of a broken home. They hail from Egator. The natives of the town believe that their nearness to the capital had robbed them of most of their traditions. There were, however, one or two such customs that linger on. They have vowed that the time has come for them to preserve some of their customs. One such tradition is the marriage of the first son in a family. The first son is normally regarded as the bloom and live wire of the family. He is naturally pampered and nurtured to be a responsible adult, so that he can take over from his father.

It is the custom of the town that the first son of a family must marry from their town, and, also the marriage should be contracted by the father at an early age of the child. This must be done before the child attains the age of three months. It was in realization of this custom that Efo who was the mother of Eka was betrothed to Joda. Joda was the infant son of a close friend of Efo's father. Both of them were very young when their fathers arranged their marriage. They were born about the same time with an interval of about one month. Children born with such a small gap are regarded as age mates. Joda was born first. His father had visited his good friend, one day, and learnt that a female child was born.

It was customary for people to extend greetings and good wishes to a newborn baby and the mother, and ask about their health. Joda's father had asked to be taken to greet the mother and the child. They were living in an outhouse. He was charmed by the beauty of the child. He was so infatuated that he did not know when he blurted out to his friend. "I will marry this one." This means that he had a son who will marry the child. The father of Efo replied. "It will only cost money." Thus with a combination of jokes and humour, serious deals were struck. It is normally taken seriously when a father chooses a wife for his male son. Even though Efo's father had another of his good friends in mind as the person he expected to propose to his child, Joda's father had spoken first. The people believe that the first words pronounced on a child this way should be binding and must be honoured, for indeed, they come from the gods.

When a marriage deal is struck thus, some rites are performed without delay. They are quickly followed up so that other families would be aware of it. This will alert them to the fact that the child's "hands are tied," which means that she is engaged to somebody. The boy and girl will from the time the rites are performed start to enjoy special privileges and rights from each others' family. Their mates will be calling them husband and wife, and, will indeed, regard them as such. No other boy or girl will attempt to go after any of them or attempt to marry them. They will be left for each other. They are expected to grow together. Efforts will be made to allow them to move about together and try to have regard for each other. When they reach school age, they will be made to attend the same school. They are thus expected to graduate together. When they reach an age when they know more about the world, the initial marriage ceremony is performed. The marriage ceremony is not a once-and-for-all affair. They are done in stages. A couple should not normally call themselves husband and wife or do any act to portray themselves as such until the final ceremony is performed. This is why a man is still regarded as a bachelor if he has not done the final marriage ceremony. He has no rights where married people are meeting.

A father uses his wisdom to know when to start the first stage of the ceremony for his son and his future wife. When he is convinced that they have reached an age they know what romance was, he approaches his in-laws to start the ceremonies. He must act quickly to avoid the girl getting pregnant unexpectedly. It will be regarded as a shame to both families if this happens. A father's interest in performing the marriage ceremony for his first son is rooted in custom. He sees his first son as himself personified. The first son is the heir apparent who must ensure that the family lineage is not destroyed. The father does not perform the ceremony for his other sons. He could if he had money but it is not compulsory. This is understandable. The man may not be rich enough to perform marriage rites for his numerous sons. Thus, other sons apart from the first will marry spouses of their choice when they are fully grown up and have saved enough money to go into marriage. Apart from the father's intervention, the first son can opt for absolute marriage as from late teens even while at school. Where he does that, the burden on his parents will increase.

If any issue is involved, the child will be given to the mother of the boy to bring up.

This traditional practice has persisted in the town of Egator up to this time. The people are reluctant to let go this tradition which they consider a very important aspect of their life. They had been passed over to them in the form of oral tradition by their forbearers. Most of their cultures which had been passed over to them have all been desecrated and abandoned in the name of civilization. They are therefore ready to cling to this last one which makes it possible for their first sons and daughters to remain at home. It is a common saying in their community to say that "They that have been consecrated with the flowers of their youth should not pollute their clean lives by marrying strangers." This simply refers to the importance the people attach to their first born. This strict adherence to their culture had not gone unchallenged especially by their educated young men and women. This set of young people had done all they could to destroy this cleavage to what they considered outdated custom.

They feel that they should not be limited by culture from exercising their freedom to choose whosoever they feel they can marry. Their argument about freedom and choice would not change anything. Anybody who argues too much or goes against their culture in anyway was threatened with banishment from the town. A lot of people had been outlawed and isolated from the town because of this.

There was one man who travelled overseas. He stayed many years there and eventually married a foreigner.

He was the first son of his parents. This means that he was betrothed to a young girl back home. His marriage to a non-native was in defiance of the culture of his people which made it compulsory for him to come home and marry the young girl. This young girl was left without hope. She had been abandoned since everybody knew her as the man's wife. All her hopes had been on this man and she never looked sideways in the hope that the man must marry her. Her people were heartbroken and did not take kindly to this. "How can this be?" they queried. This man's family was equally angered by his action. They considered his marriage to the foreigner null and void. In the alternative they wrote to the man and warned him never to bother to come home again. The man remained overseas unperturbed by the talk back home. He believed that one day he would be back home with his wife and children. That would be the only way his people would see reason. Then, it would be impossible not to accept him and his family. The man was however wrong.

He misjudged the determination of his people to remain themselves and avoid being contaminated by outsiders. His recalcitrance brought him a different type of news. His mother had suffered a stroke since she learnt that her son married a foreigner. She never recovered from the illness and died of it. The young man was duly informed about his mother's death. He knew that the custom required him to come home with his family for such an occasion. He therefore came along with his wife and some of his children. He was not very sure the type of treatment that awaited him.

But he was prepared for anything. On his arrival back in his country, he decided not to proceed direct to his home with his family. It was better to test the type of welcome he would receive. Maybe after a surveillance of the situation, he would bring his family. He kept his family in a friend's house in the next village and went home alone.

He was shocked at the treatment given to him. They were very hostile to him and asked him what he had come to do. They told him in no unmistakable words, that he was responsible for the mother's death and wondered how many more people would die for him. They asked him to leave and go back to wherever he came from. If he failed to leave they promised to abandon the corpse of his mother for him to bury alone. This sort of thing is considered an abomination in the town of Egator. The man was confused. He did not know what to do. He loved his mother and wanted to pay her this last respect. He pleaded with the people but they refused. He called for a family meeting but nobody attended. He was heartbroken himself. After staying for about two days, he knew that something must be done so that his mother would be buried. The people who would do the burial had deserted his father's compound for him and refused to commence the burial rites until he left. When the man was convinced that there was nothing he could do to change the situation he left with tears in his eyes. He went to the town where he kept his family hoping to bring them to his home if things went well. Things did not go well. He collected them and they left going back to his country of residence. He never brought his wife and children home again. He was treated as an outcast and he remained so till he died. When he died, his children assumed the citizenship of their mother's country and never returned home. What happened to the man did not prevent the young of Egator from migrating to the cities and finding their wives there. They were rebelling against their culture and shunning them while their elders remained adamant.

The marriage ceremony between Efo and Joda was performed immediately Joda finished high school. Eka was thus born. Eka had a grandmother called Fatima. She too was a beautiful woman. It was said that Eka was a carbon copy of her. She was from a poor family. She was betrothed to her husband, a handsome man who however hailed from a wealthy family. She gave birth to Efo. It was said that Joda and Efo were able to be married because of a remote linkage of Efo's mother to the family of Joda. Moreover, Efo's parents were not originally rich. They did not inherit wealth. They struggled until mother luck smiled on them and they became rich. They however became so rich that their betrothed children lived on opposite sides of life. Joda's family suffered from extreme poverty while Efo's parents were exceedingly rich. It is a well known fact all over that the children of the rich despise the poor and would not ordinarily associate with them. The association between Efo and Joda, thought awkward in the circumstances, was understandable. But it had its problems. Efo could not see herself different from the children of other wealthy families. She had been born with a silver spoon in her mouth and had received a University education. She had been worried by the type of marriage she was going into. "Had God and her parents condemned her," she thought. The marriage was contracted without her consent. She had started to argue against a culture that was to her a monster. She now realises the import of the revolt of the youth of her town when she was a toddler. She had heard all the arguments but never understood what it was about at that time. It is her turn now and the heavens seem to have descended on her head. She was heartbroken but there was nothing she could do about it. She felt that as a poor man, her husband would be a liability and she was being forced to marry this man. She was particularly annoyed with her husband's family members who pester and disturb their marriage by their constant request for help. She did not understand for how long this would go on.

Her husband on the other hand was a self-made man. He was able to obtain a University education due to his personal efforts and sacrifices. When he finished high school, he took up a job with the civil service. It was at this time that he enrolled in a University for further education. Through sheer dint of hard work and personal sacrifice and privation, he got his bachelor's degree. After his graduation from the University, his extended family saw him as the beacon of their hope. He was seen as a saviour; and specially sent by God. Now other children will follow his footsteps. Not only that; he was expected to train as many of his siblings as would be recommended to him. He would also maintain and take care of his extended family. These are some of the burdens that Efo could not come to terms with. "If he did all this what time would he have for his family," she wondered. There is no doubt that an enormous burden had been placed on Joda's shoulders. This responsibility to emancipate his family from the shackles of poverty was accepted by him with a humble mind. He never wanted to shirk this responsibility. He was willing and ready to help his family as much as he could. He however, married a high profile woman from a very wealthy family. Efo was not ready to go along with Joda if he arrogated to himself the post of Father Christmas of his family.

Joda had been pleading with his wife to try to see things from his own perspective. His people needed his help. He assured her that her income from her own family would not be tampered with. Joda would use only part of his own money to support his extended family. Efo knew that there was nothing she could do to prevent Joda from supporting his family. It was not easy also to divorce

Joda in a society in which marriage is regarded as inseparable.

An agreement was therefore reached by the two of them to live apart. This was not a divorce or a separation. It was just an agreement that would enable them keep their marriage intact without squabbles. Efo conceded to it as a form of help to her husband. As they live apart, she would be able to provide all her needs from her own resources while her husband would concentrate on his extended family. Joda could support Efo if he wished. It was not obligatory by the terms of the agreement. This had its implications. In the society in which we live, once a man is not responsible for providing for his wife, he was sowing seeds of discord between himself and his wife. He is bound to lose the respect of his wife which in turn will lead to the break-up of the marriage. Joda is now being forced by his financial quagmire to accept conditions most men will hate to accept. Every man accepts the burden of maintaining his wife. This is what makes him the man that he claims to be. He would not like his wife to look down on him. Most women look down on men who do not provide for their families.

By their accord, Efo would be living and working in another town. There was however, an arrangement for her to visit her husband, from time to time. This is a natural arrangement. As husband and wife they should be having contact. It was during these visits that Efo became pregnant. When Efo became pregnant, the family was elated. They decided to reduce the frequency of her visits to Joda's station in order to avoid any strain on the fragile pregnancy. Efo by nature was a very kind woman. Even though her family's wealth was standing between her and her husband, she knew she must help her husband. She did. She was happy at being pregnant. She doled out large sums of money to enable her husband to start buying baby items in advance. Her gesture enabled Joda to make adequate preparation for the forthcoming baby. The baby eventually came. She was a very beautiful baby girl. Her father called her Eka. This was the first name that came to his mouth. In their custom, Joda was not competent to name a child alone. The ultimate name of the child would be given by Joda's father in consultation with the elders of the family, but Joda's opinion would be sought and respected during the naming ceremony. The ceremony would be a future event. When the parents are ready, they would inform those at home and a date would be fixed.

Eka's parents rejoiced when she was born. A lavish party was thrown for friends and well-wishers of the family at their residence. Joda never wanted to waste time about the naming of the child. It was while he went to inform the home people about the birth of the child that he also fixed the date for the naming ceremony. He was told what to bring along to enable the ceremony to proceed. He bought the items including drinks.

He later travelled home with his family for the ceremony. On the day of the ceremony, Joda's father carried the baby in his hands. He held her up and then asked his people to each suggest a name for the child. This is in accordance with their custom where every member of the extended family present was allowed to give the child a name. In the end Joda's father would choose among the suggested names and the one he chooses will be the child's name. All sorts of names were given to the child at the ceremony. Joda was the last to suggest a name. He had already given the child a name which he wished could be confirmed by his people. He told his people that he would like the child to be called "Eka". He had hardly finished calling out the name when his father said "The child's name is Eka." This is a confirmation of the name Joda had given his baby. Everybody started clapping and the drinks were served. The name Eka literally translated means a 'Knot' that binds things together. Joda had deliberately chosen this name. He had been worried by the division that existed between him and his wife. He had hoped that the birth of the child would bind and cement the bond between him and his wife.

He wanted to have a solid family like his mates and colleagues whose trouble-free marriage he envied.

After the ceremony, Joda left for his base with his family. However, hopes of the child uniting the family were shattered. The wife who had hitherto been supportive had become a changed person. She wanted the whole family together and did not want to live in another station again.

She wanted her husband to assume the responsibility of maintaining his family. She wanted her proper role as the woman of the house. She knew the implication of her latest decision. It meant that Joda would no longer be able to help his extended family as he had been doing. There was nothing Joda could do if his wife insisted. The wife was merely emphasizing what custom demanded. The other arrangement reduced her to a helper rather than a wife. She had been living like a spinster while she had a husband. "This cannot happen again. It is either I have my husband live in the same house or we call off the marriage. All I want is my status to be defined now," she had said. Joda had been thinking within himself that he was finished. His wife had merely been helping out.

The revolt by Joda's wife was all he needed to turn his back on his people. He had forgotten his humble upbringing and his vow to be of service to his people.

In order to satisfy the demand of his wife and the pressure of city life he stopped going home. When he was invited home, he would give one excuse or the other. But the real problem was that he was finding it difficult to cope financially. His father was lamenting at the behaviour of his son. It was more worrisome because Joda was his first son whom he had placed all his hopes on. Eventually the man became hypertensive. He was taken to various hospitals; but he gave up. When he died his son just came as a matter of respect, but he was no longer ready to take over from him. That would have meant his leaving the city and coming to reside in their village. Joda was not prepared for that. In fact, it was either he lived in the city or nowhere else. He left for the city as soon as his father was buried. There was nobody to take over since all his younger brothers had also left to live in the city. His father's compound was overgrown with weeds and the house finally collapsed. The farmland was converted by other people. There was nobody to challenge them. The farmland became their own. This meant that Joda had no place to return to. Henceforth he became a man of the city and had no roots. He would not however accept that he had no roots. He would always claim that he was from the city. He did not see anything wrong with that. After all, so many of his fellow migrants make the same claim. But it is the same city life that engulfed and consumed them.

They were caught between catching up with its demands and adjusting to the natural ways in which they were brought up.

Joda knew that his wife agreeing to live separately was a way of helping him, but had wished that his wife would be magnanimous enough to continue to help. She was not ready to help any longer. She had developed a strong belief that unless Joda did as she demanded, she would get out of the marriage. She intended to find a man who she would regard as her equal. It was under this tension that Joda feverishly brought his wife and child to live under the same roof with him. This as matter of fact has been his supreme wish but he had been constrained by the problems at home.

Joda was soon to discover the true nature of his wife. She was a domineering and nagging woman. She had driven all his family members away. His friends had stopped coming to his house. Instead of helping her husband to build a family, she was driving the man to his grave. She would not even cook his meals. She would collect his pay packet and add to her much vaunted wealth. She would wait until her husband was out before she would cook sumptuous meals for her personal enjoyment. Soon she started to invite her female friends who would come around only when Joda was away toiling to feed his family. Unknown to him, his wife had become a different person who had no regard for him. He did not know who to complain to. He was fearful of her parents because of their wealth. How can a poor man challenge a rich man. He endured but the strains were eating deep into him. People had noticed his lean nature and had started to ask "What is wrong with you?" This is one question that was thrown at him so often these days. It is equally one question he could not answer, even though he knew that the poor relationship that existed between himself and his wife were responsible. Matters were made worse by the nature of his work. He occasionally was sent to work out of his station. This made it difficult for him to give his wife maximum love and devotion.

The child was in her third month and Joda had gone on a trip to one of the outside stations. He came back not only to his wife's cold shoulder but amidst rumours of the immoral activities of his wife. Her infidelity was being talked and debated openly. His good friend Tati had drawn him aside and told him pointedly what his wife was doing. She was bringing a man to their matrimonial home. Joda took everything calmly. He was afraid to challenge his wife for many reasons. First was the fear of destabilizing his family because a child was involved. The second was the wealth of his in-laws. He would not want to offend them lest he burn his fingers. He was however, strong-willed and would want to find out for himself. He therefore decided to set a trap for her and be more observant of his family. He soon discovered the indiscreet path his wife had chosen. He summoned courage and challenged her. She never denied anything but decided to quit the marriage. She packed her belongings and left to go to a place she believed would be out of reach of Joda. She took the child with her.

It was seven months and two weeks since the wife moved out and nothing had been done to effect a reconciliation. Joda did not even know how to start tracing his family. He laid a complaint with his in-laws and informed his family of the development. He was not keen on looking for the woman but for the child. He wanted to know that his child was doing well. While still undecided on whether to launch a full scale search and bring his wife and child back, Titi, a girl working in the same office with him started to make overtures to him. He had at first resisted the "temptation" as he called it, but was soon to realise that it was difficult to suppress nature when it calls. Titi's persistence soon melted his heart and he asked her out. It was an open relationship. Everybody was aware of it and words had spread to several places. His wife heard about it. Initially she did not appear bothered but was soon to lay a trap for them. She had reasoned that if she ever caught them together, she would deal ruthlessly with Titi and imprison Joda. She later decided that it would be better to hire the services of the Police. She preferred police to hoodlums. It is in a country where the services of police can easily be obtained to do anything on the payment of a fee. She had hoped that she would be able to cover-up her activities and even imprison Joda illegally if she involved the police. With this evil intention she went to the police station. She got the men she wanted but not officially. She just got three police recruits who charged her exorbitantly to undertake the operation. It was also decided that the operation had better be carried out in Joda's house since it was known that Titi had become a live-in lover.

The day was sunny. Joda had not gone to work. He was off-duty, so was Titi. It was probably a design by the two lovebirds to have a good time together. They had gone out to the departmental store that day to purchase some items. Efo had arrived with her gang but did not see Joda's car in the garage. She surmised that he was out with Titi. "It was still the morning hours and they would not be going to any love nest this morning," she thought. She had obtained a first class account of their movements from Joda's neighbours who at any rate were also her neighbours when she was living with her husband. She sat coolly at one of her friend's house in the neighbourhood. Joda lived in an area with a cluster of houses. She directed the policemen to hide in the flowers surrounding the houses. They did. It was not long before Joda's car pulled up. Titi was in front with Joda. The car was parked at its garage. It was an open garage. Titi was the first to step out. Everywhere was calm. It never looked as if anybody was in sight. However, there was a woman who had been sick for a long time now. She had just been discharged from the hospital. She has been recuperating. It had become her habit to sit in the shade provided by trees at the back of her house.

Titi did not go straight to Joda's house. She had gone to a nearby kiosk to buy something. Joda delayed before getting out of the car. When he did, he took time to check that the car was properly locked. He then took measured steps down the road to his abode, apparently, hoping that Titi would catch him up. It was a paved walkway to his house which was about five meters from where he parked his car. He was holding a small bag of their purchases, the food which they would prepare for lunch. As he walked towards his door, Efo emerged from nowhere. She walked briskly in the opposite direction and passed Joda midway to his house. She did not stop him but passed him before turning again to say a word, "So you accuse me of infidelity while you carry women about." Joda turned almost simultaneously so that their eyes met. He looked directly into her eyes without saying a word. At this time, Titi was coming out from the kiosk from the same direction as Joda had come. She was quick to notice Efo. She had not met her before. Efo rightly guessed too; that the lady emerging from the kiosk was Titi. Titi fidgeted a little at seeing Efo and wanted to make a detour. She wanted to pretend and sneak away as if she had not known Joda. She was unlucky. Efo had seen her some minutes earlier in Joda's car. Titi had wanted to avert any confrontation with Efo but the latter blurted out, "Honey; come; do not run." Her tone seemed to have reassured Titi. She summoned her courage and started to come in their direction. Efo left Joda and moved briskly to meet her. Her quick steps made Joda shiver. He thought she would pounce on Titi and tear her to pieces. He too moved quickly and followed Efo. The two women met at the junction of two adjoining houses. Efo was the first to speak. She did not attack Titi. The nearness of Joda to the scene had mellowed her devilish plan. She accused Titi of breaking up her home. Titi was embarrassed by this accusation. She only met Joda after Efo had gone out of his life. She was from a Christian home where high moral standards were enforced by their father. Her first thought was what her father would say if he ever heard that she broke up somebody's home. He would probably kill her. She kept quiet and hoped that Efo would agree to quietly and peacefully settle whatever she saw wrong with her association with Joda. She had wanted to placate Efo by explaining the situation. She had hoped that as a woman Efo would see things from her own point of view. Efo refused to see things the way Titi had prayed for. Joda was close to the spot. He had been watching as the two women were bracing up for a possible fistful settlement. He quickly intervened and pulled Titi out of the scene. A group of people had gathered and had been following what Efo had been saying. It was a motley crowd. They had listened attentively. Some of them knew the truth. Titi was in fact not responsible for the break-up of the marriage. She had been caught in the web of circumstances. They sympathized with her. They wanted to calm Efo and plead with her on behalf of Titi. Efo was not ready to hear anything good about Titi. To her she was the most devilish of the devils. When Joda pulled Titi out of the scene, Efo became more hysterical. "Her husband had slighted her," she thought. "He was now adding insult to injury." She followed Joda and Titi behind but changed her mind immediately. She went to one of the flowers where some of her police thugs were hiding. She beckoned to them to follow her. They did. The thugs were heavily armed. They ordered Joda and his girlfriend to raise their hands. They introduced themselves as police officers from the special branch. They showed their identity cards. They searched Joda all over the body while his hands remained in the air. They found nothing and removed nothing from him. Nonetheless, they told him he was under arrest. Titi was not touched nor searched. Joda did not resist his arrest. He knew he was face to face with law enforcement agents. It was better to obey them, even though, he did not see any offence he had committed, nor think it necessary that he should be treated this way. His thoughts raced to all tangents. His former wife as he regarded Efo should not think that he was made of wood. If she wanted her marriage back she should make restitution and come forward for a reconciliation the way civilised people all over the world do it. She should not resort to this type of crude justice. While his thoughts were still wandering, Joda said almost absent-mindedly, "What offence did I actually commit? Why are you dehumanizing my person this way? Do you not have any iota of respect for decent people?" The policemen were infuriated. They shut him up. One of them hit him on the buttocks with the butt of his gun as they yelled, "Shut up; son of a bitch. If you are decent why have you stolen madam's money?" Joda was dumbfounded. He could not understand this type of allegation. He had kept quiet in order to avoid further punishment from the officer. He however, thought that his ex-wife must have told lies to the police in order to gain their sympathy. "What money; and, how much," he wondered again in his thoughts.

Titi was already hiding her face in her palms. Joda wanted desperately to talk to her but there was no way he could. He was already feeling pains for wanting to express his opinion. He looked in the direction of Titi and caught her eyes at last. He winked at here. She appeared to have got the message. She dashed off towards the direction of the woman who was sitting under the trees unperturbed. She seemed to say something to the woman but was rebuffed. The woman never showed as if somebody was talking to her. Titi had come to elicit the help of the woman to intervene on behalf of her boyfriend. The woman's husband works with police orderlies and therefore had the right connections that would make an arrested person get bail as soon as possible.

Titi had been embarrassed by the woman and was miffed. Joda was taken away to the police van waiting in a hidden corner. The policemen pushed him into the vehicle where he was sandwiched between two armed guards, while the third, the driver was at the front, and they soon took off. The police station was not far away, just about twenty kilometres. However, on the way there was a commotion somewhere, a lot of people had gathered and under such circumstances, it was not proper for the police to leave the milling crowd. They were the law enforcement agents, who must not drive past such a large gathering without stopping to find out what was happening.

Their arrival at the scene caused the crowd to turn in their direction since they were blowing the siren. Inspector Dauda was among the crowd. He made to the police car parked at the distance. What appeared to be a commotion was not a commotion after all. It was a roadside advertisers who were using the latest heavy metal music and acrobatic dance steps to attract people. On getting to the police vehicle, Dauda looked inside and saw his friend Joda in handcuffs. He was surprised since he knew Joda to be a good and honest man, who also had a good job. The only problem he had was with his wife who had moved away. They saw three days ago when he came to the joint with his beautiful girlfriend. They had sat briefly together that day before Dauda went to a private room at the joint. Dauda demanded to know what was wrong. Why had the police officers arrested his good friend? He looked at the policemen's faces but none would talk. He equally looked at his friend who would have loved to talk, but was prevented by his police guards. By the time the police driver came back to the vehicle, he too was accosted by Dauda for the reason of the arrest.

He pushed Dauda away instead of replying to him. The irony of the behaviour of those police hirelings was that they all knew Dauda well. They knew him to be a senior officer but from a different branch. They were from the special branch. Their problem was that they were on their private duty parading in official uniform and vehicles. Dauda's insistence on knowing what his friend had done made one of the police guards jump out of the vehicle. Before anybody could guess what enraged him, he had given Dauda a slap. Dauda embarrassed was ready to see the end of this. These boys as he called the policemen knew him very well even though he was in mufti. They had not only disobeyed a senior officer by refusing to answer innocent questions, but they had added insult to injury. "This is outrageous, this is unbelievable," he thought aloud to himself. He dashed off, his private car was parked behind the crowd. He entered his car and zoomed off to his station, which was closer to the scene than that of those hoodlums. He collected his gun and asked some policemen to follow him. They did and were soon to overtake the police hirelings. They stopped them by blocking their lane. A fight erupted between both parties, in the ensuing melee, Dauda quickly went to the vehicle where Joda was and released him. Joda watched the imbroglio for a while and then escaped from the scene. He was happy at his escape. He would not sleep in those vermin infested police cells after all.

Though Joda was happy at his dramatic escape, the problem with his estranged wife remained. The police episode of arrest and escape had added oil to the fire. It has worsened a relationship that was very bad, and it was not entirely Joda's fault. Nobody actually knew that his wife was not interested in the marriage. She had not shown it. She was the cause of their separation, and she had moved out without showing any remorse. It could have been her duty to arrange for settlement. She was being jealous without showing any commitment to her marriage. Her first diabolical intention to mete out justice to Joda and his girlfriend had failed. It failed woefully but that did not make her relent in further assaults and plans.

She had a distant cousin, Asubi, well known for his thuggery. Efo had engaged his services and the boy had been laying ambush on routes through which Joda was known to pass. His aim was to intercept him and fight to kill, or maim him. It was therefore not surprising that on this particular day, Joda had gone out with a friend, when Asubi had sighted him in the car. He got on his motorcycle and trailed their vehicle. Joda and his friend had been talking, not suspecting that somebody was following them. They had driven past one 'posh' upstairs on the right. The building was fenced with concrete walls with a gate. They seemed to have remembered that this was where they were going to, so they went further to the roundabout and made a "U" turn. They turned to the right and were soon at the gate of the building. The security-man surveyed their faces briefly, before asking them who they wanted to see. "This is the embassy of the Republic of Ekleand." It was Joda's friend who replied. He said they knew it was the embassy, and requested to see the commercial attache. The security man obliged and gestured to the other security man who was standing close by to open the gate. The gate soon swung open. They were shown where to park. After parking the car, they trekked to the building. They were still at the entrance when the glass door parted on its own. This was the first time Joda was passing through such a door.

The door could open for any moving object. He was surprised but could not talk. After they had passed the door closed back. They were already inside the building. There was a bold sign directing visitors to reception. They made their way to reception. They saw a tall lanky girl with a foreign accent. She asked if she could help them. They told her they wanted to see the commercial officer. She asked if they had an appointment. They said No! She then called the officer, who asked that they be allowed in. The receptionist asked them to climb the stairs then go left. It was the 6th room on the left. They did as directed. The officer welcomed them warmly. He knew Joda's friend very well but had not met Joda before. Joda's friend introduced the two of them. They soon sat down and introduced the subject of their mission. The truth is that Joda had been living below the standard he had set for himself. He could no longer make ends meet. His friend had advised him to go into business and leave the government job. He assured him about improvement in the quality of his life and success in business. They have therefore come to see if the Commercial officer will help get connection for Joda in the new business he wanted to start. He was highly interested in importation and being a commissioned agent.

Meanwhile, Asubi who had trailed them had carefully parked his motorcycle outside the gate. He went to a nearby kiosk and bought some cigarettes. He was puffing at his cigarette when Joda and his friend showed up at the gate. Immediately the gateman locked the car out. Asubi emerged from nowhere. He stopped them. "Good afternoon Joda," he said. "Do you still remember me? I am Asubi!" Joda knew him but could not remember his name. Before Joda could say anything further, he was interrupted by Asubi who told him that he was a relation of Efo. He held Joda by the collar of his shirt and was shouting that he should come out of the car. Joda calmly demanded what it was all about. Before anybody could actually say what was amiss, Asubi had given Joda a punch in the mouth. This was what made Joda get out of the car. Immediately he was out, Asubi was jumping up and down and saying so many things which were not coherent. People had started to gather at the scene. Asubi was uncontrollable. He threatened to burn down the car. It took the concerted effort of reasonable people around to calm him down. He had claimed that Joda was owing his sister for the expenses incurred during the delivery of their child. The amount was $7,000. He wanted it paid on the spot. An agreement was however reached that it was a family affair. They should all go home and talk it out. They would meet at Joda's home by 4.00pm.

Joda had anticipated the worst and had gone to the local security agency to hire their services. Thus at 4.00pm on the dot, Joda was home with one security operative. It was agreed that the other security personnel be dispersed. Some hid under the flowers. This was because it was expected that Efo and Asubi would come in a militant way. They did.

They came two hours later in an open van loaded with about fifteen young hefty boys. Some of them were drunk and had wild manners. It was the security officer who came to open the door when the bell rang. It was Efo and her senior brother who showed up at the door first. The rest were waiting in the van ready to pounce and execute their devilish plan of tearing Joda to pieces. They had planned to murder both Joda and Titi if she was found in the house. She was not found. She had been taken to a guest house by Joda. There was a light argument between Efo and the security man. Joda had come to the door himself before Efo and her brother were let in. Soon after they sat in the sitting room for discussion, the bell rang again. The security man went to open the door. The person at the door was one of the thugs they had brought along. They had planned to be coming out of the vehicle one after the other in order to avoid stampeding the house. Asubi had not shown his face. Joda wanted to meet him face to face. But he was in the vehicle. The security officer ordered the caller back, and stood in front of the door in order to prevent any unwanted person coming to disturb again. It was then that the thugs in the van started coming one after the other. The security man was forced to lift his jacket and show his gun which was fastened to his waist.

It was when the hoodlums saw the gun that they knew that Joda had adequately prepared himself for them. He did not want to take chances with such buffoons like Asubi. He had expected them to storm his house, to terrorise him. When they discovered that he was not alone, and had a gun they became afraid. Some of them went back to the vehicle, and sat calmly at their seats.

It was not long after some of them had gone back to the vehicle when some noise was heard inside the house. It was Efo's voice. Efo was shouting all over the place. She was demanding to see Titi and asking for maintenance money. It was obvious that all her anger stemmed from Joda's relationship with Titi. She was hysterical and wanted to see Titi, with her eyes. Only then would she decide on what to do with her. Unfortunately, Titi was not in the house. She had been taken to a safe place. While Efo was shouting at the top of her voice, her brother sat calmly. He believed that his sister was actually raising dust for nothing and would have preferred if matters were settled more peacefully. He did not want to say it out loud lest it looked as if he was not on the same side with his sister.

However, he was able to persuade Efo to agree to negotiation. She did. She wanted to respect her brother whose presence actually was the spark that ignited her emotions. Eventually they agreed on the maintenance money. Nothing was discussed about another woman. Ironically Efo who had come brimming with anger about the presence of Titi in her former house never talked about coming back to her matrimonial home. She eventually left with her thugs and Joda breathed a sigh of relief. He believed that his decisive action in hiring the security agents had saved his life.

Chapter Two

Joda had resigned his appointment with the government and gone into full business. After the last debacle with his former wife he was determined to reorganize his life and make a fresh start. His business had started to grow and his child, who had been living with his wife's uncle, was coming of age. Efo had found a man leaving the child with her maternal uncle and his wife. They had been childless and welcomed the presence of the child in their midst. They had been taking good care of her. She had reached school age. Joda wanted to bring back his child to his house because of his new found wealth. He felt the child should come and live in her father's house. This would give her a sense of belonging instead of the present circumstances in which she had been living like an adopted child. He had made representations to the parents of Efo to release the child. This was in accordance with custom. In such circumstances if a man wanted his child, he would approach the parents of the ex-wife and give them a present of hot drinks and money. Thereafter, the child would be released to him. There is no further ceremony to take place if the couple were legally married. Joda did not anticipate any opposition in his effort to secure the release of his child. He had made elaborate arrangements on how the child would be taken care of. He had got a nanny and got a place in a private school where the child would attend. He then duly went to his in-laws' house with his relations to collect his child.

He was frustrated by his father-in-law who insisted that the child should finish her primary education before she could return to her father's house. This was the fourth time that he had said a similar thing. Joda was visibly annoyed at the latest ambivalence of his former father-in-law. He resolved that he would no longer stomach this rubbish from the man. To him this was the last straw. The story of their latest visit to his in-laws house had become common talk everywhere. It had become obvious that his in-laws would never release Joda's child to him. Under normal circumstances, collection of a child from an in-laws' house was not a subject of controversy but this had become a different issue altogether.

What happens when a group wants to claim a child is that they would come as representatives of the village with a spokesman. They are expected to act together. The father of the child being claimed may or may not be among the entourage but in most cases, he is there. It is expected that his presence would lend weight to the discussion at hand. His in-laws may fear his presence and concede certain aspects of the talk. Joda himself was a member of the entourage that went from his village. When they got there for the formal meeting, he did not talk but listened raptly to the deliberations. He had not contributed anything during the discussion. This was largely due to the fact that their spokesman was the only person allowed to talk on such an occasion but, he could permit any member of his entourage to talk if he so wished. What they tell their in-laws must accord with the agreements reached with the elders at home before they left.

They must talk with decorum and are not expected to do or say anything that will hurt their hosts. It was not an individual's talk per se. It was a whole village against another village. In this case Joda as the main character in the drama was not expected to say a word. He knew this and had sat quietly throughout the deliberations. However, things were not moving the way he wanted. His in-laws were clearly being stubborn and putting a lot of obstacles in their way. It was becoming clear that they were not willing to release the child. Joda was becoming restless. He wished he could take over the talking from their spokesman. But something pushed him and he decided to respect the man. He had started to talk within himself and blaming a culture that had kept him from saying anything. Even though he had been restrained by custom from saying anything, he wished that the custom could be waved aside to enable him to express his opinion and feelings in a topic that concerned him personally. He decided to break his silence and talk. He raised his hand to talk. He was told by their leader to put down his hand. He did, but continued to chew his lips thereby exposing his restless mind. As the discussion progressed, he discovered loopholes in what the other side was saying. He once again put up his hand in an effort to talk. He was again told to put down his hand. Joda found it difficult to contain himself and therefore excused himself and left the venue. He went straight to the vehicle and sat down. He was thinking how to deal with the situation.

After waiting for about an hour, the members of his village came out. They were muted and downcast. They were not talking. They all entered the vehicle and left. They opened up talking when they entered the vehicle. They were talking in very loud tones and shouting at the top of their voices. Joda never asked them the outcome of their talk. He knew there was nothing good out of it. If there was any good, the child should have come along. It was all empty promises they received. When they got home, people gathered to hear them. They merely stated that it was the same fruitless journey. "The people had refused. They wanted the child to be of a certain age before they could release her." Those who heard this were not happy at what they considered an insult. Joda stayed briefly in the parlour where the discussion was going on. He then went to bed. The next day he left for his station. He did not disclose to anybody any plans he had in mind. He had however conceived a plan in his head to kidnap the child, but felt it was not a matter for anybody to hear lest they botch or oppose it.

His idea was to hire the services of police officers and use them the same way Efo used them against him. This would put some fear in the mind of his in-laws so that they would release Eka without much resistance. They would go in a hired vehicle. At the last moment, he gave up the idea of going with hired policemen. This was to reduce tension. "The police are only interested in collecting money and do not care if justice exists or not," he thought. It was also becoming very expensive. The cost of hire of vehicle alone was more than he could bear. He therefore took a chance by approaching only a hire company. He looked for a vehicle and arranged for the driver to come to his house the following morning for the journey. It was not the business of the hire companies to ask for the mission of those who hire their vehicles. They were merely concerned with the money the client would pay. They never asked Joda what his mission was. He paid their fee and obtained a receipt. He however wanted to tell the driver of his mission so that he would be part of the operation. This would enable the driver to know what role to play at crucial moments. The driver reported to his house the next morning by 7.15am later than agreed. Before the driver came, Joda was already dressed and was waiting anxiously. The door bell rang at 6.45am. He jumped up thinking it was the driver. It was not. It was the man who supplied them bread for their breakfast.

Joda looked out through the window and saw it was not the driver. He sighed but, however opened the door. A child was called up to collect the bread. Joda went back to where he was sitting and continued sipping his drink. He was intermittently watching his wrist watch. It was 7.00am and the driver had not shown up. "What was wrong," he wondered. He had emphasized the fact that he wanted the journey to start by 7.00am on the dot. The distance was far and he wanted to be at the school before they closed. If he failed to be at the school before 12.00 noon, the school might close and his plans be derailed. He would then have wasted all the money and time for nothing. He however believed that the driver would come. He had paid them and he had the receipt. At 7.10am, the driver had still not come. Joda was getting worked up. He poured more drink into his glass. He was taking more drink than he personally thought necessary for this type of journey. He needed a clear head to be able to direct the operation. At 7.15am the door bell rang again. Joda jumped from his seat. He was sure this was the driver. He did not bother to go and look through the window as was the habit of the household before opening the door. His guess this time was right. It was the driver standing at the door. He was very apologetic when Joda opened the door. He explained that on his way he had a puncture and was compelled to go and fix the tyre. Joda accepted the apology. He had to. He had no alternative unless he did not want to go on the journey again.

They were already inside the vehicle when Joda decided to brief the driver about his mission. He felt he should do it while they were still in the town so that the driver could decide whether to follow him or not. He also told the driver that he had wanted to hire the services of some police officers but decided against it at the last minute. The reason was because of cost but he also felt since the child was staying with old and feeble people, he would not need much force to accomplish his mission. The driver listened attentively to Joda's story. He was very sympathetic to his cause. He decided to support Joda and help him achieve his goal. He felt that the fate of an innocent child should not be tied to the fetters of unsound judgement. Those people were very old and could not cater for the child, rather they would be merely using the child as a beast of burden, to clear the mess in the stable, whereas if the child came with her father, she would be treated like a princess, he thought. As they reached an agreement, they zoomed off on their uncertain mission. They stopped briefly on the outskirts of the town to fuel their vehicle. They continued to talk on other issues as well as getting to know each other. It was a smooth ride. The day was windy and the breeze was blowing into the car. Joda soon dozed off. It was the effect of the drink he had taken and the cool wind. He had a sound sleep. He had not had that kind of sleep in a long time. The only time he woke up was when they were passing an army barracks. The army had set up a checkpoint in front of their barracks which was close to the major road. It is their law that all vehicles passing through there should stop and be searched. The driver was new to this road. He did not know that such a law existed at the spot. He wanted to pass without stopping but was called to stop by a soldier who cocked his gun. He was terrified and stepped on the brakes with force and the car screeched to a halt. The noise roused Joda who used his bare palm to wipe his face before asking "What is that." One of the soldiers rushed to the vehicle. He ordered the driver out. When the driver came out, he was given a slap across his face. He was further ordered to place his two arms over his head and start leaping like a frog. He did, while the soldier was singing a tune for him. Joda came out quickly from the car and went to a more senior officer standing close by. Joda begged him for forgiveness. The senior officer ordered his man to stop it. The drilling of the driver was stopped and the vehicle was allowed to continue on its journey.

The experience which was the first for the driver scared him. He was however undaunted and believed in the righteousness of their mission; and prayed to God to see them through no matter the obstacle. Their second bad experience was yet to come. After the encounter with the army, Joda never slept again. They were now at the outskirts of the town. They once again ran into a police checkpoint. The police had demanded the vehicle particulars from the driver. The papers were duly given to them by the driver. Joda was sitting calmly in the vehicle. He was sure the papers were complete and correct. He therefore did not envisage any problem.

He was watching the policeman as he carefully leafed through the papers given to him. The policeman and the driver were soon engaged in an argument. At his point, the policeman beckoned to one of his men. He handed him the papers with instructions. Joda came out from the vehicle and asked the policeman who was walking away what was the problem. The policeman did not reply, instead he went ahead. Joda increased his steps and soon caught up with him. He demanded to know what was wrong. The policeman explained that he suspected the vehicle in which they were travelling was stolen. Joda was shocked beyond belief. This was a vehicle he had hired from a reputable company. How could it be stolen?! He suspected some mischief by the policemen and thought they were holding them to ransom in order to dupe them of money. He demanded to know the proof they had for their allegation. The police officer recalled the papers from his colleague and showed Joda the evidence of his assertion. The seller of the vehicle was different from the importer and there was no evidence to show a transfer of ownership from the importer to the seller. Joda was not happy at all. He asked the driver for an explanation. The driver himself appeared helpless. He could not explain what happened. He had been using this vehicle for almost a year and this sort of thing had not cropped up. The hire company belonged to his brother. They have a good number of vehicles in their fleet and always ensured that their vehicles were purchased from reputable dealers.

Joda was thrown into more anxiety. They were now wasting time on this. "How can I waste all this money and time just for a jolly ride," he queried. He went back to the police officers and explained his mission. He was going to collect his child from school on a prearranged agreement with the school authorities. He had paid a large sum of money just to hire this vehicle. If they continued to delay them further, the school would close and his mission would be defeated. The policeman was neither moved nor interested in his story. All he was interested in was that they had caught a potential car thief. They would have to follow him back to the station. There were more pleas from the driver and Joda but the policeman would not budge. The officer in-charge directed one of his men to enter Joda's car and take them to the station. He entered his own car and followed them. They had gone halfway to the police station when Joda asked the driver to stop. He told them that he had no business in the station. They should stop him so that he would hire another vehicle. Time was running against him. It would be a sad day for him if he had undertaken this pain for nothing. The driver stopped as he was ordered. He wanted to step out of the vehicle when the driver and the policeman convinced him of the need to go to the police station. The policeman had assured him that they would not waste much time if they understood what he meant. Joda understood. This was the language the police speak when they were looking for money. Immediately he understood that money would solve their problem he calmed down. "What is money," he asked himself. He said he would give them any amount they wanted if they would leave them alone. He wished they had mentioned this at the checkpoint instead of this cumbersome way of going about it. Their stop made the officer in-charge be much ahead of them. He went very far without sighting them. He looked worried and started coming back. He met them on the way and made another "U" turn. They were soon at the police station. The policeman that had come with Joda in the same car beckoned to the driver. They went inside the small room. The driver had no clue as to what they wanted. He told the policeman to name their price. He was told what to pay. They haggled a little. The driver excused himself to confer with Joda. Joda gave him money. He went back to where the policeman was waiting in the room. The driver soon came out. He went to the officer in-charge who had parked his car under a shed but was sitting inside. The driver greeted him. He came to Joda and they drove off to their destination.

Their plan was to go to the school and take the child away right from there.

While they were in the police station Joda had been thinking about the type of society in which he was born. He was not finding things as they should be. Everybody from the highest in the society to the lowest was contributing negatively towards the destruction of the society. Nobody cared and nobody was doing anything to change the status quo. He was very unhappy. As soon as they drove out of the police station, he cleared his throat and said, looking in the direction of the driver, "My friend, what is happening in this country?" his voice overwhelmed with emotion. The driver did not know he was talking to him. He had not talked to him that way since they set out on their journey. "My friend," Joda repeated. "I have been talking to you."

"Oh, the driver answered," sorry, sir. I did not know you were talking to me.

Joda accepted the apology and began. "This country is stinking. What can we do to clean it up. You see a situation whereby soldiers trained to defend the country against external aggression turn round to oppress the very people they should defend. What is wrong? Is it because they are idle and do not find enough to occupy their time. What could have made those soldiers want to punish us the way they did if not idleness. You also see the police trained with public funds to maintain law and order turn round to steal from the people; and break the very law they are supposed to enforce. Did you notice how those police officers were struggling to prove that a vehicle we brought was a stolen vehicle. They were doing it so that they could be given money. This car was bought more than a year ago from a reputable company and had been plying many routes without problem. But just because they wanted money, they were causing us a lot of hardship. Why did they not say that they needed money and I could have given them that."

He kept quiet after saying this last sentence expecting a response from the driver. The driver did not talk. He never knew that his master could be so much annoyed. Joda started again. "What do you say." The driver said he had nothing to say. Joda fired back as if the driver's response had worsened things. "You must say something. You must have something to say." This country can only get better when everybody has something to say. We cannot all close our eyes to what is going on and say we have nothing to say. You must have something to say and I must have something to say. You were supposed to report to my house to pick me up by 7.00am. You did not come until 7.15am. This is part of the problem of this country where everybody is not doing what he is supposed to do or is doing the opposite thing. How can we survive under that condition. Things can only get better if you have something to say and have something to do to stop what is going on. The driver who had at one moment thought that Joda was getting personal realized that the man was deeply concerned about the society. He replied in a subdued tone "I am sorry, sir, I have already told you why I did not come by 7.00am. It was due to circumstances I could not help. Something like punctures can happen to anybody. It is not the same with those army people who would punish others without enough reason. Just because we were driving through their camp they stopped and punished us. It was unfair. It was also not like those police officers who parade themselves in uniforms but are actually robbers. Such are the sort of people society does not need. The problem of this country is with leadership. Unless the leaders do something, this country will continue to suffer."

Joda had been listening attentively to his driver. He was impressed by all what he had said. He replied; "My friend, you have talked very well. Now, what do you think can be done to our leaders?"

The driver kept quiet for some time before he replied. "I think they should be removed."

Joda laughed. Then, he began "Maybe it is a meeting of minds but we have been thinking alike. I know you do not know me very well. You have not even met me before, yet we can think the same . My name is Joda. I have been worried by the stench in our society. I have been thinking that the best thing this country needs is a revolution. Our society is stinking and unless honest people can come out and carry out this revolution, we shall continue to go down the abyss.

My plans are laid out and very soon I shall be going into full time politics. I want to go into politics because I love this country and want it to be cleaned up."

The driver replied , "You are the ones we are looking up to. Wherever you take us, we go."

Joda whipped back. "In a revolution nobody looks up to another, nobody is above the other. It is a mass movement and action; we must all join hands and do something. You already have the weapon which will enable you to play a vital role. That weapon is your voting card. Ensure that when election day comes, you vote in the right people. There lies the salvation of this country." Joda had merely expressed his innermost feelings and his vow to change society. He was brought up an honest man who had been agitated by the rot in society. Just as they were still talking, they entered the town.

Chapter Three

The would-be kidnappers were now in town. They did not know the exact location of the school. They however knew the home of Eka's step-parents very well. The school was close to their home. They made several enquiries before arriving at the school gate. They were welcomed by the security men. It was Joda alone who came out of the cab. The driver stayed put in his seat. He could only drive but would not participate in other operations. The car was parked in front of the gate. The mission seemed very innocent. Joda was well dressed and looked highly responsible. There was no ground for the security man to suspect any sinister motive. Joda coolly introduced himself. He said that his daughter was in the school here. He would like to see the headmistress. He was shown to the Chief Security Officer who would direct him. Before this man; Joda repeated what he had said earlier. The Chief Security Officer apologetically told him that the headmistress had just driven out a few minutes before his arrival. The man asked whether there was any special reason for his visit so that he could direct him to another senior teacher. Joda did not bother to go to another teacher. It did not make much difference whether the headmistress was there or not so long as the security man himself would be able to call out his daughter from the class. One of the security men was detailed to go and fetch Eka. She soon came out with the security man. She was bubbling. She had heard about her father but had never seen him. Her mates had been brought up with "daddy" on their lips but not Eka. Her inability to find a man to call daddy had made a traumatic impression on her. Now that the opportunity had come, she was overjoyed. She trotted into the warm embrace of her father who did not waste time in lifting her up onto his shoulders. He kissed her on the forehead before dropping her on her two feet. He now asked "How are you," to which Eka retorted "fine". They soon engaged in reminiscences. Joda asked her daughter if ever she knew she had a father. She answered affirmatively. He then asked whether she would like to follow him back to his station. The little girl said that it must be with the approval of her mummy. Joda quickly dropped that aspect of the discussion. He realized that if there was any slip about his emotions for coming, the bubble would burst; and not only would his plan be botched, he might be apprehended and given names he would forever live to regret. A group of other little girls who were Eka's classmates gathered and were watching her; and her father as they fondly held each other. Joda was at first oblivious of their presence. When he noticed their excitement, he asked them, "Are you Eka's classmates?" They chorused, "Yes." He told them he was her father and asked them to go back to their class. Eka would soon join them when they were through. The little girls dispersed. Some headed to their class while others went in different directions. Joda now told his daughter he was about to depart. He asked that the little girl follow him to the next store so that he could buy her some biscuits and provisions. The little girl quickly agreed without any suspicion. They entered the vehicle after Joda told the security men he wanted to buy her something and would bring her back. He never did. The car kicked off after they had boarded, the girl knew a particular store where they bought provisions. It was her relation's store. She directed the vehicle to that place. Before she could get out of the cab, Joda intervened and said he had seen the type of biscuits he wanted at the other store. He had suspected the girl's innocent intention. He told the driver to stop and go back. The driver reversed to go back to the store. When they got there Joda asked the girl to remain in the vehicle with the driver while he went to buy the items. The girl agreed. Joda went to the store. He bought just one packet of biscuits and returned to the car. He gave the girl the biscuits and said he did not see the exact type he wanted. This was false. He had not asked for any other type. Joda asked the driver to turn back and turn left and go straight to the main road. He claimed he had seen the type he wanted at the junction.

The driver understood all his motives and obeyed every instruction religiously. Joda engaged the little girl in a filial conversation. They had not seen each other since he separated from his wife and the girl had not known her father. She had heard about him and had wished she knew her father. She wanted to live with her parents the same way other children did. This was why, when she saw a man who called himself her father, she was overjoyed. She had thought ever since she had met this man a few hours ago her dream of living like other children would be realized. This was not to be. Joda had come to take her away without her mother.

Her mother had a very serious affair and would soon get married to a man of her dreams.

The vehicle was moving at a normal speed. The girl had not resented the fact that the vehicle was moving far away from her school. She didn't realise the vehicle was about thirty kilometres away. She never relented about her excitement of meeting her father. In the meantime, the car had stopped to refuel. The girl looked around through the windows, every place was strange. Her father and the driver had stepped out of the car, she was alone, and this gave her the chance to think. Her senses were now coming back. "How can buying provisions from the store have taken so long?" she thought. She would ask her father when he returned.

He came back with some cans of soft drinks and some snacks. She did not ask the question that was bogging her mind immediately. She would first of all take what she considered to be her lunch. It was midday. She had her last meal early in the morning and was becoming very hungry. She finished the drink and threw the empty can through the window. The driver had come back to the vehicle. The vehicle was soon in motion again. "Daddy, when are we getting to the school?" she asked anxiously. She had hoped to receive an answer that would reassure her that they had not strayed very far from the school. Joda answered her differently. "Are you not happy to be with me after so many years? You haven't seen me before and, you should be happy and relaxed. You will soon get back to your school."

The girl remained silent after hearing from her father. Later, she started to feel sleepy. Her father glanced at her, stretched his right hand and drew her close to him. He asked her to use his lap as a pillow and sleep.

She agreed and was soon dozing off with her head on her father's lap. The sleep was a good relief to Joda. He had been talking all the way. Now he could afford to rest a bit and review his strategy with the driver. Both of them smiled wryly to themselves. They were exceedingly happy at the success of their operation. It had been very smooth without hitches. They would simply go straight home. They had reached a point of no return. There were no more stoppages on the road.

It was about 4.00pm in the afternoon and they were on the outskirts of the town where Joda resided. Joda thought it was time to tell the girl the truth about their movements. He was certain there was nothing the girl could do at that stage. He however, did not anticipate the reaction he got from her. Immediately he told her that he had brought her back home to his house for her own good, the little girl burst into tears. She continued to cry uncontrollably, and all efforts by Joda to console her and reassure her that it was in her best interest that she came home with him fell on deaf ears. She had been living like an orphan while he, as her father was still alive. The driver was also chipping in words to the girl. He told her to look at herself and see all her collar bones sticking out. "You will soon be a changed girl if you stay with your father," he told her. Nothing ever told to the girl had any meaning any more. She was no longer seeing him as a father, he had turned into a monster who must be avoided. She was praying that her step-parents would appear on the scene and rescue her. She was wailing and cursing and begging for God's deliverance. At one stage, she turned to Joda and told him that she knew that one day he would come to collect her but, she never imagined that he would come the way he had done it. She wanted Joda to go to her mummy and strike a deal before she could be released normally to him in accordance with custom. She was however, unaware of the fruitless efforts Joda had made to secure the peaceful release of his child. It was her mother in collaboration with her step-parents who had thwarted all his efforts. He felt justified therefore by his methods which he considered unassailable.

They were soon in Joda's house. The girl was reluctantly pushed into the house. She continued crying requesting to be sent back. People in the neighbourhood came to greet the sobbing child. They had heard about Joda's journey. They had hailed it as the right decision. The girl was his blood. He was capable of providing for her. He did not understand why another man should be taking care of his own child against his best wishes. She was his child. He gave her life. He alone could nurse and nurture that life. Nobody else could and nobody should attempt to come for Eka. His decision and subsequent action to bring her to her father's house was final. He would deal with anybody who attempted a counter action.

The little girl had no choice but to adjust to the new life in which she found herself. Two days had passed since Joda's successful operation and nothing was heard from her grandparents. Joda had been expecting their reaction. "I am ready," he told himself. On the third day however, at about dusk, the door bell rang. It was Joda's girlfriend who went to the window to see who it was. She saw two hefty men. She did not know either of them. She quickly went to Joda and told him. Joda immediately ordered Eka to leave the parlour and go and stay in her room. The little girl obeyed and went to her room. Joda went to the window but couldn't quite see the faces of the people. However, he opened the door, coming face to face with his nephew and the security man who had called Eka from her class when he went to get her. He welcomed them heartily, as he knew that they were on his side. He took them into his house, served them drinks before asking them their business. He had suspected they were sent by his people. The two men, however, said that they were sent jointly by Joda's family and Eka's grandparents. They had been asked to come and find out if Eka was in Joda's house. Joda admitted that Eka was with him. He then called Eka out. The little girl came out. She greeted the august visitors genuflecting as she did so. The people responded with smiles. Eka was asked by her father to go back to her room. She did. The men narrated further what had transpired since Eka was taken by her father. First, her grandfather had gone to Joda's father to complain. He had been informed that it was Joda who had collected his child and he felt that it was an insult for Joda to have done it the way he did. Joda was very happy that the man was feeling insulted by his actions. "Had he forgotten the insult he gave to me himself. Those who live in glass houses should not throw stones," he thought to himself. The two men further said that his ex-wife's father could have gone to the police but knew that he would not succeed in any case with Joda. He was a stranger to the affair between his daughter and Joda and therefore had no *locum standi* to sue. Eka is not his child and no matter how he tried he could never win any case against Joda as far as Eka was concerned.

The school authorities were also concerned about the way Eka disappeared. Even Eka's grandfather had also threatened to deal with the headmistress unless she produced Eka. It was in sympathy with this threat that the headmistress had sent a note to Joda to sign an undertaking that he had collected his daughter. He should also state that he did this without the knowledge of the school authorities. Joda never wasted time in providing this undertaking.

The two visiting men and Joda stayed very late into the early hours of the morning. The main topic of discussion was the kidnapping of Eka and how people were reacting to it. The two families had sat together with the school authorities to discuss the issue. It was at that meeting that a decision to send the two men was arrived at. Eka's grandfather had wanted to send somebody along, to represent him on the mission. This was however flatly rejected by Joda's parents, who felt that Joda might not take it lightly if he saw somebody he would not approve. It could result in unpleasant consequences.

In the morning the two men had their breakfast and prepared to go. Little Eka had been monitoring everything since the men arrived. She had approached one of them secretly and told him that she would follow them back. The men had dissuaded her from having such a thought. She did not however give up, hoping that the men would take her back to her grandparents and her school. She was missing them and the only thing God could do for her was to make it possible for her to go with the men. Immediately the men stepped out of the door, bags in hand to go, Eka emerged from nowhere and said, "I want to go with them" wailing as she said that. She was, however, told to go back by both the men and Joda. She refused and was running after the men. She realized that there was no way she could follow them. She eventually came back to the house. In the house, she continued with her crying and nobody tried to stop her. It would have been futile to try that. It was better to leave her alone. She would get tired and would stop herself.

She did, when nobody was looking in her direction or sympathized with her.

In fact, she dozed off where she was sitting on the floor of the parlour.

When she woke up, her father ordered her to go and have her meal. She refused. She said she would go hungry. Her father tried to be palliative. He cajoled her but she would not obey, which infuriated him. He told his daughter that both of them had not seen each other for several years. It was God's wish that they should come together now but, he noticed that her grandfather had mistrained her as she did not respect her seniors and elders as a normal child should. Her disobedience of his instructions was an insult for which he blamed the type of training that Eka had received from her grandparents. He therefore threatened to sue her grandparents for mistraining his child. Eka was shocked at what she heard her father say. She believed her father would take her grandparents to court. She therefore started to beg Joda not to sue her grandfather. This plea made Joda very happy. He smiled in his heart. He then asked Eka to go and have her breakfast if she wanted him not to sue her grandparents. Eka agreed and went to eat her breakfast. Joda had won. Since that day Eka lived happily in the house and Joda had been providing for her. She stopped asking questions about her foster parents. She was realising for the first time in her life the value of a father. Beyond that, nobody came to snatch her away. She started school and was doing well in school. Her relationship with her father improved after the initial strain. Her father was providing her with all her needs. She was attending a private school. Her outlook changed. She started to notice changes in her life, but, occasionally she would yearn to see her step-parents. She was not so much concerned about her mother as her grandparents. They were the only parents she had ever known. She had vowed even as a child to provide for them when she grew up.

Chapter Four

Preparation was in high gear for Joda to get married again. He was anxious to have a family he could call his own, just like all other men. He had discovered that married people were respected more in the society. They also lived a more meaningful life. His children would feel more at home if they had a father and mother in the house. It was the thought of providing a home for his children that led Joda to hire two home helps. One of them Apo was an elderly woman. She was probably in her early forties. Joda had thought it wise to bring in a woman of that age so that she could act as the mother of the house. Moreover, children from broken homes ended up being broken themselves. There was also Ari, who was thirteen years old, she would act as a playmate to Eka in her formative years. However, plans were at an advanced stage for Joda to remarry. His new heart throb was Nora, a very beautiful girl from a respectful family, in her late twenties. She too had been dreaming of getting a responsible man as a husband. She hoped to settle with that man and raise a family of her own. In all her imaginations she never believed that she would marry a man who had been married before. They used to talk about their dream marriages when they were at school. They had always called men with children second-hand. They wanted their husbands brand new. All these turned out to be child's fantasy. In the real world, the type of men they had hoped for were not available. Most of their male agemates were far behind them socially. Men tended to marry at a later age when they felt they had built a solid financial base that would enable them to maintain a family. This was not the case with females, who, were always looking for males who had made it. They called these type ready made. They expected their future husbands to take them into their house, care, maintain and love them. Any man who failed to do this was regarded by society as a failure.

It was with misgivings that Nora received the news that Joda had been married before and even had a daughter. They had been introduced by a mutual friend. Ejike was a close friend of Joda and, an intimate friend of Nora's brother. There was therefore a deep trust on both sides about Ejike's choice. Inspite of Nora's misgivings and beliefs about a married man, she accepted the offer from Joda to marry him. She was getting older and had realised that there was a time when a woman must make up her mind. Some old prejudices must be shed. She decided she would marry Joda. After all, what was important was that she was marrying him out of her own volition and nobody had coerced her. She would raise a family of her own and the man she did it with was her own business she thought.

Everybody in the neighbourhood had noticed the presence of Nora in Joda's house. She was paying frequent visits and behaving as if the house was hers. She had taken a liking for Eka whom she regarded as her own child. She however, did not like the presence of Apo in the house. She thought her to be an experienced old hag who might snatch away her husband. She reasoned that her first duty when they finally got married was to do away with Apo. She saw Ari as an asset to the house, who would help her in the house and look after Eka as well. She thought her to be such a nice little girl who had not been corrupted by the vices of the world. She would guide her morally so that together with Eka and her own children they would raise a solid family.

The marriage took place amidst pomp and pageantry. A lot of people attended the ceremony. Nora fully moved into the house after the marriage. True to her vow to sack Apo, she started to find fault with her. She would complain at the slightest good intention of Apo. Apo was clearly getting frustrated. She did not want to resign on her own. She promised to go but would wait for the new family to take the initiative, and it was no wonder that she reported for duty one morning and was told she was no longer required. Apo calmly accepted it, as she had been expecting it. She turned back and left for her home.

Nora was now in charge as the only woman of the house. She was good to her husband and kind to the children. Everybody was calling her mummy and she proved equal to the accolade. She was also enjoying her new life. It did not take long before she became pregnant. Joda was elated at the prospect of becoming a father once again. He did not wait before he started to buy baby things. He reckoned that nine months was not too far. What if on that fateful day he had gone on a business trip. It was necessary to have some of these items that would be required when the child was born. The position in the house was cordial. Joda believed he was building an integrated family. There was however a snag. Both he and his wife did not reckon that Eka did not actually regard Nora as her mother. She had been cynically calling her mummy. She was aware that Nora was not her natural mother. She was nurturing the hope that one day she would go back to her mother. Nobody noticed that she always winced whenever Nora called her to send her on a message.

Joda and Nora had always cuddled together in one bed ever since they got married. They would make love whenever they felt like it. It was 3.00am this cold day and Joda felt like making love to his wife. His wife refused. He was surprised because the wife had never before refused any of his overtures. He persisted thinking that women need the gentle pressure to give in. He was mistaken. Nora got up from the bed. She headed towards the door. Just as she was approaching the door something dropped from her body. She looked down and saw a drop of blood. She called Joda with a halting breath. "Joda, darling come, come quickly." Joda jumped out of the bed and rushed to her. He held her firmly and asked what was the matter. Nora told him to get ready and take her to the hospital immediately. She believed the baby was coming. Joda did not hesitate. He panicked before going to the wardrobe. He violently jerked the wardrobe open. At 3.00am it was not desirable nor necessary to look fashionable. He just put on the first clothes he could lay his hands on. He searched for his car keys. He saw them on the bedroom table where he kept them the previous night. He snatched them up and joined his wife who was already by the car.

Ari and Eka had heard the noise in the house. They had come out from their room to find out what was going on. Joda whispered into their ears and told them to go back to their bed. They would soon come back. Mummy wanted to see the doctor. The children went back to their room. Mummy had always gone to the doctor for check-ups. So there was nothing new if she was going to see the doctor! What the children did not reckon with was the unusual time for the check-up this time around. They however obeyed their daddy and went back to bed. Joda carefully closed the outer door behind him. There was a need to act carefully at this time of the night in order not to arouse the curiosity of the neighbours. He went to the passenger's side of the car where his wife was leaning on the bonnet. He inserted the key and opened the car door from there. He then went to his wife. He took her right hand and crossed over his shoulders in order to provide support. He led the wife into the car before going to the driver's seat. Joda used reverse gear to come out of the garage before heading towards the gate of the estate where they lived. He was stopped at the gate by the security men who did not hesitate to wish him a safe journey, and, madam, safe delivery. He drove through the quiet and lonely roads. He was soon at the hospital. He helped his wife out of the car and into the waiting room. There were about two nurses on duty. Joda requested to see the doctor. The nurses told him not to worry. They would handle the situation. It was not necessary to call a doctor for what they considered a minor problem. Joda soon gave up arguing, even though he would rather prefer a doctor to handle the situation. The nurses asked Joda to go and wait in his car. He did. He left the room after a glance at his wife. The wife bent her head. She did not show any sign of pain nor was she in a happy mood.

The hours spent by Joda in his car waiting to get news about his wife were the most anxious in his life. The nurses seemed to have forgotten that he was around and would like to be informed of what was going on. When he could not bear the anxiety any longer, he decided to go and check. He did not see anybody in the waiting room where they had been. He asked a hospital help whom he saw by the door whether she knew where to find his wife and the nurses. It was then that he was directed to the labour room. On approaching the labour room, he heard the wailing of his wife. He wanted to rush to her aid. She was clearly in pain. It was labour pains which every woman who wants to be a woman must undergo at some stage in her life. But inspite of the accompanying pains, most women would want to get pregnant immediately after delivery. This is one of the contradictions men find difficult to come to grips with. The door was locked. Joda could not enter. He thought it was needless staying out and hearing the wailing of his wife which also reverberated in his body as if it was his personal pain. He decided to go back to the car. It was better not to hear her than hearing her sobs without being able to help her. In the car he was disconsolate. He could hardly put his thoughts together again. He wished God would transfer the pains of his wife to his body. Just as his thoughts were wandering, he remembered what he read from one mystical book about the law of assumption. He believed time was ripe for him to try to apply the principles. He would assume the pains of his wife and by so doing her burden would be transferred to his body and so lessen her burden. He raised his head skyward; and closed his eyes and kept silent. He did not know how the principles would work but if he would ever believe all these mystical teachings again, this particular one should work. He was also praying to God to alleviate the pains of his wife.

After some time, he decided to go near the labour room to check the efficacy of his supplication. Near the labour room, he did not hear his wife's voice again. He was exceedingly happy. One way; or the other his prayers had been answered. He went back to the car and sat quietly. It was about 8.00am and he saw somebody rushing towards his car. It was the woman who had shown her the way to the labour room earlier. She was smiling broadly. Joda remained bland even though the first thought that came to his mind was that Nora must have delivered. She had. Joda wanted the woman to break the news to him and tell him everything. The woman got to the car. The first words that came out of her mouth was "Congratulations." Joda jumped out of the car. He pretended he did not know why the woman was congratulating him. He quipped, "What happened." The woman was still smiling and repeated herself, "Congratulations." It is a baby boy." Joda simply left the woman and dashed into the hospital. He could not find enough words to express himself. When he left the woman by his car, he saw himself in the female ward. He went straight where his wife was lying and planted a kiss on her lips. He next turned to the cot where the bundle of their joy was lying. He surveyed the child carefully. He saw his features in the little thing and nodded his acquiescence. "This is my child," he muttered inaudibly to himself. He turned to his wife and asked what she wanted him to bring for her. Both of them made a list of what was required. He dashed off once more. He went to his house first. He told the children at home about the good fortune God had brought the household. He went to his inner room and collected some money. He left to go to the market to buy the necessities.

He brought the items to his wife at the hospital before going home to prepare food for his wife. He soon returned to the hospital. They gave him a chair and he sat down beside Nora's bed. He had been informed that his wife and child would be discharged the next day. After staying with them at the hospital, he left for his house at dusk. He hoped to be back the next day to bring them back to his house. It was a celebration galore when he got back home that evening. Friends, well-wishers, and neighbours had heard about the good tidings. They had been waiting for him to come back from the hospital before they could come to rejoice with him. They came in droves and the house was swarmed with human beings. He even found it difficult to cope with the reception. It was however not the old Joda who was a poor civil servant slaving for other people. This time around, it was a new Joda who had a flourishing business enterprise. The family stayed late into the wee hours of the morning. Joda had hardly had a sufficient sleep when the maid came to remind him that it was 9.00am.

He had left word with the maid to ensure that he woke up by 9.00am to go to the hospital to bring his wife and child home. Even though he was still drowsy, sleep can wait. He would sleep later after they had come home. He therefore jumped out of bed and into the bathroom. He had a quick shower and hurriedly dressed. By half past the hour, he was driving towards the hospital. He arrived at the hospital before ten. He was presented with the bill. He paid that effortlessly. He went upstairs where members of his family were. He told them it was time to go. His wife had dressed up. She too knew that Joda was obsessed with time and would be there on time. Nora excused herself to go to the pharmacy before she left. She did not waste time. Everything was prepared before she came there. She merely collected them. She wished the staff there goodbye and joined her husband upstairs. They, later left, with Joda, carrying the baby in his two arms. He carried it as if that was the first time he was seeing a new baby. But he had got his first baby. It was then that he learnt how to carry a child. He was carrying the baby like a fragile glass. The last thing he would wish was for anything to happen to the baby. His wife was following him. They were soon down. They greeted some of the hospital workers who were around. He allowed Nora to enter the car first. He then gave the baby to her. After he had carefully handed the baby to Nora, he went round to enter the driver's seat. He drove very carefully. He did not want anything to cause any form of strain to the new baby. When they got home, Eka and Ari rushed out to welcome them. They all entered the house together.

The family continued to live harmoniously. Nora, after some time became pregnant again. A baby girl was delivered almost in the same pattern as the first. There was so much trust and love between the couples and in the entire family. They became the envy of everyone. However, fate was to become cruel to this erstwhile peaceful family. Ari was coming of age. She had grown plump and roundish. Most men would turn twice whenever she passed. Joda had noticed the outstanding features in this young girl. He was however not lustful and never imagined himself going so low to have anything to do with a small girl who called him daddy. In fact, she was the playmate of his own daughter. Things took a different turn however. It was in the late morning. Nora who shared the same bed with Joda had got up and had gone to the bathroom to wash the baby. Joda was still in bed. Nora had asked Ari to go to her bedroom where Joda was sleeping and bring her new pomade she had bought for the baby. She had forgotten it when she got out of the bed. Ari went straight to the bedroom and pushed the door open. She did not knock. Incidentally Joda had just got up. He had removed his sleeping apparel. He was standing naked and sorting out the clothes to wear. He was oblivious of the presence of Ari. He heard the noise when the door opened but he thought it was Nora. He was shocked when he heard, "Sorry Sir." He turned quickly and there he was naked before little Ari. The girl wanted to run back but Joda recovered enough to ask her not to go. He quickly grabbed the bed-cover. He first of all covered his frontal frame and later used it to cover his entire body. He called Ari to come near. The little girl did. He rubbed her ear and told her not to worry. He warned her not to tell anybody what she saw. The girl who had been panting, managed to smile. She said, "Thank you Sir." Then she went to where the mistress told her to pick up the pomade. She picked up the pomade and left. Joda watched her all the time she was in the room. As soon as she closed the door behind her, he shook his head and smiled. He had started to think how attractive she was. He wondered if it would not be worthwhile if he took a chance. A deluge of thoughts had taken hold of Joda. "So it is a man like myself who will eat this meat," he thought.

There was, however, the need for Joda to hide whatever feeling that had overwhelmed him since Ari entered his room. It would be a serious matter if Nora ever knew what he was thinking, or, what happened in the room. He tried to suppress his thoughts and feelings. He forgot everything about the whole episode and continued to live a normal life with his family. Ari was affected more. She had grown extra shy because of what she had seen. She was rather shy and afraid that she must have offended her master. If her master told their mummy that she did not knock on the door before entering the room, her mistress would kill her. She continued to live with guilt, unable to tell anybody anything. Joda ignored her completely but that was for some time. He had been biding his time. He had developed a lustful desire for Ari. He had forgotten all he stood for. It was no wonder that he had correctly timed the situation,, when his wife would be going to the market. Eka would be at school while Ari would be at home to look after the baby until the madam came back.

After some months, Joda had planned to go on his business trip as usual, but he made a detour when he knew that everybody had left the house except Ari. He came home pretending he had come to collect what he had forgotten at home. He first of all went into the room. He later went to the cot to look at the baby who was sleeping peacefully. He hesitated for a while before calling Ari into the room. He had already planned what to do. Though he appeared to be putting on his trousers, he did not have any underwear on. He had a bulging trousers. He was sitting on the bedroom cushion chair, and did not waste time in asking Ari to come close. He held Ari by the hand and before anybody could wink an eye, the little girl was sitting on his lap. He played intimately with the girl but never made love with her. He later warned her never to let anybody know what had happened. He did not leave the house until he had extracted assurance that she would keep silent. He gave her money and promised to buy her things. This was the litmus test he needed before he plunged in.

This day had marked a turning point in the life of both Ari and Joda. Joda's clandestine amours pilgrimage to his house whenever Nora was away continued unabated. He had not yet made love to Ari. He was still afraid that Ari was a virgin and he thought that if she felt hurt during any love play, the cat would be out of the bag. He was however mistaken. Ari had been having sexual intercourse without letting her foster parents know about it. She was fully aware of the game being played by Joda. Her only problem was that she felt exceedingly shy to do it with a man she called daddy. However, she was waiting for Joda to make the first move. A wave of desire had also permeated her being since she first saw him naked and subsequent close contacts. Moreover, Joda had been buying her presents. She had started to eat special secret snacks and biscuits. Her life had changed. She was looking down on Nora.

It was difficult for Nora to observe the changes in Ari. She had absolute confidence in Joda. She had boasted to her friends that she had her husband in her handbag. The changes in Ari's confidence was showing in her body as she now ate special things provided by the master.

Joda's plans received a boost when the family was informed about the death of Nora's aunt. She was asked to come home so that she might join other family members in paying her aunt last respects. This means that Nora would leave the house for some days. This had been Joda's wish. He had wished for that day when Nora would be out of the house and stay out for a long time. This would enable him to be alone in the house with Ari. That opportunity had been offered by the message from home. Even though he sympathized with the loss of the old woman but he believed that death was inevitable and no matter whosoever that died, life must go on. Nora was badly affected by the news of the death of her favourite aunt. She had been very close to the woman. She regarded her as much as she did her own mother. She had therefore been adversely affected by her death. It was with heavy heart that she prepared and left for her home in the countryside. She planned to stay seven days. She had implicit confidence in her husband, and believed that he would take care of their house before she came back. He did take care of the home actually but not to the expectation of Nora.

It was during this period that Ari and Joda had the house all to themselves. The old adage had it that when a child eats what keeps her awake, she will sleep. When to make love to Ari had been a very big problem to Joda and Ari. They would now eat that thing that keeps them awake. Nora was out and would stay out for sometime.

Joda never wasted time in executing his plans. He had already sensitized Ari when Nora was around so that the girl was aware of what to expect when Nora was out. It was therefore not surprising that Ari was the first to take the initiative. She had prepared dinner that night. Joda had taken the table as was his habit. Ari came behind him and placed her two breasts at the back of his shoulder blades. He turned and gave her a broad smile. He left the food he was eating and was getting up when Ari ran into her room. He pursued her. She again ran and he continued pursuing her until, he caught up with her. He held her by her two hands and smiled into her eyes. He whispered into her ears that he would see her in the night. The girl nodded her head affirmatively while still smiling. The deal had been struck. That day in the night, Joda invited Ari into their matrimonial bed. She did not hesitate to take the place of Nora. They stayed until about 1.00am when Ari sneaked back into her room. From that day on Joda was inviting her daily into their room. They would go to bed after the children had slept. Ari used to prepare the children for sleep very early so that she would have enough time to stay with her master. In the morning, they would pretend as if nothing had happened. In fact, it was this time that Joda was finding fault with Ari. He was also scolding her. All this was a ruse. Ari was behaving in strict compliance with the instruction given by Joda that under no circumstances must another person hear of what had transpired. Their nocturnal play continued until Nora came back. When she came back the amorous couple reverted to their old ways. Joda was not coming near his home during the day as he used to do. He pretended that he was too much preoccupied to be coming home. Nora was still dazed and exhausted by the death of her aunt and the burial ceremonies. She needed full rest. The keeping of the household still rested on Ari who was doing a good job of it.

It was early in the morning one day when Nora saw Ari spitting repeatedly. As a woman, Nora was alarmed. She decided to keep quiet until she confirmed what was happening to her. Her suspicion was not misplaced. Ari was becoming lazy. She was not waking up to clean the house early in the morning. She was oversleeping. Nora had assured herself about Ari's condition. She would however wait until the pregnancy showed up in the stomach. She used to hear her elders say that "One cannot cover up pregnancy with bare hands." She had made up her mind that whenever the pregnancy came up, she would tell her husband to take Ari back to her natural parents. It never occurred to her that her dear husband would be a suspect. This was the last possibility she would want to hear. Her own mother had been a victim of a morally depraved man whom she first married. She had advised her children to be very careful before they got married "Look before you leap. Do not let any man touch you anyhow," she had told them.

After about three months, Ari's stomach protruded. It was obvious even to a child that she was pregnant. Nora called her into her private room and asked her who was responsible. She refused to say. She was crying throughout. Nora tried to persuade her to tell her but she would not. She left her. When Joda came back from his business trip that day, Nora told him. Joda did not utter a word. Nora left the room where they were talking. She returned with Ari. She asked her to sit down. She then continued with her question. She insisted that Ari tell them who was responsible. Ari refused bluntly to say who was responsible for the pregnancy. It was Joda who asked Ari to leave the room. She did. After she had left the room, Joda suggested that the best thing was for them to take her to a doctor to abort the pregnancy. Nora did not like the idea. She favoured their sending the child back to her parents. Joda succumbed to her wish and the girl's parents were invited to come and take their child. It was Ari's parents who now threatened to kill her unless she divulged who was responsible for her condition. Ari said "It was daddy's." Her daddy in question was Joda himself. Joda was speechless. Nora was dumbfounded and could not believe what she was hearing. Her mind raced to the traumatic experience of her own mother.

Her mother had told them why she was forced by circumstances beyond her control to marry two men in her life. Her first husband who she had loved and trusted was a demented man.

Kodie was Nora's mother. She told her children the following story. "I was about nineteen years old when my husband met me. I had not known any man by then and I had no boyfriend. I was sent on an errand by my mother. I was returning home from the errand when this young man saw me a few meters from our house. He smiled when he saw me but I did not reciprocate. All of a sudden he ran into one of the houses along our street. He came out with another young man from that house. I did not think anything wrong when I saw them looking at me. I took it that; maybe, they were admiring my person. After all, most young men will always admire women who appeal to them. I entered our house. I was however surprised when a few days later, that same young man came to our house with an elderly man who was introduced as his uncle. The surprise turned into a shock when my father informed me after they had left that the young man had come to seek my hand in marriage. I did not hesitate in telling my father that I was not interested. But the man's uncle happened to be a close friend of my father. They mounted pressure on my family which eventually led to my first marriage. Even though the man was a stranger, I had agreed to marry him because of his family. I did not envisage that the man was a beast who would never do without anything in a skirt.

Our marriage was like honey initially. The man showed me maximum love which culminated in the birth of my first child. The baby was a girl. Things went sour when my younger sister came to live with us. She too was a very young girl who had just finished her high school. She was living with us pending the time she would secure admission to attend the University. She could also start work whichever came first but ultimately go to school. Unknown to me my beloved husband was making amorous overtures to my own blood sister. My sister never reported this incident to me. She was afraid that if she told me, my marriage would be wrecked.

She kept it to herself but eventually succumbed to the pressure of my husband. According to my sister, they used to make love whenever I was away, and at times, when I was at home. My husband would sneak out of our bed later in the night under the pretext that he was going for a pee. He would tiptoe into the room where my sister was. He would have her. After sleeping with my sister, he would have nothing to do with me. We used to stay for several weeks without having sexual relations. I used to wonder how he was coping that long without a woman. I was suspecting he kept women outside. I did not, in my wildest imagination, think that the woman outside was my sister.

The cat was out of the bag when my sister became pregnant. She even refused to tell who impregnated her. It was our parents who extracted the truth from her. She told our parents that the father of her forthcoming baby was my own husband. I could not bear the shame. I did not consider it necessary to continue with the marriage. I therefore left. I left my first child behind because according to our culture the child belonged to the man since we were fully married. My sister wanted to terminate the pregnancy. She was advised against taking such a step since she would put her life on the line. She kept the pregnancy. However, nemesis was to play a cruel one on my sister. She died while delivering the child, who also died in the process.

After my experience, I made up my mind not to have anything to do with men again. I never allowed any man to get close to me. I went back to school, and inspite of my misgivings, I believe fervently that marriages are made in heaven. When my present husband who is your father made the first moves, I rebuffed him and even insulted him. The day I gave in to him, eventually, I was cursing both himself and myself. But as you can see, all men are not the same. There are still men with consciences. Your father is a very good man and I pray that all of you will get spouses that will give you a peaceful marriage. Look before you leap, do not allow any man to touch you any how."

That was how Kodie married her second husband who is the father of Nora and her other siblings. She had urged her children not to allow the same fate to befall them. This was not to be for Nora. She had been muttering "Why me, why me," since Ari spilled the milk. She had thought to herself that her life was finished. She would never live to bear this shame. It was no wonder that Nora took an overdose of pills. She was rushed to the hospital where the doctors confirmed her dead. The parents of Ari insisted that Joda must marry her. They did not want the shame either. The two children of Nora were evacuated from the house. They were taken to Nora's parents in the countryside. Joda and Ari were joined as husband and wife. Nora was mourned by her friends and neighbours. Some believed that she was wrong to have taken her life. Others believed that she had no choice and had acted rightly. Whatever was anybody's opinion, life belongs to God. We should therefore not resort to self-liquidation.

Chapter Five

Joda's business was growing in stature. He had diverse interests in import and export real estate, contracts and supplies. He was however very secretive about his conduct of business. Most of his wealth seemed to have come to him like a windfall. Nobody knew how he got his money to expand his business as rapidly as he was doing. People who knew the intricacies of business thought it was impossible to generate within a short time, the necessary working capital needed for the type of investments Joda was making. Bank loans were not easily come by. This was because of the stringent rules and collateral - required by the banks before they could give out loans. Joda was not the type they saw capable of getting loans. He was from a poor home and therefore had no inheritance. His success was a subject of gossip by everybody. A business associate had died in mysterious circumstances but nobody took notice of it or even thought Joda was connected to it. He was a dashing young man who was determined to make a mark.

The story nobody had verified was that the dead associate was a land speculator. He was responsible for connecting Joda to landowners. He had signed an agreement for some plots of land at the time Joda was developing his real estate. Joda later discovered in the deeds some clauses he thought were unfavourable to him. He did not bother to ask his colleague for renegotiation. He approached him quite alright, but asked him to bring his contract documents. His associate obliged. Joda took the agreement and squeezed and put it in his mouth. His associate was gasping breathlessly as he chewed the documents. Joda never said anything. He chewed and swallowed the entire agreement. Curiously the agreement he purported to have brought was a fake one which he abandoned on the man's table. After he had chewed and swallowed the agreement he sauntered outside and went off in his car. His associate did not know what to make of the whole episode. He was however prepared to guard his interest in the land. He approached his lawyer who advised him to fence the land and ensure that Joda was never allowed to build on it. The associate hired thugs to guard the land. It was therefore amazing how one day the associate came on routine inspection of the land. He saw a human skull which he thought was unsightly. He took his shovel. In an attempt to remove it he collapsed and died. After his death, the only documents available for the ownership of the land were the ones Joda produced. He assumed ownership and built some of his houses on the land.

Joda's new-found wealth was being envied by his colleagues who started business at the same time with him but had not made it. People were therefore relieved when one day the local newspaper splashed on its front page - "A notable business Tycoon nabbed for armed robbery, Joda in the net."

The newspaper reported extensively how Joda and his gang used to wear masks and ambushed motorists who they robbed of their money, goods and other valuables. Luck ran out for them when they laid ambush in a lonely expressway for a truck. The truck was carrying troops who were going for military exercises. They were well armed. There was a shoot out. The soldiers had an upper hand. Several of Joda's men were killed, some including Joda escaped while others were captured. It was during the course of interrogation of the captured men by the police that it was revealed that the leader of the gang was Joda. Police investigation further revealed that this gang had been responsible for the various robberies that had been going on in the highway. People were not surprised to hear that Joda was involved. They had been doubting the source of his wealth which they considered out of this world.

They were, however, shocked to learn that Joda was released. He was not released on bail but discharged from police custody because there was no evidence to link him to the robbery. This was not the first time this had happened. His gang had been caught several times before, but each time they were arraigned before the court, Joda would buy over a poor and unknown member of his organisation to stand trial for him. The poor man would be given a large quantity of money that would remove him from the poverty line forever. All he needed to do was to agree that he and not Joda was the gang boss. He would be jailed for about five years. Thereafter he would come out to enjoy his money. He would be supported during the trial by Joda who would use his wealth and influence to make sure that he got minimum jail terms. Joda had succeeded this way in the past because he had not actually been mentioned personally. But the suspicion was always there. The setting this time around was different. He was mentioned. And he had gone to the police cell. However, there was always Judas in every organisation. A corrupt police officer was bought over by Joda. The officer had agreed to allow Joda to swap another man as the culprit. Joda had been released for mistaken identity. This was how he was let off the hook to the consternation of the public.

Joda had however been disgraced even though, he did not go to jail. His disgrace did not deter him. He had become a hardened criminal. He had vowed to pursue wealth to the last breath of his life. His circumstances of birth and the deprivation he suffered during his childhood, and adolescent years, and the loss of his first wife because of poverty had combined to make him pursue wealth relentlessly. No matter what people might say about him and his wealth, he believes that the end justified the means. What matters was abundant money and not how you got it. This philosophy was regrettably sanctioned by Joda's society where people were not judged by how they came about their wealth. The more money you had the more you were adored and respected. Joda did not see himself to be different from the rest. He wanted to be rich first and make restitution later. People who were against him were those who could not make it and did not know how to go about it. He knew people who had stolen millions only to use their ill-gotten wealth to buy political power. He did not believe in hypocrisy. He was never caught again but that did not mean he gave up armed robbery. Since the last bitter experience he had decided to be staying away from the robbery scene.

Joda's import business was also growing. He had sought joint venture with his foreign associates to construct a bridge across a well known river. The government had required tenders to show evidence of some technical expertise before they could be allowed to collect mobilization fees which runs into several millions. Joda had therefore asked his partners to send one of their experts to come for the formal meeting with government officials. An expert in the construction of bridges was sent. He was duly received by Joda at the airport. Thereafter the foreign expert was driven to the estate where Joda lived. He was given one of the guest houses where he would stay until he finished his assignment. The man had come with a large amount of money and was visiting a country in which foreign money was regarded as hard currency. This was due to its scarcity and value. It was badly sought after and the people who have it are regarded as special people. Their wealth in hard currency was seen by the society as a sign of status symbol. This foreign expert was not used to the country. He had come naturally with little knowledge about the country he was visiting. The night he arrived Joda threw a lavish party for him. He invited guests including officials from the embassy of his guest who stayed with them during the party. The foreigner did not know the character of his host. He had not met him before. He was merely serving the interest of his home company which had sent him to this country. His host was well regarded in his company back home. He had no cause therefore to fear this man.

During a private discussion with his host, he had brought out his briefcase which he opened before him. He had taken some documents which he used to expatiate on a topic under discussion. His host had seen wads of hard currency neatly packed in his briefcase. They were brand new and occupied more than half of the box. Joda's heart went up when he saw the money. He had surmised that the money was up to a million dollars. He was right. The visitor did not want to take chances in a foreign land. More so when he was visiting it for the first time. He had collected the money so that he could take adequate care of himself in case his host failed to deliver. Joda's mind had thought of so many things when he saw the money. He wanted by all means to relieve his guest of the money. He would do it by all means even if that would mean the loss of the contract to build the bridge or even if that would lead to the death of his guest. He knew how he would convince his foreign partners of what happened. He even thought of killing the man himself and dumping his body on the highway. All this crossed his mind while his guest was busy doing all the talking which Joda was no longer listening to. He would occasionally make, "em, yes" to make his guest believe that he was listening and understanding what he was saying. They had glasses of wine on the table. Joda was gulping and pouring more into his glass while his guest was taking very little. At a stage, during their discussion, the foreigner suspected that Joda was not listening. He might have drank himself into a stupor. He felt Joda was not following what he was saying. He glanced over his shoulder and eyed Joda. Their eyes met. He noticed that Joda's eyes were red and heavy. He muttered, "Oh, you're sleeping."

Joda retorted, "Oh no, go on." The foreigner said, "OK." He gave Joda a paper to read. Joda took it and browsed through it.

He could not actually read because of the drink he had been taking. He pretended he had read it and gave it back to the expert. The foreigner cut off the talk. They decided to retire for the evening. They had agreed that later in the morning, the next day both of them would drive to the secretariat where they hoped to discuss with the government officials. This was not to be. The expert had gone to his room. He was staying late into the night to study more of his documents.

All this time, Joda had kept a close watch of his room. He continued to observe the room until the lights went off. Joda then went to his own room. He dressed in a long flowing dark robe. He put on his masks and took his gun. His estate was fenced round with dwarf walls. There was a gate and Joda had employed some security men. They stayed mainly at the gate but patrolled around the estate during the night. Joda did not want to walk straight to the foreigner's house. He went out through the back door and then tried to scale the walls into the back of the house which the foreigner occupied. He had misjudged the security men. These men were very observant. One of them was hiding somewhere oblivious of their master's intentions. While he was snuffing his tobacco, he saw a silhouette of a man climbing the wall. He quickly dropped his snuff bottle. He moved closer. He took aim with his gun. He had seen the figure clearly but could not see his face since he wore a mask. A shot rang out. Immediately the other security men heard the shot they ran towards that direction. They were there in time to see their colleague cocking his gun again for another shot. The man climbing the wall had clutched his chest before falling to the other side of the fence. They all rushed through the gate. They met him. They ripped open his mask with a pocket knife. They were stunned at what they were seeing. They saw it was Joda. He was already dead. They continued looking at themselves and at the lifeless body of their master lying before them. One of them sneaked out and started to knock up residents of the estate. They started trooping out in large numbers to behold what had happened. Some even got up on their own. They were roused by the noise. Those who saw it never knew what to make out of it. The foreigner never knew what happened and he did not come out during the night. He had slept very late. If it were not for fate that had decreed events to happen, this way, he would have been the victim while Joda would have carted his millions. It was not yet his time to die.

A small crowd had gathered in the morning. They formed themselves into small groups and were discussing in low tones the events of the previous night. The security man that fired the shot was unconcerned. He was not ready to discuss with anybody. He went back to his residence across the road. His wife sheltered him from anxious intruders. Some of the other security men who remained at the scene were recalling and narrating their experiences to the people. They had, all the while, been under the illusion that their master was above board. They were mistaken. They could now make certain deductions about the life style of their master. They said they could remember an incident in which two police patrol vehicles stopped at their gate one day. They were in exasperated mood and were prepared to shoot any of them. The police told how they have been pursuing another car which had been used as a getaway car after a robbery. The car had disappeared around their estate. They were sure that the vehicle entered through their gate. The security men denied any knowledge of any car entering their estate about that time. The only car that passed about thirty minutes ago was their master's car. It was unthinkable that the police officers could be referring to their master's car. The policemen insisted on their demand about the car. They even described the car and its colour but the guards could not understand what they were saying. When the police realized that they were not getting the desired co-operation from the security men, they left with threats to blacklist that estate. Joda was thus saved by the obstinacy of the guards. The fact is that unknown to the security guards, Joda had many cars. He frequently changed into other cars. There were some of his cars that were not known to the guards. He never brought some of his cars home. He had not used any of the cars with which he was well known to commit robbery. He had not also attempted to bring any of the cars he used in robbery to his home. The incident that happened last night had given deep insight about the man called Joda. They would resign en-mass. Some tenants in the estate also opted to pack and move out from there. They would not like to be associated with this man again.

Quiosi, the foreign visitor went to sleep very late. The effect of this and the drinks he took was showing on him. They weighed him down. By early morning when people were preparing to go to work, he was still in bed. He had been sleeping very deeply and calmly when the telephone buzzed. At first, he did not hear it. The phone continued to ring. Quiosi thought he heard the phone. He turned on his bed and believed it was a dream. He continued with his sleep. He was about to enter into another deep slumber when the persistent ringing of the phone jerked him awake. He opened his eyes. The phone was still ringing. He muttered to himself, "Who might this be that is calling so early." He seemed to have remembered "It must be the boss," as he called Joda. "Maybe he wanted us to finish up our discussion of last night which was interrupted by sleep." He picked up the receiver and said "This is Quiosi, can I help you?" The voice at the other end identified himself as the commercial attache at the embassy. Quiosi was surprised and wondered why the commercial attache would be calling so early. They met at the party the previous night.

The attache did not want to waste any time. He told Quiosi. "I want you to get ready immediately and report at the embassy. The Ambassador would like to have a word with you. A vehicle is on its way to collect you. You should come with all your belongings.

Do not get in touch with your host. Just get ready." He did not give Quiosi chance to say anything before hanging up. Quiosi knew from the tone of the attache that he had no time to waste. Immediately he dropped the receiver he dashed to the shower. He acted in such a lightning manner as if the inaudible voice of the attache was urging him on. It was. While he was getting ready he was hearing his voice saying get ready and report at the embassy immediately." Quiosi got ready and waited for about ten minutes before the vehicle from the embassy arrived. When the door bell rang he rushed to open the door. It was the chauffeur from the embassy. They exchanged greetings. He collected his briefcase and followed him to the vehicle. When he came out, before he boarded the vehicle, Quiosi saw a large crowd in the estate. They gathered in small groups and were talking among themselves. He was a stranger and could not make any meaning of what was happening. He did not ask the driver since he believed the driver was not in a position to know. Both of them entered the vehicle and drove off.

They did not talk to each other until they got to the embassy. They arrived about fifty minutes later. The slight delay was caused by a traffic hold-up just before they entered the major highway. The attache and the other staff of the embassy had been waiting anxiously. They were relieved when the vehicle pulled up. He stretched out his hand and greeted Quiosi and offered him a seat.

The ambassador, a stately built man was a seasoned diplomat. He did not want to do, or, say anything that would make Quiosi nervous. He knew that he had already been kept in suspense. He was therefore looking for a way to break the news to him so that he would absorb it. He talked about Quiosi's mission to the country and discussed business generally. He talked about business failures and lost revenues. Quiosi did not understand exactly why the ambassador should invite him to meet him only to start talking about businesses. He was a businessman and had no time for diplomatic niceties. He felt that the ambassador was wasting his time. He should get straight to the point so that he could go back and meet with his host. The ambassador noticed his anxiety and restlessness and then hit the nail on the head. "My friend," he began "Your business trip to this country is botched. Joda was shot and killed while he was about to kill and rob you last night. You should consider yourself lucky to have escaped from the jaws of death." As he talked, Quiosi was gasping for breath. He was staring at the ambassador and found the story incredible. Joda was highly regarded in his home company and since he arrived he had been overwhelmed by the man's hospitality. He did not know what to say. He asked for a cup of coffee. This was given to him.

As he was taking his coffee the ambassador told him that arrangements were being made to take him to the neighbouring country from where he would take a connecting flight back to their country. A feedback was soon received from his counterpart in the neighbouring country. Arrangement was concluded and agreement reached on the phone.

Quiosi who had been shaken by what happened was given a room at the embassy. He would stay there till the following morning when he would depart. Two security men were assigned to guard him. Quiosi stayed the longest day of his life at the embassy until the next morning. He was driven to the airport in an embassy vehicle from where he left to the neighbouring country.

Chapter Six

It was while in the civil service that Joda learnt about the society in which he lived. He was in his early twenties when he finished from the University. He had been working there with a high school certificate. He was employed as a junior officer and therefore did not know much about what was going on. He obtained a university degree and was upgraded to a senior officer. His eyes were opened to the rot in the service, when he was working there. After graduation he had hoped he would work hard to contribute towards the development of the society. His lecturers at the university had always emphasized the need for people to contribute something to society before they died. This was well implanted in Joda. His humble upbringing had made him a disciplined man.

Rather than realise his dream he was frustrated by the level of corruption in the service. He learnt the hard way that vice can be extolled and rewarded, while virtue and honesty can be condemned and even punished. He remembered vividly an incident of a man who was his immediate boss in the office. Both of them had worked in various departments. While working in the stores, he had watched in utter disbelief how his boss brazenly allowed suppliers to bring in materials and remove the same items after they had been recorded as received. Production was low because the inventory level was not being maintained. At the same time the company was spending enormously on purchases. Nobody was questioning what was going wrong. The management was busy blaming the prevailing glut in the economy. He had many cars of different types and his lifestyle was out of tune with his earnings. He had solid arrangement with the suppliers whereby a greater percentage share of the scum was reserved for him. He in turn had a godfather who he made returns to. This godfather threw his weight behind Joda's boss while the company was dying piecemeal.

Joda and his boss also worked in the accounting office. While there Joda saw how his boss was charging suppliers a percentage of their bills before they could be paid. Any supplier who failed to pay was sure that his bill would never be paid. A supplier must pay in cash in advance if he ever hoped to get his money. Joda knew of one supplier who committed suicide because he could not get paid. He had borrowed money from the bank to finance the order. He had hoped that he would be paid in good time to enable him offset the bank loan and the attached interest. He also hoped to make a handsome profit. His money was tied up because he could not produce the extra cash required by Joda's boss. In the end the accumulated interest had quadrupled and he was owing the bank more than double what he originally borrowed. The bank was after his neck. They had obtained a court injunction to declare the man bankrupt. His assets were seized and a liquidator had been asked to sell off the properties and recover the bank loan and interest. The man found it difficult to feed both himself and family. He sought refuge from his enormous problems by taking his own life. It was heart rending for Joda that his boss who he regarded as both a murderer and a rogue was promoted. Inspite of all these sad experiences, Joda was never influenced to become a criminal. He never had any regard for his boss. He resolved that he would never commit any criminal act just because he wanted to get rich.

However, things were to turn out differently for Joda. He had been seconded to government owned Company as a Branch Manager. He was to relieve the incumbent who had proceeded on course overseas.

In this new office they would collect cash from customers. They would keep this cash in an office safe until it was paid into the bank the next morning. Joda knew the danger of keeping cash in the office. He had come here to make a name and show that not all men are bad. Within this his new office there were some bad people. They had conspired to take advantage of Joda's newness to the office to steal the money collected the very first day he reported for work. Coincidentally that very day close to a million was collected. The normal procedure was that the receiving cashiers would hand over cash collected to the manager at the close of work each day. It was the Manager who would keep the money in the safe from where the bank officers would sign and collect them the next morning. The Manager would keep the key. Joda, though, satisfied with the arrangement nonetheless, decided to work late that day. He waited in the office after receiving the money until every worker in the establishment had gone home. He then went to the safe where the money was kept and carefully removed all the money. He took the money to a cabinet in a different room. He securely locked the cabinet and took the key home. At about 3.00am in the morning, some of the bad boys in his office struck in the office. They wore masks and knew their way around. They tied the security guards and went straight to the Manager's office. They had brought strong instruments sufficient to break open the safe. They succeeded in blasting open the safe but to their chagrin they could not find any money. They were terrible disappointed. They ransacked everywhere in the Manager's office for the key but could not find it. They left without the money.

In the morning, the staff reported for duty as usual only to discover what had happened. They were stunned. The Manager came about an hour late. People were already discussing and pointing an accusing finger on him. When he arrived and discovered what happened, he took it calmly. He invited the police. The police did their normal investigation. He then told them what he did. He had suspected this type of thing and had removed the money to some other place. A report was sent to the head office. His honesty was duly acknowledged in a letter of commendation signed by the Managing Director. Beyond that, however, nothing was done to promote him. Rather during the evaluation exercise, others were promoted because they had godfathers. He was not promoted. This experience also proved yet another turning point in his life.

"The society is rotten," he used to say to himself. "Does it mean that people at the top do blind Management," he thought. However these and other vices that plagued the service and were condoned and abetted helped to make Joda develop a heart of steel. He believed that he alone could not reform the society. The only option was to grab wealth in what ever way he could. That was the only way the society could recognise and reward him. He hoped that after he had acquired enough wealth he would go into politics just like his contemporaries. He would make his mark there and have a shot at the presidency. If he succeeded in his new line of thought it would be better to start reforming the society right from the top. But this was not to be, as the cumulative effects of his negative life led to his death before he could achieve his aim.

After Joda's death his relations wanted to conceal what happened. They even wanted to hide the fact that he died. They took him to a private morgue. They wanted the world to believe that it was another man that died. That Joda was very much alive and healthy. He took some days off to have a rest in his private resort home. He would not want much public attention. They bought over a local but a popular newspaper to fake an interview with Joda ostensibly from his hideout. This was all lies designed to becloud the public. The supposed interview was published as requested by Joda's family. People were enraged that their favourite newspaper could give in to that type of pressure because of money.

They called it blood money. From then on people started to boycott the paper. The paper was losing sales and was on the brink of finally fold-up. The Management was alarmed. They recalled their recent closure for nearly a year. The newspaper had in the past published articles and editorials critical of the government. The government had issued several warnings to the Management of the paper to change. The paper refused to heed the advice of the government because those articles were what made it popular. It was a very popular paper with mass circulation. People loved bold newspapers and business was booming. The government sent armed men to guard their premisses to enforce the decision. Their machines were filled with rust while the best of their workers were seeking for employment elsewhere. It was therefore unacceptable to the board that after that humiliating experience they should continue to lose sales. "This is a trivial matter," one of them said. The board decided to invite the editor and other top executives to appear before it. They had decided to relieve them of their duty because they had not acted in the best interest of the Company which was what was expected of them. When the executives of the paper appeared before the board, the Chairman recited 'The reviewed Company policy' after the closure. He followed it up by telling them that their services were no longer required. The aim of establishing any business is to make profit and not to engage in acrimony and greed.

The effect of the firing of the top executives of the newspaper was to show the next day. A young school graduate was promoted; and given the mandate to resuscitate the paper. It was therefore not surprising that the paper carried in its front page the next day the death of Joda. It had photographs of where he fell to the ground with mask and also when the mask was removed from his face. This was to the embarrassment of the family of Joda. However, the public was jubilant at the change of heart by the paper. The sales that day outstripped the expectation of the newspaper's management and the demand was still coming. The newspaper had bounced back to life.

Sales had returned to normal and the workers were coming back to the establishment.

The family of Joda had little, or, no time to arrange to bury him. They now made a formal announcement about his death. "He died quietly in his sleep," they said. They knew that this was not true. They further went on to say that he had lived a good life and the role he played on earth will be difficult to be filled. Indeed! This accorded with Joda's philosophy of finding money by all means. He had done it in the belief that the end justifies the means in this corrupt and accursed society. His relations are now echoing the same thing at his death.

A date was fixed for his burial. A church service was held for the repose of his soul. During the service the officiating pastor stated that he was sure Joda having lived a good life, would be received in the bosom of the Lord. Those who attended the Church seemed to have acquiesced to this hearsay by the pastor. The pastor had been given money. People established churches these days in order to make money. They do not care who brings the money. But whoever brought the money was a man of God who is thoughtful. He has donated money so that the work of God would be continued on earth. No matter how he acquired the money the good Lord was using him to further his cause on earth. This is why the corpse of Joda was blessed with holy water after he had been eulogized by the pastor. Many important dignitaries attended Joda's burial. Some streets and landmarks were eventually named after this man. His philosophy of the end justifies the means had also been fulfilled at his death. A sole administrator was appointed to administer his estate. He was a fiftyish old academic. He was expected to act in the best interest of the instrument that appointed him and to the benefit of the children of the dead man. He did not do either. He acted in his own interest in utter disregard for the law. The children of Joda were finding it hard to cope with the harsh economic climate. The administrator was taken to court and subsequently jailed. This was what one man termed a society being rotten from head to toe. Nothing was spared. Nobody was spared. It is corruption everywhere.

However, another administrator was appointed. He was a professional in the field. He resuscitated the fortunes of the estate and Joda's children were able to enjoy the proceeds from there.

Chapter Seven

Efo was Joda's first wife. She was from a wealthy family, and had been disenchanted at the idea of marrying Joda who was from a poor home. The disparity in their standards and style of upbringing led to the break up of the marriage. Eka was the product of that association. She was very small when her parents broke up that she did not realise what happened. She had moved from one foster parent to the other. She was living with Joda at the time of his death. Efo had hired assassins to kill Joda after their separation. She had been trying to do this because of jealousy. She failed in her several attempts but eventually decided to stay on her own. She did not care about him again. She was not aware of Joda's new found life which led to his death. Even though she had been at dagger's drawn with Joda, she was hurt by his death. She mourned Joda as if he was still her husband. She came on the day of the burial. She put on the traditional mourning dress. At the ceremony she was the cynosure of all eyes. People were always glancing and pointing towards her direction. She never cared. She knew she was there to mourn a man who had played a very important role in her life. Joda was the father of her first child. It was Joda who made her realize herself as a woman. No matter what was their problems in the past, all was gone now. The man is dead. Nobody speaks ill of the dead. The culture of her people also says that nobody should speak ill of the dead. The souls of the departed should be allowed to have their eternal rest. These were the thoughts that brought Efo to Joda's burial. She had reunited with her daughter who was also at the burial. Eka was seen by her mother as a permanent bridge that had linked her family and that of Joda. Her father had wanted her to be a knot that binds relationships together. That was why he gave her the name "Eka." Efo planned to take Eka back to her place after the ceremony. The burial ceremony was taking place in the city and not in their village which is the natural place Joda could have been buried. But he and the modern day youths had repudiated the way of life of their people in preference to the city life. They have been applying the customs of their ancestors with modification, in a way that will make their grandfathers chew their lips in regret.

It was after the burial ceremony that Efo and her relations approached the family of Joda for the release of Eka to her mother. They had pleaded that the child should be allowed to go with her mother now that her father was dead. They knew that by custom the child belonged to her father. That was not in dispute. They were concerned about the welfare of the child. It is only her mother who can give her the love that she needs. Joda's kinsmen did not oppose the idea of Eka going with her mother now that her father was dead. They, however, demanded that she should be brought to them from time to time so that she would know her people. An arrangement was then made as to when Eka was expected to come home to see her people. She was taken by her mother. She however did not take her directly to her house. She gave her to her childless uncle to bring up. Eka would continue her education in the uncle's house. Efo had taken Eka to her uncle's house because she was not fully married. She wanted the child to be away until she settled down. Then she would be able to bring her to live with her. It was not long after. Efo was introduced to a man. His name was Okin. He was a slim tall handsome man. He had just returned from overseas after staying about fifteen years. He had been working there after completing his university education. Okin had stayed overseas for so long that he had lost touch with home. He had been living like a stranger in his country. Everything did not appear normal to him and everybody behaved in a way that always elicited condemnation from him. He had become an odd fellow and had been thinking of going back abroad. This was the time he got introduced to Efo at a wedding of a friend. Okin was from a rich family. He was not thinking of any permanent relationship with Efo. He just wanted a fling and then dump her. But Efo saw everything in a different way. She saw Okin as a dream man. She had thanked God for giving her such a handsome, rich and educated man. They had started moving in together but had not yet planned for any marriage. Okin was not in a hurry to marry. He did not take his relationship with Efo seriously. Efo thought differently. She believed from the inception of the relationship that they would marry. She had been working towards it. She had told herself after the break-up with Joda that she was not desperate for a man. She promised to take her time before choosing the next man. This time around she had been swept off her feet by the emergence of Okin in her life.

Initially they regarded their love for one another as a private affair. Each kept it in his mind what his real intention was. With time their love started getting stronger. This was the wish of Efo. Okin was responding fully now. She was very submissive and ready to do anything Okin wanted in order to cement their relationship and get him to propose to her. It was while this was going on that Efo suddenly became pregnant.

She told her heart-throb, he accepted responsibility in good faith, and they decided to get married. Okin had proposed at last. They knew that they must hurry up for whatever they wanted to do. The first step was to inform their parents. It is customary that when a boy and girl are in love and are willing to marry, investigation is conducted about each other's family. That was how Efo and her man were told to wait for some time to enable the inquiry to be made about their families. Each family will conduct its own inquiry and will announce its decision its own way. In some cases, it is enough for a family to just say "I do not think the thing will be possible." This puts a final nail on the couple's ambition.

The inquiry on the intention of Efo and her man was fully conducted. It however revealed a stunning story. Both were blood related, they were in fact cousins, who did not know much about themselves. They were prohibited from marrying each other, and were devastated by the news. Confused, they doubted the inquiry and thought they were being deceived. They however made up their minds to marry. The result of the inquiry would not deter them. They were in love.

They believed that what mattered most was that they were in love with each other. They hoped to give their people enough time to rethink. For now, however, they would abort the pregnancy until their people agreed to their wish. They were convinced that their people would agree eventually. During their years of growing up they had learned that a hot soup must be licked gradually. They were however mistaken and their decision to abort the pregnancy was fatal to their hopes. Their people adhered strictly to their customs. They had offered prayers to their gods and ancestors not to allow the pregnancy to stand. Once the pregnancy stood and a child was born, it means that a blow has been struck to their custom. The child would have no future as everybody would do all that was possible to do away with the child. Their pride would be wounded. It would even be impossible to argue against the relationship because a child was regarded as the foundation of any marriage. Once a child is involved it is difficult for a man not to treat the mother of his child as his wife. His relations too will find it difficult not to honour the man's wish, and respect his wife. A child therefore is the taproot of any marriage.

When Okin and Efo aborted the pregnancy they had killed their hope of getting married without realizing it. They had put themselves out of reckoning as husband and wife. Their people heaved a sigh of relief and believed that the relationship would crumble by itself once a child was not involved. They did not care much again if the two lived together as long as they did not produce children.

They believed that one day the two "sinners" would get tired of waiting. Then they would pack it up.

The couple lived together for so many years hoping things would change. It did not change. They started living in seclusion because society did not approve of what they were doing. They were waiting for their people to get tired and approve their relationship while their people were waiting for them to get tired and pack up the relationship. It was their people who would occasionally get worried. They would send emissaries from time to time to persuade them to do away with their association because it was an abomination for them to continue to cohabit. Their parents were also worrying them to terminate the relationship and find new spouses. They remained adamant and continued to live together in defiance of their people.

When Okin and Efo noticed that their people would not yield any ground in their desire to get married, they decided to travel abroad and live, and, then get married where they will be far removed from the searching eyes of their people. They decided to travel in a manner that would make it impossible for people to suspect there intentions. Okin would travel first and would not let anybody except his wife know where he had travelled to. He would later invite Efo to join him. Their plans and intentions were kept close to their chest. They believed it would work.

Immediately Okin travelled the parents of both parties rejoiced. They believed that such a separation was vital for a rethink for each of the couple. They were wrong in their assumption. Okin had been away overseas for nearly a year. He had been communicating with Efo. He was still very much interested in the relationship because he loved Efo. He had been assuring her in all his letters that time was not yet ripe for her to come over. He would surely tell her when the time comes.

The invitation finally came. Efo packed her belongings and went to join Okin. They continued to live together. This time nobody was disturbing them because they never let anybody know their whereabouts. The people at home did not know which overseas country they went to. They refused to communicate with anybody at home. They were living in a world of their own. They eventually got married over there. They however refused to make babies. They knew that they had formidable opposition at home. And they knew that one day they would return to their homes. They had only married in order to meet up with some immigration requirements. Okin had full residence permit but Efo did not have that. She had only come on a visitor's visa. They have renewed the visa several times. In order to avoid further harassment from the immigration officials they decided to get married. That was their ultimate hope. They believed that their long sojourn abroad would soften the heart of their people. They would start making babies whenever they returned home and have secured full consent of their people. For now any babies they make would be social outcast and misfit. They wanted to avoid that.

They had hoped that their years abroad would douse tension generated by their relationship. It never did. They stayed abroad for nearly ten years before coming back. They knew they would face their people's wrath when they came. But they believed that would be for some time. They came back and continued to live together in what their people considered a taboo! They were neither deterred nor daunted. They still believed time would vindicate them.

It was obvious that their continued recalcitrance would spell doom for both of them. Their people's view on the issue was final. This led Okin to give up. He vowed not to continue to wait for time. He told his mistress that the time had come for them to bow to the wishes of their people. He loved her but there was nothing he could do to marry her. He knew that his people believed strongly in their way of life which they regarded as being superior to any imported idea.

He resigned his appointment and moved out of the house where he had been living with Efo. He went to another town to live, found himself a new job and was working there. It was in this new town that he met Ela. They fell in love and got married. Efo wished Okin all the best when he was leaving. She even attended his wedding. Okin had many issues now and Efo used to visit them regularly. The thought of Okin did not leave Efo for a very long time. She had found in him the important attributes she needed in her man. They both came from the same social background but there was nothing she could do now. They had to bow to the wishes of their people.

She would be living alone but the search must continue. Searching for a husband is a lifetime preoccupation for a woman. Any woman that is not attached to a man has less respect. If she needed respect she must have a man, she will bear his name. This will distinguish her from unmarried ones who fall easy prey for men. She would not want to be seen by men as a chaseable commodity. Even though, Efo was searching for a man, but she was not desperate for it. She did not want to go out of her way to get a man. She believed that for every woman, there was a man. She would wait for the opportunity.

The opportunity came at last. It was a middle-aged man. The man who had been married, had a serious misunderstanding with his wife, and they separated. They did not have any children. It was stated that after they separated, they tried every possible means to effect a settlement but the woman's wayward life which contrasted with the man's gentle Christian life, made settlement impossible. The man's search for a new wife, took a memorable turn the day he met Efo. It was a chance meeting. Both of them worked in the same company. They had gone to the staff canteen for lunch, and had coincidentally sat together at the same table. A conversation developed between them and the man learnt more intimate things about Efo, who he had been seeing from a distance, previously. He was surprised at the way she expressed loneliness, because they had thought her to be a married woman. She had been commanding respect the way, only married women did, but one quality that distinguished her from other married women was her manners and the dignified way she carried herself, and her colleagues used to gossip among themselves that she must have come from a rich family. However, wealth and manners do not guarantee escape from loneliness; but rather help isolate the rich from the rest, and make them yearn for the life of the common man. This was what was affecting Efo. She had no husband and was feeling lonely. There were a lot of men around, but pride would not let her condescend to pick a man.

Efo relaxed when she was discussing with the man at the canteen. She observed that the man was intelligent but maybe he had some problems. When they finished their meal, both of them walked shoulder to shoulder to the administrative offices. They talked on many issues but never discussed anything amorous. They however exchanged telephone numbers before going to their respective offices. They promised to call each other. It was Efo who called first. It was during lunch the next day. She wanted to go to the canteen with the man. The man accepted to go with her. They met in the reception lounge and walked together to the canteen. They discussed extensively. This became their regular habit. People had been noticing two of them going to the canteen together. Some did not read any sinister meaning to it. This was due to the fact that Efo was widely respected and known to be married. On the other hand her new companion was not well regarded and nobody thought it possible that such two extreme people would have anything in common. This is a wrong notion held by society.

All human beings are the same and no matter anybody's social standing people should interact with one another.

Money as they say is not everything. Efo is realising this fact. She is finding happiness in the company of a poor man. Ordinarily the man would also not have bothered how a rich woman spends her time. Their association was developing into a closer relationship. They were being seen going outside the company premises for their lunch. At the close of work Efo would pick up her man and drop him off at his house before going home. The man eventually proposed to Efo after they had carefully studied each other. Efo did not waste time in accepting the offer. She had surmised in her mind that the man's status was not important. She was getting old and the previous two attempts in getting a man of her own had failed. Wealth, the symbol of her pride was also not considered too important at this stage of her life. She had known more about the world and life. If she fully understood life at the time she got married the first time, the marriage could not have broken up. She was too young and wealthy, and these had swelled her head. She therefore believed that she lost her first marriage to youth.

This is not the time for recrimination but she had learnt her lesson of life. "This marriage will be the last. I am going to make it work," she told herself.

People were duly informed of the impending marriage between Efo and her new man. A lot of people expressed cynicism about it. "Will it work, will it work? Is it not Efo we know too well? Will she be able to stay with one man?" they continued to say. While people were having their say, Efo knew what she wanted. She had already blamed her youth for the loss of the first marriage. The second attempt was a mistake. She did not know that Okin was her cousin. That relationship was doomed to fail right from the start. As far as she was concerned this is only her second marriage. Okin's experiment was not a marriage. During the wedding, she participated and followed the ceremonies. This was unlike the first marriage which she did not quite follow because of her age. After their wedding Efo went back to her station. She was now a married woman. They were living a modest life inspite of her wealth and previous beliefs. Though the man was not from a wealthy family, he was well educated with a university degree. Efo was happy. She now had a company and was no longer feeling lonely.

It is now three years since they got married but had no issue. In their society the kernel of any marriage is a child. Any woman that fails to deliver a child is seen as having led a bad life before she got married. They have tried everything possible to see if Efo would get pregnant but have not succeeded. They have tried both the Orthodox medicine and spiritual churches but to no avail. Efo did not know what caused her latest problem. She was afraid that if she failed to get pregnant, she would lose her husband. This is a possibility she did not want to think about, because this will mean returning to her lonely days. Moreover, it would become news that she is not capable of bearing children. This will make prospective suitors stay away from her. She therefore was praying hard to her creator. She was now getting closer to God. She has developed a deep interest in spiritual matters. In her new held view, marriage and children are more important than wealth, and she prayed to God not to disappoint her.

In one instance she was told by the pastor of the spiritual church that her inability to get pregnant was witchcraft; and small devils. She needed thorough cleansing to wash away all that was troubling her. She should therefore get ready to follow the pastor and other anointed people to the river where all their sins would be washed away. Efo was ready to do anything provided she got pregnant. She therefore prepared herself as the pastor had directed. The cleansing and bathing would take place by 12.00 midnight. When Efo got to the place, she met a lot of members of the congregation.

She knew some of them. This gave her reassurance and removed fear from her. She trusted the pastor. They went to the river bank. The pastor and one of his assistants went to the middle of the river from where they were calling those that were to be bathed in small groups of two or three. When a person is called for his turn, he is expected to pull off all his clothes and enter the river in the nude. The pastor will then use a small open container to scoop water. The person being cleansed will bend her neck while the assisting pastor will press the centre of her skull with his palm.

Nobody is sure why this ceremony was being carried out at midnight. Some have speculated that the reason was that the holy scripts said so, others held the view that it was because it was being performed in the nude. The point remained that the church had been creating a scenic view for people living around the river. Unknown to the authorities of the church, the nearby residents had been converging around the bushes near the river and had been feasting their eyes on nude celebrities who perform this ceremony. Even though it is purported to be carried out at midnight when there is supposed to be darkness, street lights and other flood lights from a nearby airport had always shown the people clearly. Some laser lenses were used to take photographs of the nude people.

The day Efo was there to bathe and be cleansed was not different. Her photographs were taken while she was stark naked. Her nude photographs appeared in the local gossip newspaper the next working day. It showed her nude. She was standing before the pastor and his assistant with her head bowed. Some mischievous person delivered the newspaper on her husband's desk the following morning. He brought it and kept it on his table. He did not ask to be paid for the newspaper. He did not want to be identified either. When Efo's husband saw the newspaper, he was furious. He rushed to meet his wife. He had not been aware that his wife had been trying secretly to seek help so that she would be pregnant. The man had been assisting the wife to be treated by the orthodox medical doctor. But not this one. His wife had exposed herself to the whole world. The man was not happy and demanded full explanation from his wife. The wife was embarrassed. She did not understand how her nude picture got into the papers. She knew that she had offended her husband. She could not utter any word for a very long time while her husband was fuming. When she thought that her husband had cooled down, she knelt down and begged him for forgiveness. She explained that she needed help. The pastor and his congregation had assured her that bathing in the river would surely cleanse her of all her sins and enable her to get pregnant. She said that they had quoted the passages in the holy book where it is written that all ailments are rooted in sin and before they could effectively be cured, the sins must be washed away. They had also cited cases of those who have been helped this way. "They are no proud mothers." Her husband listened raptly. When his wife had finished her confession, he drew her close to himself and kissed her on the forehead. He went back to his office. He did not make any further fuss about it but continued to live a normal life with his wife. He knew how he would ward off curious inquirers. He however warned his wife not to do it again. His wife accepted and from that day she stopped going to that spiritual church.

Efo was still desirous in curing herself and getting pregnant. She was now going to the clinic to meet a specialist. It was on one of such visits that the doctor told her that she would never get pregnant in life again. Her Fallopian tube, which leads to the uterus had been blocked by an operation during an abortion. There was no way they could reopen it. Efo was shaken, she remembered what happened to her when she aborted the pregnancy of her cousin.

After the abortion was performed, she was bleeding profusely and was unconscious for about twenty-four hours. She was placed under intensive care before she was revived. It was that abortion that was now ruining her life.

Even though she believed what the doctor had told her, she

was not willing to give up. As a woman who is closer to God and knows his ways, she believed that a miracle can still happen. "To God, nothing is impossible. Those who have faith will surely experience the kingdom of God." She still remembers these quotes. They had formed part of her personal philosophy. That is why she had been praying hard. She called her husband one night and confided in him. She told him that, she would start to attend another spiritual church. She assured that this time around she would do everything possible to protect herself. Never again will she be found in the nude or partake in that type of ceremony. Her husband agreed and allowed her to resume at one of the nearby churches. He however warned her against acts that would bring disrepute to the family.

Shortly after, her husband was nominated to attend a three month course abroad. He got ready and left. His departure afforded Efo the opportunity to get closer to God. She was, at times, sleeping in the church premises. She wanted to free her mind from the material world. Other women with similar problems were also sleeping in the church premises. One night while sleeping in the podium on a very cold night, she felt somebody's hand on her body. She shouted and got up. "Who's that?" she said.

The pastor replied, "It's me. I have come to share the word of God with you." Efo relaxed when she heard the voice of the pastor. She felt confident that nothing would happen to her. She was blank about any ulterior intention the pastor might have. The pastor stayed very long discussing her problem. He started to make such visits every night, until one night, he told Efo that he saw a vision. He saw her with pregnancy and eventually a baby boy. The Lord had revealed to him what would make her pregnant but she must follow his instructions. She was anxious to hear more from the pastor and pressed for it. The pastor then threw the bombshell. "The Lord had revealed that you will get pregnant, my daughter, but you must submit yourself to the man of God. It is only he who can make you pregnant. Your husband is profane and you will never get pregnant through him." Efo like all other members of the church did not doubt their pastor. In fact, they trusted him more than they trusted themselves. She wanted to get pregnant by all means in order to secure her marriage. She told the pastor she was ready. The pastor ordered her to kneel down. She did, and the pastor prayed to the Lord to accept and grant the wishes of his daughter. Thereafter he told Efo to remove her clothes. She did. The pastor slept with her. He continued to sleep with her every time Efo came to sleep in the church premises.

Her senses came back to her when the month passed and she did not see any sign of pregnancy. Matters got worse when the pastor made another stunning revelation. He had told her that God had revealed to him that all her problems would be solved if she could leave her husband and come and live in the church for full church service. Efo was exceedingly annoyed. She had started to doubt the motive of the pastor. The pastor was sure of his own motive. He noticed that Efo would doubt his latest revelation. He then told her in an intimidating manner that he wanted to marry her. If she ever has hope of getting a child she should leave her husband before he came back from his training. Efo was not prepared for that. She told the pastor so. Efo reasoned that she must have got into wrong hands again. This pastor already had a wife. If he wanted more women, he could acquire them; why should he be hiding under the refuge of pastoral duties to destroy people's homes. Efo left the church and never went back there again. She stayed at home hoping that her husband would not hear this latest assault by the pastor.

It was while still hoping and waiting that she received the news of her husband's death. She was devastated. "What have I done, what have I done," she muttered. She did not understand what could have killed her husband. He was a very healthy man who rarely fell sick. She got ready and travelled with some members of her family to go and bring the corpse home. It was while overseas on this mission that she heard how her husband died. The story had it that it just started suddenly. A group of them had been on this course. The course was into its second month. They used to visit a lot of places of interest in the host country as a part of the training. They had gone on one such trip. They returned to their hostel late in the evening. As was their custom, once they came back from such trips, everybody would go into his room. Her husband had gone into his room. He brought out his bottle of apple juice. He poured some into the glass. He put on the television. He wanted to relax with his drink and watch a local film. He had just sipped the juice when he suddenly clutched his lower abdomen. Other colleagues were in their respective rooms and did not know what was happening. The rooms are such that it is not possible to hear what is happening in the next room. There were no telephones in the rooms. But there was a common telephone in the passage way. All the inmates used it when they had the need. It was while Efo's husband was thus crying for help that a colleague unknowingly entered his room. He had come to borrow one of his video cassettes. He met him in an almost unconscious position. He called out his name twice. He asked what was wrong. He received no response. He rushed out and went to the telephone. He called the ambulance. People from the Red Cross arrived within thirty minutes. They took him away and rushed him to the hospital where he was seen by a doctor immediately. He examined him and diagnosed his sickness as appendicitis. The doctors said that the appendix had burst. They also made it clear that, he had only a marginal chance of survival. A greater percentage of patients with ruptured appendicitis dies. He would be lucky if he survived. He was not lucky. The operation was carried out in the early hours of the morning. He died in the process. Arrangements were made and his corpse was brought home. He was accompanied on his last journey by Efo and her relations. He was mourned and buried later.

Chapter Eight

While Eka was living in her father's house after she was kidnapped by her father, her playmate was Ari. The age gap between the two kids was not much. They therefore were seeing themselves as equals. However, events took a different turn when Ari became pregnant by her father and suddenly became Eka's stepmother. It was difficult for Eka to call Ari "mother". Her father subsequently evacuated her and took her to a boarding school. After her father had died in a very disgraceful way, her mother came and took her to her uncle's house. The was where she continued her schooling.

In the new neighbourhood there lived a lanky tall man called Anode. He was handsome and charming. He was married to a foreigner. They had a child. Anode was a notorious sexual adventurer. He was well known to the foster parents of Eka. In fact he was a friend of the family who came and went as he liked. He was a shift worker in one of the reputable companies in town. He was thus off-duty some days and stayed home. During those off-duty days, he used to help neighbours bring their children from school. He was highly regarded for this kind gesture. This regard had made it possible for people to overlook his sexual escapades which had destabilized many homes.

Eka had just turned nine. She had not known anything about the world. She was attending school like other children of her age. After school, she would wait under a shade for her parents until they came and picked her up. On days that her parents failed to come she would join other neighbours in their vehicles. This had become routine for her. It was therefore not surprising that this cloudy day, Anode had pulled up and Eka jumped into his car. There were other children in the car too. They used to join Anode previously. Anode took them home. He had dropped all other children first. He had gone to Eka's house but the foster parents were not in. He decided to take her to his flat. He hoped the little girl would remain there until her parents were back. The cloud was getting darker over the roof. This was a sign that there would be a very heavy rain soon. It had started to drizzle in some parts of the city. It was, however, windy down Anode's residence and very cool. A thought had flashed in Anode's mind. It was about his wife. She was away in her country with their child and they were not expected back until next month. He had thought how they used to spend their cold days and nights. He wished his wife was around. She was however not around. Anode was still engrossed in the thought about his loneliness when a different thought crossed his mind. He went to Eka sitting down in the single cushion close by. He lifted her up and touched her cheeks. In the process of playing with the little girl he defiled her. Eka had enjoyed what Anode did to her. She wanted more. Anode did not want to go too far. He had done it playfully and because of the cold and the flood of memories of his wife. He realized that Eka was a playmate of his son, and had started to regret even attempting it. He wanted another way in which he could pet Eka and make her forget what he had done to her. He went into his pantry and brought out a box of cookies. He took a handful and gave them to Eka. She accepted them but did not eat them. She put them into her schoolbag. She was not ready to eat them yet. Her mind was set on the act Anode had done to her. She wanted more of it. It was sweeter than the cookies. She begged Anode that they should continue the act. Anode was not ready to do so. He however knew that he had added fuel into the fire. The conflagration would continue to burn in Eka. He did not know how to quench this fire, since he had not reckoned on the reaction he was getting from Eka. He was surprised and confused. He wished that her parents would just come back so that he would take her home.

While Eka was begging for more Anode was feeling guilty. In order to placate Eka, he carried her on his lap as he would his own child. He rubbed her hair and whispered into her ear that he would do it with her another day. His promise of doing it another day reassured Eka. She agreed and stopped begging. They stayed in Anode's house for a considerable length of time. The rain which started earlier had subsided. Anode opened the window. He looked in the direction of the house in which Eka lived. He noticed that there was movement in the house and one of the windows was open. He knew that Eka's foster parents were back. He asked her to come and go home. They went downstairs and he took her home. He had told her not to let anybody know what had happened if she knew that they would do it again. Eka agreed to all he said. When Anode brought Eka home he was warmly thanked by her parents for his kindness. He later left to go to his house. He was happy at his accomplishment but a nagging fear remained with him. "Will Eka actually tell somebody," he thought. In this area it would be regarded as an abomination to have sex with a nine year old girl. The point remains that this was not the first time Anode was undertaking such a dangerous venture.

He had two outstanding cases against him. One was the wife of his best friend. He had admired this woman before she got married to his friend. He had tried to befriend her then but later abandoned the idea when he saw that she was engaged to be married to his former classmate and friend. During their wedding he had participated in the ceremonies and played a very active role. Thereafter, he became very close to the family. Both the husband and wife trusted him to the extent that whenever they had any misunderstanding, the aggrieved party would normally invite him. They would accept whatever verdict he gave on the issue. This showed the depth of trust reposed in him. His good friend was a salesman who travelled a lot. Any time the friend travelled; his wife used to visit Anode and his family quite freely. It was on one such occasion when his friend travelled that Anode told his wife to come to his office. He had told her that he had something very important to tell her. His friend's wife had no reason to doubt, or, reject the invitation to come to the office. She went. When she came to the office Anode was already waiting. He told her that his office would not be conducive for what he wanted to tell her. He asked that they go to some place. The woman agreed. She had no reason not to.

Anode took her in his posh car and drove her to an hotel. He had reserved a room there. The woman was surprised at the type of place Anode had brought her just because he wanted to tell her something. Her thoughts, however, did not tell her that Anode would attempt to have an affair with her. She was waiting for the surprise Anode would give her. She obediently and effortlessly disembarked from the vehicle and followed Anode. He was a trusted friend of her family. He would not kill her. He would not sell her and he would not attempt to do anything to her. She regarded him as she regarded her husband and have been enjoying maximum protection from him. The type only her husband usually gave her. She therefore kept quiet as Anode collected the key of the room from the reception. They went upstairs and Anode opened the reserved room. Both of them entered. Anode locked the door and left the key in the door. They took their seats on the cushions.

It was at this time that Anode opened his eyes and told his friend's wife of his admiration for her. He told her to remember, that even before she got married, he had been making moves to her. The woman was dumbfounded. She did not believe what she was hearing. Anode continued with his sermon and pleaded with the woman to allow him to have her. When Anode finished talking, the woman told him she was prepared to oblige him but it should not be that day. She asked to be given some time to think it over because of the special relationship that exists between Anode and her family. She gave hope to Anode that ultimately he would have his way. She even quoted some verses in the Bible which says "Ask and it shall be given unto you, knock and the door would be opened for you." When Anode heard these words from her he was very sure that he would succeed. He decided not to press further. After all, he had asked and he had knocked. Anode called for drinks but the woman refused to drink. They thereafter left the hotel. Anode took the woman back to her house before he went back to his office. He was excited at the prospect of succeeding in having this woman. He had told himself several times that he could have married this woman if not because his close friend was faster that he was. He continued to pester the woman for a date. He was now promising to buy her any car of her choice if only she would allow him. He had considered it the greatest thing that would happen in his life if he could go to bed with the woman. Unknown to him, right from the first day, the woman had told her husband what happened. Her husband had doubted her and told her she should not tarnish the image of his intimate friend. He believed that women have a way of spoiling the friendship of their husbands if they do not like the other man.

The wife was not happy the way her husband was doubting what she told him. Anode had continued with his pestering, when an answer was not quick to come; since they visited the hotel. The wife eager to prove herself, and in order to persuade her husband to take some action, advised her husband to set up a trap if he doubted her. He agreed. They hatched an entrapment plan. The woman then went to Anode to give him an affirmative nod on his request. The day she came to Anode, she was very humorous and was in buoyant mood. The type Anode had not seen her in years. She entered Anode's office. He was alone. She called him "Darling". Anode's head got swollen on hearing the word. He knew instantly that the door had been opened for him. The woman then told Anode, "Everything is in your hands." Anode understood what she meant. Anode then said, "I hope it will be in your house, when is he travelling." The woman agreed it would be in her house and told Anode when her husband would travel. They both agreed to meet in the woman's matrimonial bed. This is in accordance with Anode's wish to have her right on that bed. The woman left Anode's office escorted briefly to the door by him. He did not want to be seen with the woman for now. He wished her goodbye. She got home and relayed everything that transpired between her and Anode to her husband. They laughed. The husband arranged to pay Anode a visit. It was a friendly visit he used to pay them whenever he was about to travel. He went to Anode's house. They talked as usual on different topics. None of them said anything about the visit of the man's wife to Anode. The man told Anode about his travel plans. Anode wished him a safe journey and promised he would take care of the home. The man smiled viciously in his heart "Take care indeed" his small inner voice told him.

Anode in keeping with his promise had given the woman a large sum of money. This was to enable her to prepare a special meal and buy the best wines for their date. The woman did as agreed. The woman's husband did not actually travel. He was hiding in one of the houses in the neighbourhood. He had been there for some days now. He had gone there in advance of the date between his wife and Anode. This was to remove any suspicions on whether he travelled or not. Anode could hire anybody in the neighbourhood to spy for him on whether the man travelled. It was to obviate this that the man took up residence in another man's house, while he kept a close watch on his own residence.

On the agreed day, Anode arrived as planned. He was bubbling with confidence. He was sure the coast was very clear. He did not reckon with dishonesty in human beings. He brought his car close to the residence of his friend and parked in front of the house. He was well known in the neighbourhood. Nobody suspected anything since he was well known. The woman was waiting and looking out of the window. She opened the door before Anode could ring the bell. Anode tried to kiss her on the lips but she turned her right cheek. Anode did not read anything sinister into this. He took it as normal. They entered the bedroom. That was where the woman had prepared for two of them. Both the meal and drinks were served. Anode had been drinking heavily. The woman did not drink at all. The drink had helped stimulate Anode. He was right in the mood when he blurted out amidst the drinks. "Today is a turning point in our lives. I will take you abroad. I will buy you a car of your choice. I will sack my stupid wife and I will marry you." The woman did not say anything but listened intently. After saying all those things, Anode started to remove his clothes. He asked the woman to do the same. She agreed. She removed all her clothes except her pants. Anode was totally naked. He was high with drinks and excitement. Both intoxicated him. While in that mood he stood up and raised his two hands to the ceiling and asked the woman to enter into his embrace, so that hugging thus, he would take her to the bed. It was at this juncture that the woman excused herself. She told Anode that she needed to visit the toilet before the action. She left the room. She went to the outer room. She gave out the sign she formulated with her husband. The signal was well taken. She went back to the bedroom. Anode was already lying down in his nakedness on the bed. The woman did not waste time in joining him. She laid her frame beside Anode. She still had her pants on. Anode did not mind her pants on for now. He was busy and voluptuously caressing her forehead and neck area. Just then the door jerked open. It was the woman's husband with four other neighbours. They ordered Anode to get up. He did. They told him to kneel down. He did. They were thus playing with him while he remained naked. They eventually sat him down on the floor and beat him mercilessly. His entire body was bruised. He was begging them to forgive him. He offered them monetary compensation, or, a car, or a house, whichever they chose. They would not however listen to him. They knew that they may accept some of these things. But they were not in a hurry to do that. They wanted to torture and disgrace him first before he would be asked to pay compensation.

Anode sat down like a man. He raised his two knees and was holding them with his two clasped hands. The effect of the wine he took had cleared from his eyes. He was regretting everything. He had attempted on a few occasions to catch the eyes of his intimate friend to see if he would sympathise with him. Today was not for that. He had committed a crime against his friend. As far as his friend was concerned, their friendship did not exist any longer.

It was then that the people sent a secret emissary to his wife. His wife was a private secretary in a large company. She was told that some people were looking for her. They were standing outside the building, they wouldn't go inside. She excused herself and went to meet them. She greeted the two, who she'd never met before, they looked quite respectful and greeted her back. "Are you the wife of Mr. Anode," they asked. "Yes," she said. "Your husband had a very serious accident, you must come with us and help take him to hospital." On hearing that, her mood changed... her eyes turned heavy... Her own words came back to her mind: "I have told him so many times to drive carefully but he would't listen. Look at it now, I am done."

She asked the men to wait for her. She said she would be back in a minute. She went inside and gave her boss the message. The boss was very sympathetic. He was a very understanding elderly man. Mrs Anode then asked to be excused from work for the rest of the day, and left with the men in their car. They brought her to a familiar place. It was the house of her husband's friend. "Oh, it was his friend who helped him and took him to his house," she thought. She was thanking her husband's friend in her heart for being a good friend. She did not know she was there for a different purpose. She saw her husband's car. It was neatly parked in front of the house. There was no damage done to it. Her thought wondered again "Which car did he have the accident in. Who drove it." She was to learn who drove the car soon. They rang the bell. The door was opened from inside. It was her husband's friend. She was about to greet him, before she stretched her neck and saw her husband on the floor. She burst into tears and was asking repeatedly "What happened, what happened." She rushed to her husband who could not utter a word. The other people in the room who had been holding her husband captive in the most despicable way were watching the drama with amusement. They were enjoying what they were beholding. It was the final humiliation of the sexual adventurer. His wife was wearing a skirt and blouse dress. Her thought told her she could have offered her husband a dress if she had anything extra. She thought of occasions she used to have even head scarf. Today is not that day. She wanted to drag her husband up and shield him from the view of other people. That was not to be. She was shouted down to "Leave that beast alone." The words came from her husband's intimate friend. What was happening was not only a shock, it was unbelievable.

They sat the woman down and told her every bit of what happened. She was still sobbing but listened to what they were saying. She was sorry for everything. Her husbands' infamy in sexual matters was no longer new. But never before had he been so much publicly disgraced. She was finding it difficult to bear. She broke down in tears. She however, realized that she needed a heart of steel to surmount the present problems. She subsequently stopped crying. She begged for forgiveness for her husband. Her pleas melted the heart of his captors. They had thought that the woman would have, there and then, disowned her husband. They were surprised that she wanted to take him home. They praised her courage and love for her husband. They decided to accord and treat the woman with respect. She deserved it. The husband was still sitting on the floor unable to say anything.

They thought within themselves that this must be a wonderful and special woman. Most women would not take it the way this woman was taking it. Their reason for inviting the woman to witness the humiliation of her husband was to disrupt Anode's home. They wanted the wife to take a final decision and quit the marriage. Their plan had failed. The woman was still begging to be allowed to take her husband home. She promised they would come back another time for eventual settlement. The woman was allowed to take her husband home. She was warned and given conditions for settlement. She agreed to all the terms for the release of her husband to her. She promised to come back. In order to intimidate her more and ensure that she brought the man back, she was shown the nude pictures of her husband. They were taken while he was posing in different ways. They were therefore warned against making up stories and denying what happened. They were told that if they attempted any denial the photographs would be handed over to the press. The woman drove her husband home. His clothes had been soaked in a bowl of water. He managed to put them on like that. They got home and the man changed his attire before he was taken to the clinic for a medical check-up.

This was a shameful story of Anode's past. He has not given up. His defilement of Eka had confirmed this. It had continued unbridled. Nobody suspected that he was having an affair with Eka. The little girl was enjoying what she was getting.

Chapter Nine

As the years went by she grew older. As she grew older the more she was enjoying the act. It was at 16, while in her final year in the primary school that their hideous game reached its climax. Anode had eloped with Eka. The schools were on long vacation. Anode was off duty on this bright day. They had stayed together as usual. Anode had suggested to Eka that if she would agree to follow him, he would rent an apartment for her. She would stay there so that he would be free from both his wife and the girls' parents. He promised to give her "That thing" in its sweetest form. The little girl agreed. They then planned what to do. Eka would ask her foster parents to allow her to visit a distant relation and spend some time with them. The holiday was too long and boring. Her foster parents agreed. They did not see anything wrong in her going to spend part of her holiday with a distant relation. They arranged for her to go. The girl would be able to travel on her own. She has reached the age to do that. It was Anode however who met her at an agreed spot and conveyed her to her destination. They both had agreed that she would visit the relation but would spend only two days. Anode would then collect her to go to the place he had rented. She was collected by Anode after two days after she had left her relation's place. She told her relation that she was going back to her foster parents.

They believed what she was saying.

After about seven days her relations visited her parents. He was asked about Eka. He told them that she left his house more than a week earlier. Everybody was surprised. "Where is she? they chorused. A search was mounted for Eka. The police were duly informed and they issued their bulletin declaring Eka a missing person. They requested anybody who knew her whereabouts to report to the nearest police station. All media houses were also informed. It was being carried on the news, on the radio every hour. The television was showing pictures of Eka intermittently. They said she had gone to visit a relation nearly a month ago and had not been seen. The newspapers also published the picture of the little girl. Eka had been seeing herself in the television being declared wanted. She was enjoying what she called a joke. Anode had also been showing her newspapers where her photographs were published in an effort to locate her.

Anode was a married man but he did not find it difficult to fake an alibi to his wife before disappearing mostly during the nights. He was known to be a shift worker and nobody would raise an eyebrow if he told them he was on duty. To consolidate his gain and to make sure that his plans were ahead of other groups, he hired a paid informant. This man was a very good friend of Eka's foster parents. He used to visit them often but stopped for some time now, when he lost his job. He had no job now and would do anything for money. Anode hired him to spy on Eka's parents so that he would pre-empt whatever plans they had for locating Eka. That was how this hired informant reappeared in her parents' house. He was welcomed as an old friend of the family. He told them that he heard what happened and had come to sympathise with them. From then on he was always in the house and even offered useful hints of what should be done. The people accepted some of his advice.

It was when confidence had been established between him and the child's parents that he suggested that they should sponsor him to go and look for the girl at her mother's place. He wanted to use this to extract the address of Eka's mother. Her mother was living with her new husband in a different town. The girl's parents reflected this suggestion because they knew that the girl's mother was hospitalized in another town. The little girl knew about it and could not have been visiting her mother. She did not even know where she lived. The rejection and revelation appeared to have botched the informant's plans. He reported back to Anode and Eka. Anode insisted that he should go back and mount more pressure. The girl could still travel to her mother's place to see other people. The informant went back as instructed. His intention to get the address of Eka's mother was for them to take the girl to her mother's place to make it look as if she went on her own. The pressure was mounting on them and they knew they would very soon be caught. Her mother being out of town would suit their purpose.

The informant had not succeeded on the first occasion in extracting the address. They were however not ready to give up since taking Eka and dumping her in her mother's place was their only hope of escaping from the arms of justice. The informant went back. He was ready to hide under the tension generated by Eka's disappearance. People had been coming to sympathise with the family. He had been there on several occasions. His presence was no longer in doubt. He is regarded as one of those who had shown great concern. He was regarded as a good friend of the family. Nobody thought him to be dubious. They were wrong. On this last visit he volunteered to go to Eka's mother's place himself if only they would give him the address. They did. They had come to the conclusion that it might be good after all to visit all places that might provide loopholes.

It was an innocent mistake to have given the man the address. It is all he cared for. He had not been coming to sympathise with them about the missing child. He knew where she was. He had been a paid informant and was discharging his duty. His assignment was to get the address. He had got it and the next thing was to go to the abductor and collect his fee. That night they hired a vehicle which took them to the town where Efo resides. She was away. They dumped Eka in her house. They went to a different area in the town where they slept till the next morning. In the morning they travelled back to their home. Eka was welcomed by the people in the house. From that day she continued to stay in the house waiting for her mother's return. The informant never showed up in Eka's grandfather's house again. He too, had disappeared, even though it was obvious to everybody that he was overstaying. They had expected him back two days earlier but nobody had seen him.

Meanwhile Efo had been discharged from the hospital. She went straight back to her place of residence without calling on her father or uncle. She was surprised at what she saw. She met Eka. She was aware that Eka was declared missing. "How did you come here Eka," she queried. Eka replied that she found her way to the place. This was all lies. She was regurgitating the lies she had been told to tell. Efo did not want to cause more anxiety to her people. The next day she took Eka back to her parents. Everybody was surprised. There was however jubilation that she was seen. Her mysterious disappearance had caused people sleepless nights.

A good game was played by Anode and his paid informant. They thought they had outsmarted everybody. But this was not to be. God had his own mysterious ways. Immediately the police learnt that Eka had been found, they came to her foster parents and took her away. They told them to leave the girl with them for a few days. They wanted to interrogate her and establish the basis and reasons for her action. They used different gadgets on the girl. They gave her gentle torture and applied lie detectors. After about three days of what to Eka; was hell, she confessed to what had happened. She told the story of how she had been having an amorous affair with her abductor at a very early age. The man had deflowered her. She had liked the act and continued to go to the man. The man suggested she run away from her home and come with him, where he would put her in his private house. The little girl had agreed because she was enjoying sex too much. When she was in her hide-out, she had seen herself in the television and heard her name on the radio as a missing person. She had wanted to come out but her abductor refused. She told of how the idea to take her to her mother's place was conceived by her abductors and the paid informant. She also disclosed that there were in fact four informants whose roles were to ensure that too much noise was not made about her disappearance. At the end of her story to the police she was taken back to her foster parents. A search was mounted for Anode and the paid informants who undertook the journey to her mother's place. They were apprehended after three months of a comprehensive search. On the day of their arrest, they were beaten mercilessly by the police and booed by the people. They could have been lynched by the mob but for the police protection. They were subsequently charged in court for kidnapping.

Chapter Ten

Anode's wife returned from her vacation abroad to hear this heart-rending story about her husband. She concluded that was the last. She would take it no more. She packed her things and left the house as a first step to leaving the country. She rented an apartment from where she continued with her work.

Anode's wife was an exemplary wife. She had lived for her husband alone while they were married. Things had started to change. She was thinking differently now. "Why should I give myself to a man who never cares about my feelings." She was thinking of the best way to pay Anode back, for all the injustices he had done to her. She did not know whether to go out and start picking men indiscriminately, so that her husband's jealousy would be roused by the stories he would be hearing, or, whether to just take on one man and stay quietly. She decided to do the latter first because it was more healthy to do so. After all, she had broken off her relationship with Anode and there was no going back. Not after all she had suffered in his house. It was not long after, she got a companion. He was an unmarried young executive. It was the man that rented the apartment where she was living. He also provided all furniture and household items in the house. They had not discussed marriage. The man was still living separately but was frequenting the house. He would stay there very late into the night every day before going back to his own place of residence.

Meanwhile Anode had been looking for a way to bring back his wife. He had been to the flat on several occasions to plead with his wife to come back but the woman was not ready to hear any such thing. Anode had found it very difficult to bear. He had been thinking of renting a house in the vicinity so that he would be closer to his family. It was while lurking in the vicinity, that Anode one day, saw a man enter his wife's residence. He wanted to rush in there; and confront the man, but on second thought decided against it. He had guessed that if he dared make any scene before his wife, that would be the end of the marriage. He therefore took it calmly and waited for the man. The man stayed very long and, each hour that passed Anode's heart went up. He was thinking within himself, "So I am here, while another man was in my house eating my food God forbid." But there was nothing he could do about it. He is now realizing the pain of going after other people's wives. He could now see why his intimate friend was out to disgrace and destroy him for going after his wife. He could no longer blame them for the humiliation they gave to him. "They were right," he reasoned. It is painful. Even though it looks ordinary but is always very painful for a man to see his wife being taken by another man," he concluded to himself. Many men have committed murder because of this. It is a lesson Anode is learning the hard way. He waited patiently until the man came out of the building after several hours. He quietly approached him. He introduced himself and told the man to leave his wife alone. The man gave him a perfunctory look and went his way. He entered his car and drove off. Anode felt snubbed. He decided to find out more about the man. He came out to the main road and flagged down a taxi cab and paid the driver to trail the man. He wanted to know where the man lived. Apart from knowing where the man lived, Anode was prepared to find out everything about the man: That was why he came back in the morning of the next day in time to trail the man to his office. He discovered where the man was working. It was there that he hired an informant. It was this informant who told him about the young man. He then decided to approach his wife with the information he gathered about the man.

His wife was the first to see him through the window when he arrived at her residence. She did not want to take chances about his mission. Their son was sleeping. She quickly called the police before Anode could come up. He was still at the door when the police arrived. His wife told the police that he was a thief. The police whisked him away to their station. They ignored his protest that the woman was his wife. They cautioned him and mocked him "If she is your wife why should she invite the police to arrest you." Anode's explanation about a family quarrel was scoffed at by the police. He was put in the cell until the next day when he was brought to a more senior officer. It was this senior officer who in a fatherly manner weighed Anode's side of the story against what was recorded in the police books. He decided to invite his wife for a more thorough investigation. The woman arrived in response to the invitation. When she was coming she brought along their little child.

Immediately the woman entered the officers' office, the little child saw his father. With a child-like enthusiasm he shouted "Daddy, daddy," and ran to the chair in which his daddy was sitting. His father lifted him up and planted a kiss on his forehead. Mrs Anode was ashamed by what she was seeing, and realized that she must have made a mistake by bringing the child along. She stood askance with mouth agape unable to utter a word. The police officers looked at themselves watching what would follow next. Father and child continued to play while others looked on. The child was asking the father where he had been and when he would come home. Immediately he asked this question Anode looked up and focused his gaze on his wife. She looked the other way, not wanting to betray her emotions. The officers were satisfied about what they were seeing. They had realized that it was a family affair. They cautioned and advised the woman not to drag the police into what was purely a family affair. They asked the couple to go home and seek a family settlement in the interest of the child. Mrs Anode, even though she saw herself betrayed by what happened; was still fuming with anger and concluded that her decision on her relationship with Anode was final.

Anode and his wife had not talked to each other since they met at the police station. They had been asked by the police to go home and settle their family matter. As they came out to go, Anode's son was still clutching his father's hands as he used to do his toys. His mother would have liked him to leave Anode along so that they could go home but that appears to be wishful thinking. The little child had not seen his father for a long time and was not prepared to let him go. He wanted all of them to go to the vehicle together and drive home as they used to do. Daddy would drive and mummy would sit in front while he would be in the back. His father and mother knew that there was nothing they could do but to go their separate ways, unless they found a way to convince their son why they should not go home together. Both of them had kept silent all this time, but they were approaching the vehicle, and that silence had to be broken. The vehicle was brought by Mrs. Anode. It had been with her since she moved out. As it was the only vehicle of the family, Anode had been moving about in public transport. As they approached the vehicle they knew something had to be done. It was Anode who opened up. He winked at his wife, and suggested that they went to a restaurant and talked for a while, after that he could excuse himself and go. In suggesting this as a way out, he had also hoped to use the opportunity of being alone with his wife, and in the presence of his son, beg his wife for forgiveness. This is something he had planned to do before the police arrested him. Surprisingly, his wife agreed to his suggestion. She had to. If she did not agree, it would be difficult to convince their infant son why daddy was not coming home with them.

Immediately they arrived at the restaurant, Anode rushed in to book a private room. The restaurant hardly offered such a place, but Anode told them that he had come with his family and needed maximum privacy. He was obliged and given a reserved room. He then took his wife and son to the secluded room. He ordered the food and as soon as the steward closed the door behind him, Anode knelt down, his eyes full of tears that refused to streak down his face and started to beg his wife to forgive him. His little son, not knowing what was happening, or, why his father knelt down, also went down on his knees beside his father, and joined his father in begging his mother. He was perhaps being propelled by a biological factor in him which makes him prefer what his father was doing to the passive roles of his mother. All male children do the same. At home he prefers to sit on the chair his father sits on. Any time the father comes home from outside, he would abandon whatever he was doing, or, whoever, he was with to follow him to the inner room. Since the separation, he had not been the same again. He would always go to the window and look outside in the hope that daddy would surely come back. His hopes had not yet come true. There was a day, his mother's lover knocked at the door. He rushed to open the door thinking it was his father. When he saw his mother's friend, he slammed back the door on his face, saying "Mummy is not in."

Today, it was quite refreshing to see him in a melodrama with his father, for which his mother nearly burst out laughing. She just managed to hold herself. She had enjoyed the scene and would have liked to take all of them home, and forget the past. But, no, she still bears a grudge against her husband for all the humiliations of the past. Although she had enjoyed everything, she looked at her husband and said, "This is not necessary. Get up and we can talk." She did not believe her chauvinistic husband would stoop so low for her. Anode hesitated before getting up. He was followed by his son who now went to sit on his lap. He then said, "In the name of God, I beg to be forgiven. I know I must have injured you badly. I know I have sinned. You have tolerated me beyond belief and I know you must have made up your mind, but I want you to forgive. Remember the good old days and even the bad old days. We started this journey together and have seen the best and worst together. I remember your suffering for me. Remember the fate of this little thing in our hands. Remember he has a future and that future is very important to us as his guardians. That future rests in our hands. What ever we do and whatever we say, we must recognise his future. Remember we vowed to be for each other." The wife cut him short. "Is that so?" she said. "So you know that we vowed to be for each other and you have been living for other women. It is a pity, but that is not what I have come here for." Anode was a bit halted by the statement of his wife and both of them kept quiet for a while. Anode was getting restless. He knew the danger of losing out. If this opportunity slipped by, it would be the end of the marriage. His wife had not shown any sign of yielding an inch. He became worried and was thinking of what to say and how to say it. A person may have something to say but the way he says it may kill a beautiful talk. He was thinking of what to do. There will never be a chance like this unless he orchestrates another visit to his wife and gets arrested. But that in itself will never create another opportunity like this. In the present case his wife lost on technical ground and would be wiser, the next time around. He was getting desperate. Anode bent his head downwards and focused his gaze on the floor, unable to know what to do or say. He braced up, and raised his head. He then called his wife by her maiden name. He knew that she loved to be called by that name. To her anybody who calls her by that name, loves her. Anode wanted to appeal to her sentiments. Immediately she heard that name she smiled but was quick to tighten her face. "Give me a chance. Anode began. "I promise that I will be a changed man. Just give me a chance." As he was finishing saying these words, they looked in the direction of her son and observed that he had nodded off. Anode wanted to go and lay him on the couch in the room, but his wife got up and took him from him. She took her handbag along and told Anode that she would call him later. She opened the door and left without further words.

Anode sat there for a long time after she had left, unable to know what to do. He was full of thoughts and they were weighing heavily on him. He ordered more drinks. As he drank his thoughts were becoming wild. He had no other companion in the world except the walls and cushions that were in the room. He was becoming more confused. He decided to go home. He got up, still thinking how his hopes of reuniting with his family were dashed. His legs wobbled and seemed unable to carry his small frame. He staggered but soon held himself firmly to the ground; and succeeded in pushing himself through the door. He came out to the main hall where so many people were drinking. He did not bother to look sideways, kept a straight face and did not want anybody to identify and greet him. He was just not in the right mood to greet or chat with anybody. He made straight for the outer door and saw himself outside. A rental car was close by. He boarded one and went home. Once at home he went and opened his private box. He brought out a large book and made some entries. Thereafter, he went to one of his lockers and brought out a gun. He loaded it with bullets and went to sit on his bed. He pointed the gun at the side of is head and pulled the trigger. He fell on his bed and died a few minutes later.

Chapter Eleven

Eka was cautioned by the police and released to her foster parents. Although she continued with her schooling as a day student in a nearby secondary school, she was not interested in any thing except men. She was out to explore the world. In the secondary school, she came in contact with girls who think the same way she does. Their stock in trade was to find men at all costs. They would sneak out from school in search of men. On certain days, Eka would not come to school at all but would go with a man and come back to lie about what happened in school. The teachers had been complaining about her behaviour and the rate at which she missed classes. It was not surprising that she failed her final examinations. The school refused to allow her for a resit. This meant that she would have to go and find work. She was not bothered by her failure or by her inability to secure a certificate with which to work.

Her joblessness made her idle and her idleness made her vulnerable. She was surrounded by riches but that was not all. She started to follow different men. She was not selective about her men. Her most memorable experience was a journey she made by train. She had been invited to a wedding of a relation. She decided to travel by train since the distance was far. She thought the train journey was the safest and the cheapest. She went alone. The train was overcrowded. People were even perching in the passageway. It was a night journey. They left about 10.00pm and were expected at their destination by 7.00pm the next day. Although Eka had become adventurous and daring since her scandalous experience with Anode, she did not expect that an ordinary train journey would provide her with such exciting experience as she had. It was a casual meeting with Dan. Both of them could not get seats in the train. They were standing next to each other. It was night and they could not see each other well. In the morning they saw themselves and took admiration for each other. Dan spoke first. He had said. "I cannot understand why these people will always overload the train. Do they want to suffocate us. Eka was quick to respond. She did so because she liked Dan's face and would like to get closer to him. She said, "I don't know, stupid people." Dan was experience in the game of love. He had spoken those words in the hope that Eka would respond. If she responded that would provide Dan with a basis for further talks with Eka and starting a date. If however Eka did not reply, Dan would just keep off. He would conclude that Eka could be difficult. She was not difficult. She talked and from there conversation developed between them. They later decided to go to the passageway and stay. They later made love in the bath enclosure. It was the most exhilarating experience for both of them. She had read a story of a woman who confessed to making love in the train but she never knew she would experience it. Thereafter, their journey continued on a special note. Wherever the train made a stop at a station, they would come down holding hands, as if they took off from home together. This led to gossip and envy among fellow passengers.

They did not bother themselves about the gossips. Throughout the journey, Eka was praying in her heart that Dan would never have cause to leave her. She knew that most men were out to conquer women. After they had preyed on their conquest they abandon them only to search for another victim. Eka wanted a sort of permanent relationship with Dan. She wanted to be his girlfriend and she told him so. Dan did not object to Eka's request but he knew that she was infatuated. He had wanted a train fling. He had a wife and children as well as other girlfriends. He, however found it hard to break a woman's heart. He acceded to Eka's request in the hope that time and distance will make their friendship impracticable. He was mistaken as he was actually underestimating what the little girl could do. They got to their destination safely. They met on several occasions within the town as they had planned. Dan later went back to his station. Eka would be coming later. They agreed on how they would meet to continue their relationship. When Eka and Dan were together, it did not occur to Eka to ask Dan what he was doing. She did not even care. She was more interested in the man that what he might be doing. She collected his address and car number and colour. She was determined to track him down. She would do it in such a way that Dan's wife would not know.

Immediately she returned from the wedding she stayed only two days before travelling to find Dan. His home was not too far. It was the next town. She knew the estate Dan described for her. She went there. It was a fenced estate with security men at the post. She believed that if she stayed at the security post, Dan must pass through there. She was sure. Unless he was sick and bedridden, he must go to his place of work or something must drag him through this gate. She was right. Her strategy worked. She stayed at the security post for about five hours. She had started to lose hope, and was thinking in her mind the next strategy to adopt. She even considered calling his house. She had reasoned that if she called and a female voice picked the phone, she would drop it without saying a word. But she also thought she could be lucky and Dan would be at home and pick the phone up first. In that case she would just tell him to proceed to the gate and pick her up. She had not decided what to do when a black Sedan pulled by the gate. She knew at once that was the car Dan had described to her. She quickly stood up and blurted out "Dan, Dan." She was just lucky Dan was driving himself today. He had a personal driver who in most cases drives the car. Dan turned his head and saw Eka. He moved a little bit and then parked. He came out. He embraced Eka and told her to jump in. She did. Dan reversed his car. He was going for lunch. But lunch would not be at his home again. He would take Eka to the place she would sleep and two of them would have their lunch there.

Dan is a middle-aged man in his late thirties. He is one of the newly rich men. He parades himself as an investment banker and a commodity broker. People deposit money in his phoney bank. They are paid outrageous interests. He leads a high profile life and has some connections with drug dealers. Eka wanted to be closer to him and had asked him to give her work in his establishment. Dan was reluctant. He would prefer Eka stay in her parent's house and visit occasionally. Eventually the two of them agreed that Dan should find work for Eka in another establishment. He would then rent an apartment for her. Eka promised not to do anything that would disrupt Dan's home. It was on the basis of this agreement that Dan sent Eka with a note to his business associate and friend. He knew quite well the job they were going to give Eka was related to drugs. When Eka got to the place, the boss interrogated her. It was discovered that the boss was well known to Joda. He would not do a thing like that. He did not want to use the daughter of his friend to push drugs. He thus turned down the request to employ Eka. She remained unemployed. It was not long after this disappointment, Dan was arrested and jailed for some shady deal.

Eka returned to her home. She had started to learn the lesson of life. For a young girl the price to pay for love can be very high. The road to obtain that love is equally thorny. It can bruise those who trod the path. It can even kill, yet it remains one of the most desirable things in the world. It may be easy for some to obtain but very difficult for others. Those that are usually successful in love are not necessarily the best in society. A dull girl can be very successful in love and marriage while a very brilliant girl may find it extremely difficult to get a man. Eka could not tell whether her upbringing was affecting her love life. Her mother was separated from her father. She has since then had two relationships which failed. Her father had three marriages including the marriage to his housemaid before he died. Can these then be the reason why Eka is tumbling from one relationship to another. It may not necessarily be so. Her friend had advised her that she was still too young and should not dissipate energy about failed love. These things happen that way. It is all trial and error until one achieves his goal. Eka bought the advice of her friend. She joined other girls of her age and started to pick men up on the road. They were enjoying their lives.

Eka was standing by the side of a popular road junction. She was hoping that a car owner would pick her up. They knew where to stand and men would hustle for them. She was right in her guess. It was not long before a sapphire blue metallic saloon car pulled by her side. There were three men inside. Two of them including the driver were sitting in the front while the third was at the back. They were all young and in their late twenties. The one sitting at the back was casually dressed. He wore just a shirt over white jeans. He put on dark sunglasses. The fellow sitting in front with the driver was the one who stretched his hand to open the car door for Eka. He closed the door after Eka entered. He then quipped. "You are beautiful." His mates laughed and Eka uttered inaudibly "Thank you." They then drove off. They were drinking some canned drinks and munching nuts. They hid it when Eka was about to enter the car. After she had entered and they had exchanged greetings they resumed eating the nuts and drinks. Eka was sitting directly behind the guy who opened the door for her. It was the same fellow who turned and offered Eka a can of soft drink and some nuts. Eka initially refused. She was probably shy to join them, in eating the snacks. She was however persuaded to be part of them and enjoy whatever they had. She agreed. She accepted the snacks and was throwing the nuts into her mouth one by one, and at the same time sipping the drink. Eka was now developing special confidence on the man sitting in front of her. The man had been talking and would frequently turn to look Eka in the eyes. She often smiled back at him. There had been a tacit agreement of where the groups were heading to. Eka had entered the car on the understanding that the men would take her on a date. She had hoped to meet a lonely man who was looking for a girl's company. Instead she had met these three guys. The initial confusion of who among them would be her boyfriend had been overcome by the trust she had on the man who was doing all the talking. After she had finished her drinks, she felt a bit drowsy. She thought she must have over loaded her stomach and would soon fall asleep. She was used to using food as a sedative. Anytime she wanted to sleep very soundly, she ate too much. Within an hour she would be in bed, but that was when she was at home. She knew that her present drowsiness was being caused by the extra drinks she had taken. It was not long ago she took her lunch. The drinks had made her over eat. While still thinking of the effect of food on her system, she dozed off. Immediately the man sitting by her side noticed, and told the others with a sign. Both of them turned in Eka's direction, and they all laughed. Unknown to Eka, they had drugged her drinks. These were hired operators. They were abductors operating for a fee. They knew that Eka would sleep for a very long time. They belonged to a semi-religious organisation who used Jesus name as a charade to confuse people. Right inside their establishment they engage in clandestine activities. They kill and main for money. This organisation was not known. Neither the police nor the ordinary folks knew about it. People had been under the mistaken illusion that the compound used by the organisation belonged to a religious group. They had been seeing only decent people living in the magnificent buildings within that estate. The truth is that the estate was owned by a reputable member of the society who pretends to be very religious. The man had carefully selected members of his organisation as tenants. They do their normal work in other business establishments but return to the estate to engage in crime. They trained young people who commit the crime while they share the spoils. The estate was built on a very large expanse of land and cordoned off. It was difficult for unwanted people to come in except through authorized gates.

This was the estate to which Eka was brought. She was still sleeping when they arrived on the estate. Her abductors neatly parked their car at the parking lot; and then carried Eka through a tunnel that leads to an underground bunker. She was just dumped at an outer enclosure. This group had finished with their own assignment. Another group would take her inside the bunker. The bunker was used as living rooms for victims who were kidnapped. It was comfortable inside and was equipped with modern gadgets. Before Eka was taken inside, she was undressed and left only in her pants. This was the modus operandi of the organisation. All inmates who are newly captured, must be naked until after they had been screened by the oracle. Eka was still in deep slumber at the time she was undressed. The barber would come later to shave off all her hairs. It is the barber that would remove her pants and leave her stark naked like other inmates.

At the time Eka was taken into the bunker all eyes turned towards her direction. She was carried to the right. That was the female section. They had two sections for both sexes. They were separated by a thin veiled partition. They could easily converse across the partition. All of them were naked. There were no chairs nor beds. There were only mats spread on the floor. Any inmate could sit or stand as he or she wished. Eka was laid on the floor where she continued with her slumber. The barber soon arrived for Eka. He was a stern looking man who was very business like.

He does not smile. He knew his job. He entered and banged the door behind him. Everybody kept silent immediately he entered. He went straight to Eka, plugged his electric shaver and within twenty minutes her body became very smooth. All the hairs on her body including the pubic hairs were shaved off. This made it difficult to recognise her at first sight. This would make her look like her inmates whose bodies looked smoother than glass. It was while they were shaving her, with other inmates looking that Eka woke up. It has become characteristic of the inmates to feast their eyes on the nakedness of a newcomer. Immediately Eka woke up she did not quite realise herself, or where she was. She looked around her and all she could see were naked women. There were noises coming over the partition of male voices. She wanted to extricate herself from the man holding her and get up but she could not. She was not yet over from the effect of the drugs. And she would find it impossible to overpower the stranger who was shaving her. With a feeble voice she said, "Leave me alone." Only the man huddling her heard what she said. After she had been shaved, the man left the apartment. Eka sat there looking morose, unable to make any meaning of what was happening to her. She sat down there for a very long time without talking to anybody. She heard the women sitting and standing around her talking in low tones. She was too weak to even ask them to tell her what was amiss. She later slept again.

She woke up the next day. The effect of the drug had started to ease off. She had been regaining her strength gradually. They brought her tea and four slices of toasted bread. She accepted and ate them voluptuously. She was clearly very hungry. She had not eaten anything since she nodded off after taking the canned drink in the vehicle. After having her meals, Eka moved closer to a woman sitting to her left. She wanted to talk and find out what was happening. She did now know how and why she came to this sort of place where there were only naked women. She was feeling embarrassed and ashamed. Eka had a high pitched tone betraying her emotion. She was quickly stopped by the woman she was talking to. The woman used her right palms to cover Eka's mouth. She then whispered to her in a low tone. "Do not worry, I will tell you everything when the atmosphere is clear and nobody is listening." Eka instantly kept quiet moping like several others in the room who were just moping without talking.

They knew where they were. They need not talk too much. This is a ruthless organisation, engaged in all types of crimes at the same time. The victims are abducted and brought to the organisation. They are inducted and deployed into its operations. Those who accept or qualify to work exclusively for the organisation are brainwashed and deployed to various duties. Some of the most appealing women are kept as concubines of the leader or his assistants. Those who however refuse to work for the organisation, or are found to be unfit are killed and buried inside the common grave in the compound. They could never be traced again.

The dungeon where Eka was brought to was a primary stage. The inmates there were newly captured people. They would be made to have a full experience of what hardship is before they were taken to the next stage which was the screening by the oracle. It is only the oracle that can pronounce somebody fit or unfit for the work he will be assigned. The inmates are herded around dusk with a black piece of cloth tied across their eyes. They would hold each other's shoulder blade in a single line formation while the person leading would be in front with guards following behind. When they get to the small shanty house being used as the oracle's place, they would be ushered in one after the other. There is a line drawn with a white chalk at the entrance to the house. A victim normally enters the house with his back while still blindfolded. Once inside the house, he was shown where to say until the oracle comes out, when he would be asked to go and kneel down before him. The priest would then make further consultations. A voice would be talking from where appeared to be the ceiling. It would be in a language only the priest would hear and interpret. Some victims were pronounced as being possessed by evil spirits and should therefore be sent away or killed. Some of them were sent out in the night and left on the highway where they would be rescued. Such victims usually found it difficult to tell people their experiences. This is because they are ashamed or they did not want to be ridiculed. They did not report to the police because they did not know the location the organisation is. They were taken in the night and throughout their stay there they lived in a bunker. On a few occasions that they came out of the bunker, they were blindfolded.

If a victim is pronounced fit by the oracle, he is taken to the last stage which was a meeting with the leader of the organisation. It is here that the first initiation rites are started. They would be talked to by the leader who would select his personal staff from there. In some cases, he selected his female concubines also. The final stage was when the victims were given cloaks to enable them dress like nuns or priests. They would use these dresses to attend their rituals late in the night.

It was about 1.00am Eka was still sleeping. Somebody tapped her on the back. She turned. She did not know what was happening. The person tapped her again, saying "Wake up." It was in a low tone. This time she became conscious of somebody wanting her to get up. She sat up. It was the woman who blocked her mouth when she wanted to talk to her. The atmosphere was clear now and she wanted to discuss with Eka and tell her where she was. This was about the time the guards slept. It was at this time that some of the daring men escaped. They had killed some guards in the process. Some women also escaped with the men. It was a matter of courage and strong heart. The consequences of failure were usually very grave. There was a case of four young people who attempted to escape. They had killed a guard and took away his gun. They wanted to use the weapon to defend themselves and if possible shoot their way to freedom. They were apprehended and executed before all the inmates to serve as a deterrent to all others. After that cold blooded and chilling murder; the incident of escape had become less. Eka used her bare hand to wipe her face. This was a sign that there was still sleep in her eyes. She then went to sit near the woman. The woman began. "What is your name?"

"Eka," she replied. She then asked, "Where are you from?" Eka told her where she came from. She in turn told Eka her name and background. Eka could recollect how she was picked up by three men who gave her a ride. She could not remember any other thing except her present circumstances. The woman told Eka about how she was abducted. She was a divorcee. She had one child from her former husband. She had been going out with another man who promised to marry her. Her former husband had been jealous of her relationship with her new man. He had been pestering her to leave the man. It was he who then arranged for her abduction. She was alone in her flat late one morning. She was preparing to go out when she heard a knock at her door. She opened the door. She saw four young men. They did not waste time or ask questions. They just pushed her down and gagged her mouth. They tied her hands and legs and put her in the boot of their car. They stopped somewhere on the highway and brought her out from the boot. They then injected her. She slept. She arrived where she was in the same way as Eka. It was about seven days ago. She had not been screened.

She went on to tell Eka; that they were between the devil and the deep blue sea. There was no escape for them except by divine intervention. She believed in God and in miracles. She knew that nothing would happen to her. She was however worried about her child and her man. They would be worried about her sudden disappearance. If only she could find a way of sending them messages. She told Eka about the organisation.

After she had finished her story, Eka started crying. The woman was consoling her. She advised Eka to have faith in God. They would not die, she assured her. Eka was terribly confused. She was again confronted with the high price a girl pays for love. "So I will die," she muttered. The woman who heard her answered her, "No my dear you will not die." It was almost 2.30am when there was a sound of footsteps. It looked as if somebody was coming towards the door. They knew it was one of the guards. They quickly hit their bodies on the ground and covered themselves pretending as if they had been sleeping. The flashlight appeared on the wall but the guard did not say anything. He closed the door and left. The two women did not talk again. Eka had been fully briefed about what was happening to her. She has resigned herself to God and fate just like the other women and men who had fallen victims to this outlawed organisation. In the morning they woke up and were herded to their common place of bath and other necessities before being brought back for their breakfast. They were being invited one by one for their screening. Once any member is called out for the screening, she would never be seen again by others. If she is alive that will only be known when they meet again during future assignments. If however she was recommended for slaughter, nothing would ever be heard about her again.

Later, about midday, Eka's friend was invited for screening. It was her turn. She bade Eka goodbye. It was a goodbye from her heart. Something within her had told her that she would never see Eka again. Tears almost flowed from her eyes. She did not know whether she was the one who would fail the screening and be killed or whether Eka would be the one. She wished she knew the actual position, but it was very difficult to decipher her inner voice. She left with prayers to God to preserve her life. Her prayers were not answered. She had a date with fate. She did not quite reckon with the circumstances of her coming there. Her former husband had tipped off the organisation. He had paid them a large sum of money to deal finally with the woman. She went for the interview.

She begged to be spared but nobody listened to her. She did not stay long. She was taken to the back-yard and slaughtered. The guards took her body to the common grave.

It took another week before it was Eka's turn. Her name was blurted out. "Eka, Eka." She got up quietly and followed her caller. They did not take her to the oracle. She was brought to a partially illuminated room. She saw all her interviewers very well. She was asked about herself, and she told them. They asked her if she would like to work for them. She agreed to do so. She was then passed to the next stage which was the meeting with the leader. The meeting took place in the posh and heavily furnished room of the leader. Immediately the leader saw Eka, he smiled. He salivated but hid his feelings. He knew he was a leader and should not betray his organisation with his emotions. He wanted Eka to himself. He ordered the guards who brought in Eka to leave the room and close the door behind them. They obeyed him. They knew how he behaved when he wanted to add a new concubine to his harem. He asked Eka who had been fidgeting to calm down. He asked her to sit down in a cushion chair close to the one he was sitting. He asked her about herself and background.

During the course of interrogating Eka, he discovered that Eka was the daughter of Joda, his bosom friend and associate. People in the crime world have some linkages. Joda was a notable man who acquired wealth by all means. His daughter had fallen into the hands of another gang world. The leader shook his head affirmatively when he learnt about Eka's connection. He surmised that there was nothing wrong in keeping the daughter of his dead friend while she worked for his organisation. He subsequently directed that Eka should be taken to one of the special apartments and given enough money to change and buy new clothes. She should be given employment in the public relations department immediately. All his instructions were obeyed. His lieutenants knew that Eka would become one of the mistresses of the leader. Eka soon took up her new position as both the mistress of the leader and a worker at the public relations department. She was a very close confidante of the leader and the workers respected and avoided her. She wielded so much power and authority. It was when she settled down properly that she discovered that her new place of abode was in every way related to her father's estate.

It was also while working that she learnt that not all who failed the screening were killed. Some were preserved to serve the oracle. She had been very much worried about her friend. She did not hear from her nor had she seen her after her screening. She was tempted to ask the leader but something in her prevented her from doing so. It was just like the time she wanted to ask her friend about where they were and she gagged her mouth. This time around an invisible hand was gagging her mouth when she felt like asking the leader about her friend. She had gone to the oracle and surveyed the faces of those serving the oracle but could not find her friend. It was while searching for her friend that she came across one of her abductors by chance. She invited him to her office. She is now their boss and could use her special relationship with the leader to seek a revenge. She did. She discussed with the young man and extracted every detail about him and his gang. She then recommended to the leader that they should be killed. The leader wanted to satisfy his mistress. He accepted her recommendation and the young men were killed on trumped up charges. Eka was highly elated. She had got her revenge at last. She however knew that she would not be in this organisation forever. She did not like the place. She hid her feelings about the place. She knew she was a young woman. She was inclined more to the things spiritual than to work for a gang world. She therefore plotted her escape. She was well known in the organisation. Among the leader's numerous mistresses, she was the most favourite. This is because she was the youngest and she was the daughter of the friend of the leader. She knew that these two factors were working for her. She could exploit them fully.

The rules for leaving the organisation to go outside were very strict. It was very difficult for people who were abducted to go outside the compound. The compound is a world of its own. Everything a man could need could be got there. There was therefore no need for anybody except the founding fathers to go outside. All others were normally escorted to go out if there was any reason why they should be allowed to go. Normally, they were not allowed.

Eka has been working seriously on her escape. It was therefore not surprising that one day she dressed gorgeously and drove herself to the gate. At the gate she was allowed to go. The Chief Security Guard merely asked her to come back quickly without even seeking clearance from the leader. They did not realise that Eka was going never to come back. Thus it was in the second month of her abduction and disappearance; that she showed up once again at the foster parents home. This was Eka's third kidnapping.

In the organisation, there was an outrage at what happened. The leader was fuming with anger. He wanted to execute all his security men but wiser counsel prevented him from carrying out his devilish plan. He trained a new set of security outfit, and redeployed the old hands who had betrayed his cause.

Meanwhile Eka was being urged to report her ordeal to the police. She was reluctant to go to the police. She had been tortured during her first voluntary disappearance with a man. This time is different. She had not realized the difference between the two cases. The disappearance was not voluntary. This was forced on her by people, she did not know. But she continued to remain adamant. People believed she would be saving the society from amorphous crime organisation if she could open up to the police and tell all she knew since she operated at the highest echelon of the organization as a mistress of the leader. The police was eventually invited by Eka's parents who did not want to waste any more time in busting such a crime organisation. They took Eka away. The assured her that she would not be tortured or harmed. She should only explain to them how the organisation was structured and what they do. Eka was petted and she told everything the organisation was doing. She told how she was kidnapped. The kidnap story was almost the same for all the victims who were taken away forcibly and injected or sedated. After her story to the police, she was taken home and from then on she was given extra protection by the police. The police believed that the organisation might be at the trail of Eka either to abduct her and take her back to their headquarters, or to kill her so that she would not divulge anything about the base. They were right in their suspicion. Not long after the escape of Eka, the most modern vehicles were being seen around the vicinity of her home. It was the method of the organisation to use the latest models of cars to attract girls.

They had failed. Eka had learnt her lessons of life and love. She was not prepared to enter any vehicle in search of love. Moreover the police was protecting her.

The police armed with Eka's story started to infiltrate the organisation. Their master plan had been made.

They assumed the role of wealthy business men. They would carry large sums of money and engage in such businesses where they hoped the members of the organisation would extort the money from them. They eventually penetrated the organisation. They sent back words to their headquarters and heavily armed reinforcements were despatched. After one day's operation the organisation was smashed. Key members were arrested. It was not easy to arrest the leader. He was heavily fortified. The security network weaved around him was more than the police had heard and imagined. On the day of the operation he went underground. But eventually his underground bunker was destroyed with dynamite and he died in the process. It was a successful operation in which a major crime organisation had been smashed. Only a very few captives died. Majority of the others were released unharmed.

Some of them who were naked were given clothes by the police who took them home to their various places. Eka became popular after the destruction of the criminal organisation. She had hitherto been referred to as the daughter of Joda, the criminal and had lost many an opportunity because her family was stained by the circumstances surrounding her father's death. She hoped and prayed for the restoration of his name.

Eka's good nature was inherited from her parents. Inspite of the present ordeal about her family's name, her father was not born a criminal. He was born into a humble family. He rose from the grassroots by sheer dint of hard work to earn a degree. He developed lofty ideas bout how to reform and clean up the society. He was however disappointed and frustrated by the same society. That was how he turned to crime to acquire wealth, because he saw, that was the only way to survive. Before he turned to crime, Eka had been conceived and born. She did not inherit any criminal blood from the father. Her mother was also born into a wealthy and a respectable family who have nothing to do with crime. Eka therefore was born with clean blood. It is not surprising that God is using her to reform the society.

Chapter Twelve

Efo had been beset by a lot of problems. Her second attempt at marriage had failed. She had been told that she would never get pregnant again. But she was still hopeful that one day a miracle would happen. Her only daughter had been groping about unable to find her bearing in life. After her daughter's latest ordeal at the hands of kidnappers, she decided to bring her back to her house. She wanted Eka to be nearer her so that she could teach her the righteous way. She believed that her daughter's problems were caused by lack of proper direction and parental care. The girl had consequently grown wayward and desired only material things. All this should stop. She did not want her daughter to fall into the same mess that she found herself. Every parent would want her child to do better that he has done in life and avoid his own pitfalls. It is exactly the same wish that Efo had for Eka. Moreso, now that Eka is her only hope of continuity on earth, at least until the miracle happens.

Efo is a firm believer in spiritual matters. She had been going from one spiritual church to the other in search of a solution for her problems. She had not found any. Matters were made worse by her experience at the last church she attended. The pastor there had defiled her and had even wanted her to leave her husband in order to marry him. Her saviour from that experience was that she was a woman of strong character who wanted to save her marriage.

The behaviour of that pastor had dampened her enthusiasm about spiritual churches. She had stopped attending any for some time after that incident. But the death of her husband had renewed her hope in the Lord. She wanted to go back to church. But the question that always came up in her mind was "Which church, which church?" She could not find an answer to this question which confronts her any time she thinks of going back to the church. She had lost confidence in these churches because they had not performed what they were preaching.

The answer to the question finally came one day. It was in the form of a dream. After the day's activities she went to bed as usual. She felt tired that day and was having a deep sleep when suddenly a wide screen appeared before her. There was an enclosure and there was a large number of people gathered there. She saw herself standing in the pulpit and addressing this large congregation. She was robed in white clothes. There were other people standing beside her ready to do her bidding. They would come from time to time to whisper something into her ears. This was followed by the appearance of an apparition. It was also a woman and dressed in a white overall. This was almost the same dress Efo had. The figure had a crucifix in her right hand. She was very angelic. The figure had told her that she had been "Anointed to carry God's message to the world."

When Efo woke up from her sleep, she was bemused and remained transfixed for a very long time. She lay on her bed thinking; "What it was all about." This was unlike herself who used to wake up early and rush to do her morning chores. The only meaning she could ascribe to what had happened in the dream was that the Lord had answered her questions. She should go back to the church. However she told some of her friends about the dream. Most of those who heard it believed that she should go back to the church but should first of all seek the interpretation of the dream. There was a notable pastor in the town who was good in the interpretation of dreams. She was advised to seek his views. She did. The pastor listened intently to her dream. After she had finished narrating it, he told her in simple words that she had been called to the service of the Lord. The interpretation seemed vague to Efo. She did not quite understand what it was to be called to the service of the Lord. She sought for explanation. "What do you mean pastor?" she said.

The pastor smiled and told her that the Lord wants her to go and minister to souls. "A lot of souls are wandering in the wilderness. They need to be saved. The Lord wants you to help in saving those souls. You should therefore go and get ready. Sell your belongings and come forth and engage in pastoral duties," the pastor concluded. Efo sat there in silence. She had mixed feelings of what she was hearing from the pastor. She doubted his sincerity. She thought she must have fallen into the hands of another dubious pastor. She was still engrossed in thought when she blurted out "Myself, church, myself to become a pastor or own a church." She believed that the pastor was a fake. The pastor seemed to have read her mind when he told her. "Do not doubt the words of the Lord. The kingdom of God belongs to believers. Unbelievers will be condemned to perdition, go and get ready."

Efo was flustered. She could not utter more words. She thanked the pastor and left.

She was still confused about the interpretation given to her dream. "What is a church and who can establish one?" These are new questions coming into her head. She had read the history of the churches. She cannot fully explain why she went into the spiritual churches. She came from a Catholic family. She had been brought up to be a Catholic but she had derailed and found herself in these churches. For effect, she believes that she gains more from these churches than the one she was brought up. Her greatest problem remains "Who can establish a church." Even though there is a proliferation of churches these days but the Bible which everybody uses as authority says that in the beginning there was only one church. It was stated that this church was established by Jesus Christ. It was probably during the feast of Passover when he called his disciples together and they partook of the meal of bread and wine. Jesus Christ was the Lord made man. This means that the only church that existed in the world at the time was established by God himself. Dissension came during the reformation. It was Martin Luther and his group who felt that the church needed some reforms. They were not satisfied with some of the things going on in the church. They then pulled out of the church and started to protest and attack the church which they had hitherto belonged. Their decision to pull out was attacked by another set who felt that reforms are better carried out from inside. This was the beginning of schism in the church. A final blow was delivered to the true church of God when the king of England sought the permission of the pope to marry another wife. His wife could not give him an heir to the throne. He felt that he needed a successor so that his lineage would not be closed. The pope refused to grant his request. He pulled his kingdom out of the Catholic church and established his own church. That was how the church of England came into existence. However the church of England was modelled after the Catholic church. In other words it was not established for the personal gains of one individual. It was recognised as one of the established churches. It can therefore be said that accounts of how the protestant churches came about were well documented. That is not so with the later day churches. Nobody knows their origin or how they came about. It was not even known which among them came first. It is believed that they are an offshoot of the protestant churches. It was equally believed that many of these churches sprouted in America in the 19th century. They were copied and replicated in Europe before the present day wonder churches. It is common to find these churches in every hamlet in all parts of the world.

It takes nothing to establish a church. All a would-be pastor needs is just to know how to speak in public. Even if he does not know, he will learn in the course of time. It is cheaper to start a church than going into business since very little capital is required to start. Thus, all, a poor folk who wants to make it in life needs, to own a good business is a Bible, a bell and a white robe. Any shanty apartment would do or he can start in an open ground. It does not require any special training on pastoral duties. Every pastor interprets the Bible either the way it suits his purpose or the way he understands it. Their aim is identical. That is to make money by exploiting the spiritual hunger of people, and live well. That is why churches are being established as if they are political parties. Somebody had suggested that these churches are more of one man businesses than houses of worship. They deceive people into believing that they are out to evangelize the world while their standard of living remains above average. A semi-illiterate pastor who is a school drop out; rides in the latest car models, wears designer dresses, sleeps in the best hotels around the world. His counterpart who had graduated from the university can only make it, if he resorts to robbery. This was what happened to Joda. He struggled to earn a university degree but discovered to his chagrin that a degree is not, all in all, these days. What mattered was raw cash and abundance of it. He joined the bandwagon and paid dearly for it.

University graduates also find it difficult to come out openly and establish churches of their own, even though many of them fully identify with these churches. It is on very rare occasions do graduates enter the business of preaching and teaching. If Joda had taken up just a Bible and a robe, he would have been alive today. He would equally have made his wealth and remained a respectable member of the society. Even his desire to reform the society could have been better done from the pulpit rather from the polity.

So many pastors have given accounts of how they were called

into church ministry. A certain pastor related that he was an armed robber. He was on his way with his gang for an operation. They were going to rob a bank. They accidentally passed a place where a crusade was going on in an open ground. They decided to go and witness what was going on before they could continue on their journey. They were instead converted on the spot. He is one of the revered pastors today. There was another pastor who confessed that he was engaged in all sorts of crimes previously. He was a drug pusher, a con-man and an armed robber. He too had attended a crusade with a friend. They had dubious intentions. They had planned to attack the preacher and relieve him of what he had. When they got to the crusade ground, they were carried away by the holy spirit which pervaded the entire area. The effect of the holy spirit could be felt at about twenty meters around the field. They became converted and forgot about their evil plans. They became believers. From that day on they gave up crime and took up the Bible. Today they are successful pastors.

There are numerous accounts of why and how there are many pastors and churches. These accounts are varied and as many as there are pastors. But an inference must be made. There is something inherently wrong when an armed robber or a drug pusher gets automatically converted to carry the Bible. He must have seen that there is more gain to be made from preaching than the risk of armed robbery. Majority of those who have churches of their own are driven by the monetary and material benefits. There are, however, those who go into pastoral duties because they have the true calling. They were rich and wanted to use their wealth to serve God and humanity. These are few and their selfless service is being depraved by the overzealous many who are out to grab money by all means. Like their business counterparts, these evil churches are out to protect their financial interests. Their members are brainwashed into donating a percentage of their incomes to the church. Others are convinced to renounce riches. They consequently sell off their properties and donate the proceeds to the church. They start living the ascetic life of self denial and poverty. The irony of the situation is that while the pastors are living flamboyantly and lavishly, erstwhile wealthy members are dying in penury. These heartless pastors go a step further. In order to ensure that the gap between them and their members are maintained, they make their churches look as if they are cults. Religion is used as a smoke-screen while other diabolical activities are going on. Members are detached from the actual world. Most of them lose their senses and are unaware of what they are doing. It is even difficult to convince those members that they do not know what they are doing. Many of them lose their lives in the process because they are made to believe that they must die for the Lord. Their leaders are ever ready to maintain the status quo. They resist any attempts to make them lose the newly acquired power and wealth. They are intoxicated by this power.

There are reported cases of mass suicide or mass murder that have taken place in many countries in the name of religion. Mass suicide occurs when the government or its agencies attempt to break the cocoon into which cult leaders have encased their members. These devilish leaders would rather prefer to die than face the wrath of justice. But in dying they take innocent lives along. It is a very sad and wicked way of using the name of God. Those cult leaders who commit murder are even more wicked. They kill others but would like to live. Only a devil can do this.

It had remained a mystery how these pastors achieved their aim of brainwashing their members, many of who are highly educated and successful members of society. An answer may be found in the question "Why do people leave the established churches to these new churches. What do these spiritual churches offer that the older churches do not offer."

There are a lot of educated and wealthy members of the society who attend the spiritual church. They even support and sustain them financially. These people are not fools. They must be gaining something from these churches to stick out their resources. The uneducated, semi-educated and poor folks who remain adherents must also be gaining something. The fact is that the older churches have proved inadequate in satisfying the spiritual needs of the people. They have thus created a spiritual void in the lives of their congregation. It is this void that the wonder churches are striving to fill. In the past, the Catholic church used to keep its members ignorant of what was going on. Church goers were not allowed to know what the officiating priests were doing at the alter, and therefore were, unable to follow the mass itself. You have to be a trained priest to be able to read and interpret the bible. Everything was shrouded in secrecy. The mass was rendered in Latin which was alien to the people. The hymns and songs were in Latin and only very few were selected into the choir to sing the verses with the priest. Most members of the choir did not understand the hymns they were singing. They were mere parrots chorusing what they were taught.

The 'wonder churches'have revolutionized church and spirituality. Everything that was previously thought impossible is now being practised in the churches. They have shown the people that they too can be active participants in the matters of the church. They involve the people and carry them along. All members own a copy of the Bible. Members knowledge of the Bible provide a check on the pastors. During their services, members open chapters and verses of the Bible and read along with their pastor. Whatever the pastor says is verified. If he quotes a passage from the Bible, members verify it on the spot, and know whether he is talking the truth. Members also quote the verse of the Bible freely. Pastors are spurred to study the Bible deeper and thoroughly so that they would not be ridiculed before their members.

It is the involvement of the people that had made a significant difference between the informal churches and the established ones.

In the older churches, members leave service feeling empty and not fulfilled, while in the spiritual churches, members acquire inner peace through the reading of the Bible. It is this inner peace that make members believe that some miracle is happening in their lives. These days it is the older churches that are striving to catch up with the spiritual churches. They are losing members to these new churches and are looking for new ways of attracting and retaining their members. They have thus introduced the use of brass bands during service. They now clap their hands and even dance while songs are rendered in local languages. The mass is now said in the local language so that the congregation can understand and follow what the priest is doing. Some new breed priests have established what they call charismatic groups. They attempt healing and comfort the lonely. This has restored the confidence of those members still within their fold.

The fear of Armageddon or doomsday is also driving people to the new churches where they hope to reap spiritual fulfilment. They feel their souls will be saved more in the spiritual church so that they can enjoy life after this one. Nobody wants to hear that he will die forever. It is better to die and stay somewhere and then come back to continue one's mission on earth. They may go to spiritual churches because they are lonely and needed an outlet to socialize. There is that desire to belong and socialize. The wonder churches organise Bible study sessions where members meet to know each other better. Most members got their spouses from their church. There is that close and personal handling of members problems which reassures them. They are encouraged to bring forward these problems which the pastor and his extension staff try to solve personally. Some of these pastors know that it is not always that God intervenes to solve peoples' problems so, they offer their advice and comfort the people. If a man knows that his problem will be solved either by prayer or by associating with others, he will rather prefer to go to that place because it offers some hope. He will shun the place where nobody cares about his problems. He may call it a waste of time because nobody recognises him.

The 'wonder churches', however, go beyond acceptable limits because their ultimate aim is acquisition of wealth for the founders. They exploit the weaknesses and hopes of their members and eventually betray those hopes. They make these churches personal properties and discredit other churches. They indoctrinate and brainwash their members into believing that their belief in Jesus is all that they require to solve their personal problems. It is in an attempt to solve personal problems that members are made to believe that they have spiritual problems too. The solution to material problems must therefore start with the solution of spiritual problems. "It is when a man is free in spirit that he can be free in the physical plane." They claim to perform miracles. These miracles are performed daily. All, a man needs to receive his own miracle is to just come to the pastor. This is deceitful because miracles do not happen everyday. An event can only be called a miracle when it is difficult to explain how it occurred. But for a man to claim to be performing miracles by the snapping of his finger is downright dishonesty.

Such people are dupes who should not be relied upon.

A miracle can happen to anybody. It can happen to a man who had not read a copy of the Bible in his life as well as the pastor. It is the condition of one's mind or prayer; his plight in life, previous lives and experiences that determine whether a miracle can happen to that person. It can happen as a result of the present supplication or a previous prayer. If a person intercedes on behalf of another, he must be spiritually endowed and uplifted. It is not something a fraudulent pastor shouting at the to of his voice can claim to achieve by misinterpreting the Bible.

These pastors' hollowness had on several occasions been exposed. Their claims to perform miracles had been tested by people and found to be a fluke. There was a certain man who suddenly discovered that his small son had a hearing problem. The small child could speak but could not hear other people. His father got worried. He rushed the child to the hospital. The ear and throat surgeon advised him to tread softly after he had examined the child. The surgeon advised that the child could still hear. The father should wait for developments while bringing the child to the clinic for regular check ups. The father, however was restless. He told so many people and was advised to take the child to a spiritual church. He accepted the advice and rushed his son to a pastor. The pastor assured him that his son's problem was over since he found his way into his church. The man was relieved. He believed the pastor. The pastor then prayed for the boy. He clapped and danced but for over a year the boy's condition refused to improve. At the same time this same pastor was mounting the pulpit every Sunday and claiming to be performing miracles. He urged people to bring the sick and the afflicted. That he was capable of healing all of them. When the boy's father got tired of waiting for a miracle that was not forthcoming, he took his child and left the church.

There are numerous instances of dying people being rushed to these churches. The pastor would always claim to be capable of reviving or curing the patient. But in the end the person would die. The pastor offers no apology to anyone. He believes he does not force people to come to his church.

Some pastors are very crafty people who are out to deceive their members. These members are very gullible or so much troubled that they would always believe these fake pastors even when they know that they are telling lies. Some of these pastors start their deceits by crying for the sins of the world. Every other person except themselves are sinners. They ask their members to join hands with them so that they can use their tears to save the world. Members are told to dedicate their lives to God if they are believers. When they are thus convinced about serving God to the exclusion of any other interest those of them who have wealth or property will be asked to sell them and donate the proceeds to the church. "It is more blessed to give than to receive," they will be told. If such a member should ask for the return of his money he will be killed. These churches kill and cover up their sins, yet there is nowhere in the Bible where it is written that murder is a way of serving God. In some cases they kill both themselves and their members in pursuit of nonexistent verses of the Bible.

Chapter Thirteen

Efo had been engrossed in thought about spiritual churches, their origin, activities and what people thought about them. She knew many people did not believe nor accept that spiritual churches were true churches.

She had questioned her own ability and prowess to establish and run a church since the revelation of what the Lord wanted her to do. The pastor had recommended a pastoral college to her. She must attend the college if she wanted to acquire the necessary skills that would aid her in her new profession. She had been thinking about this and knew within her that she had serious doubts about the whole thing. Inspite of her misgivings she got ready and moved into the college. To her there was no going back. Let the will of God be fulfilled.

In the college she met people with similar callings. They had all been called by God to serve him. They had come to study the Bible and other courses. They were taught the art of public speaking and how to win souls for the Lord. Special sessions were devoted to the teaching of the Bible so that they could master the book.

At the end of the course, she established her own church. She did not ask people to contribute money so that she could build the church. She was born into wealth. She did not go into the pastoral duties to acquire wealth. She went there because she was called by God to serve humanity. She used her own money to build a massive building which she used as a church. She equipped it with her own money. She also built houses within the church premises for her pastors. Her church was regarded as unique because first, she was a woman. Women were not known to own churches. It was rare to find a woman who owned a church. Most of the other women who attended the same pastoral school with her joined other churches as assistants. This was therefore the first time that a female was establishing her own church and having males as assistants. Secondly, Efo did not make any financial demands of the congregation and she never stipulated that people should donate a certain percentage of their income to her church, or sell their property and donate the proceeds to her church. She therefore, stood alone in an arena that was filled with dupes and questionable characters.

Since Efo passed out of the pastoral school, many pastors had started to use television as a means of preaching. She did not believe in it and had questioned their motives. She had reasoned that people who did this had some other motives other than preaching and saving souls. Her suspicions of their intention was proved right when some of these pastors started asking people to donate money by post. The aim of engaging in tele-vangelism is therefore to reach out to more people. It is good for business. There are wealthy people who may find it inconvenient to come to the church, and may need the services of a pastor, and consequently be a good source of income to the church. She confined herself to preaching in her church and holding occasional crusades in open fields. Her church became very popular and people flooded to the place. She held about four services every Sunday because one service alone was not enough.

Even though she never asked for donations, people still donated money and property out of their own free will. It was not her style to ask for donations. She made up her mind right from the time she was going into church ministry that she would run a special church which would gain the confidence of the people. She was determined to prove that not all spiritual churches were bad.

When donations started streaking in she appointed a committee to manage the income. This committee managed the resources and reported to her. The activities of this committee was audited from time to time to ensure that no impropriety was going on and ensure probity in the financial affairs of the church.

In what appeared to be the first scandal that rocked Efo's church, the committee was discovered to have misappropriated the funds of the church. Efo was annoyed but she learnt her first lesson in her church ministry. She believed that she had mistrusted people who she regarded as close associates. She had carefully selected members of that committee trusting that they were men and women of integrity. She was disappointed. She dealt with the situation in her own special way. She directed that the findings of the auditors should be released to the entire congregation. She wanted to disabuse their minds about a possible linkage of her name to the shady deal.

She had been living above board and did not want anything to dent her image. After exposing the actual position to the congregation, she dissolved the board and recommended its members for excommunication. This was done as a deterrent to others. Her decisive action was hailed. Confidence was restored to the church. She appointed another financial committee. This time, she was lucky to appoint men and women of proven integrity. This new committee had given the church a healthy bank account. Other humanitarian services were established because the funds are available to finance them. They used their resources to support the needy, and give scholarship to the children of the poor. A sick bay was established within the church premises. The sick were brought there to receive free treatment from the church doctors.

The charity and humanitarian aspects of Efo's church had

aroused envy among other churches who regarded her success as not being good for business. They felt that if she was not checked, she would just swallow them up. They had been holding meetings on how to meet the challenge posed by Efo and her church. They resolved to form an Association of Pastors and churches to regulate the practice and proliferation of churches. They invited Efo to their inaugural meeting, but excluded the established churches. The reason for excluding them was not stated but it was obvious that they felt that they did not practice the same brand of Christianity as the established churches. On their part the established churches did not regard them as churches and would not have anything to do with them. Efo rejected their invitation.

She resolved that she would have nothing to do with that type of association. She did not want to gang up in matters concerning spirituality. She was called to serve God. She believed that religion should be free and a private affair. Each person should feel free to practice it the way he deems fit. Efo's refusal to attend the meeting was a big blow to the pride of the members of the association. They decided to send delegates to go and persuade Efo to join their association. The delegates arrived and pleaded with Efo to join them, but she refused. The delegates reported back to the Association and it was resolved that they would collectively and variously do all in their power to destroy Efo and her church.

Chapter Fourteen

The refusal of Efo to parley and fraternize with the association of pastors was the beginning of her problems. She refused to associate with them because she felt that she did not have the same objectives. She was called to serve God and not to make money. What those other pastors were doing was well known to the people. They stole, killed and took people's wives. She however did not reckon with the determination of the association to deal with her.

It did not take long. The day was a normal day. Efo went to work as usual. The day was very busy and hectic. On such days she used to close very late. She was feeling tired so she decided to close around 10.00pm. While in the office she used to attend to the problems of members. Their problems seemed endless enough to exhaust anybody. She attended to very few people. The problems were mainly spiritual, monetary and social. Whether on a service day or not she had made it a rule that she would close by 11.00pm every day. Those members that she could not see that day would have to come back another day since she was there every day. Some troubled members spent days on the church premises waiting to be attended to by the leader. Some of them had come from very far distances and would not want to undertake the trouble and expenses of going home and coming back another day. They made adequate preparations before leaving home that they would sleep in the church premises if the need arose. Others who were from within the vicinity also made arrangements to sleep in the church compound. Their case is due to anxiety. They want to be attended to as soon as possible. They may feel that they require urgent solution to their problems and therefore require urgent attention. They therefore sleep in order to be in front of the queue the next day. That is why there were always people in the church premises. But their squatting in the church premises even though tolerated by the church does not, however make it the duty of the church to protect and provide for them. They stay at their own risk. However the church had provided a modest security network to guard the property of the church. It is true that members benefited by the extended security services, they are expected to leave the church premises immediately after services if they have nothing else to do.

Efo normally treks home after work each day. Her home is about a hundred meters away, within the church premises. She does not want ostentatious life, and trekking would afford her the opportunity of walking under the breeze while meditating on the days job. She was usually accompanied by about four aides. They were trusted members of the church who also live in the same neighbourhood with her. She built the houses for them.

They had set off for home after closing. They were walking in silence. This was one of the days Efo did not normally talk to anybody while walking.

This happens so often. Silence enables her to pray. This is so if she wanted to reach out to someone who needed help. Some members used to have bad cases and she used to continually pray for them in order to alleviate their sufferings. There are days when she does not pray. On such days they would converse while walking home. Efo naturally did not talk too much. She therefore used to listen to members of her retinue who were talking. She could interject by saying one or two words. This was very often in a very low tone. Efo had been praying since they left her office. They were not anticipating any problem on the way. They have not had any since the church started. They had cut a straight and narrow path from the church to their homes. It was shorter. The street lights were very far away and could only provide dim lights to the centre of the field where they were walking. The light was sufficient to enable them to find their way. The church compound was a very large expanse of land. Efo had deliberately acquired the land. Her plan was to expand to the vacant areas later, when the church started to grow and they needed more structures. It was a good business decision. If she had allowed non-members of her church to acquire the adjoining plots of land, that would create a problem when they wanted to expand in future. The compound was fenced with concrete walls. There were trees planted by the sides of these walls to provide shades and beautify the place. The lawns and grass were well tended. All around the walls there were bulbs stuck on the top to provide light. A security organisation was contracted to ensure that the property of the church was safeguarded. It was expected that nothing would escape their notice.

Efo and her retinue were about thirty meters from her house, when suddenly she stumbled and tripped over a middle-aged man lying horizontally in front of them. She fell down immediately. So did one of her companions. The other three were walking slightly behind and barely skipped over the body of the man. They ran in different directions into the dark open fields to no place in particular. Each was running as far as his legs could carry him. Their heads were blank and their hands were whirling in the air in a manner that could win an Olympic gold. Suddenly not knowing what they were running for they screeched to a halt as if being controlled by an invisible force. Still gasping for breath, they yelled out to each other calling themselves by their names "Where are you."

Another added "Where is the evangelist, where is the evangelist."

"Maybe she is in the house," he answered. They again ran towards the house.

Efo and the man who fell with her got up immediately after falling and started to run. The man ran far into the darkness. He did not actually know the direction he was running in. Efo ran but could not go far. She ran as far as five meters towards her house before falling down again. This time she could not get up. She was exhausted and could not talk. She lay there almost lifeless. It was about ten minutes later that the others gathered their nerves and came towards the dead man to look for Efo. They had tried to look for her elsewhere but she was nowhere to be found. They had thought she ran to her house. When they rushed to the house, they were told she had not returned. They started to fret. "Where is she, where is she?" they chorused. They were unaware that she was lying somewhere like the corpse that had frightened them.

A search party was organised to look for Efo. More people especially the security personnel were mandated to find Efo by all means. Efo was found lying about five meters from the corpse. People were terrified. They thought that she had passed away. They hurriedly lifted her and rushed her to her house. Many people who heard what had happened had started to gather around her house. Many were crying. In their frenzy they forgot to check properly who was lying on their path. That would have to wait until they knew what was happening to their leader. The church doctor was called in. The doctor administered first aid on Efo and assured that there was nothing very serious to cause alarm. "She had had a shock and would be alright in about an hour's time, he said. The doctor's words calmed down a lot of people. They started to re-group to go back to the spot where the whole thing started. They wanted to check whether the corpse was still there and who it was. They wanted to find out everything about everything. They left with their search lights. They had thought, the fracas was the handiwork of a mischievous truant who wanted to play a dirty game. It was not. They also thought it could be that the man was not dead after all, and could be a drunkard or even a destitute seeking the special attention of their leader. None of these deductions was true. It was a real dead person, that was lying down there. He was well dressed and very neat. That meant that he was not a destitute. Their surprise was that such a seemingly responsible person could just be lying down in the centre of the field dead. They suspected fowl play. However, they were not there to determine the cause of death, even though the doctor had gone with them. They were there primarily to determine whether the man was playing a trick. He was not. They were satisfied but sad at the whole episode, a man dead, their leader in a coma, and their premises being used as a dumping ground. "Some people must have done this job of dumping," someone among them said. They left the man there and went back to their leaders' place. They then called the police to formally report what had happened and the presence of a corpse in their premises. They were shocked at what the police told them. The police had told them that it was not only a corpse but there was another corpse in another area of the compound. The police also queried why they were making a second report since someone who claimed to be acting on behalf of the church had reported the existence of the corpses at about 10.00pm. This police feedback was the more surprising because at about the time the first report was made, the leader was closing from the office. That was before she left the office. The existence of a corpse was only discovered some minutes later when she tripped over it. Something must then be going on. Who made the report. This is the question they found very hard to answer. They also wondered where the second corpse was lying. They immediately organised a search. It was later found behind a concrete pavement near the church building. Nobody touched it nor did they attempt to examine it closely as they did the first one. They were content on seeing where it was. They barricaded the place until the police came in the morning. The police arrived at dawn as they promised. They checked the security system in the compound and took some photographs. They also took samples of the soil before removing the corpses. They took the corpses to the general hospital for autopsy.

It was the members of the association of church pastors who had deposited the corpses in Efo's church compound. It was one of a series of ploys they had planned to impugn and malign her character and destroy her church. It was they who first reported to the police about the presence of the corpses. They had pretended in their report to the police that they were concerned members of Efo's church. They wanted the police to investigate the matter urgently and absolve them. That was why the police were surprised at the second call.

The police came back to the church and arrested several members of the church. One of those arrested for questioning was the leader of the church. The discovery of the corpses had generated tension in the city. People were anxious to know what had happened and who were responsible. Some members of the association of pastors had come forward to pose as the relations of the dead people. They demanded that justice be done. One of the ways they wanted justice to be done was the trial of the leader of the church and payment of a large amount of money. They insisted that if she was found guilty which they had planned she would, she should be given life imprisonment. They believed that if Efo was thus incarcerated, her church would disintegrate.

They were however, mistaken in their hopes. The autopsy had been performed. One of the victims was found to have died from poison. He had taken some drink which led to his death. The second person was found to have died by a stab wound at the back of his neck. He must have been dead for days before being brought to the compound. The result of the autopsy did not stop the police from taking the case to court. They had been under pressure from the Association of church pastors. This body whose members had posed as relations of the victims had done everything to intimidate the police into action. They had accused the police of collaboration; of deal making and shoddy investigation. They wanted the case to be prosecuted so that recompense could be made. The police on their part knew that they were not getting enough facts about who killed the dead people. A man was found dead by poison. This was not provable in a case of murder since the person who administered the poison could not be ascertained. Unless it could be proved on balance of probabilities or beyond reasonable doubt it was a useless case. In the second case a man was found to have been stabbed in the nape of the neck and he died. Although the wound had started to heal, it killed him days before he was found. A circumstantial case could be made but there are a lot of questions.

The police however, wanted to discharge their duties no matter who was involved. They did not believe in favouring anybody. They consequently charged the members of the church to court. The case was protracted. During the trial, the judge was receiving anonymous phone calls asking him to ensure that justice was done or else he would be one of the corpses. The judge was a man of impeccable character. He was noted for his fearlessness. He ordered an inquiry into where the calls were coming from. The calls were found to have been coming from the residence of one of the members of the association of pastors. It was also found out that the very first call that informed the police about the existence of corpses at Efo's church also came from this phone. The owner was a pastor of a nearby church. His arrest was ordered by the judge. This was done. He was charged in court. During his trial it was discovered that the two dead men were dissenting members of his church. They had been staunch members but they had quarrelled over money. The quarrel was tearing the church apart and members were leaving to join Efo's church. This did not go down well with the man who ordered their execution. The man who was stabbed to death was killed a few weeks earlier. What happened to him was well known to the members of their church. His family had threatened reprisals. They were conciliated with a very large sum of money. They agreed that the body should be used to bring Efo to her knees. Because of the scandal which rocked the church about the killing of the first man, the leader contrived to kill the second man by poison so that nobody would be blamed. It would be said that he died after a brief illness. His corpse was taken to Efo's compound as a way of roping in the leader and destroying her church. It was a conspiracy of the association.

This case had therefore decided Efo's fate. On the day of judgement the judge told Efo "Woman, go in peace, the good Lord has decided the case in your favour. This shows that you have been doing good work in the name of the Lord. Those who seek to destroy you will themselves be destroyed. It was Socrates who said that "Nothing happens to a good man." I also say to you that nothing happens to a good pastor. You should therefore go and continue with your good work with the fear of God. You are discharged and acquitted and I want the law enforcement agents to provide you with security." All those present at the court chorused. "As your Lord pleases" before shouting "Halleluiah." Members of Efo's church were rejoicing everywhere. Their leader was very high. The jubilation continued until they got home where members were trooping in to thank their leader and give praise to God. They believed that God in his infinite mercies had wrought one of his miracles. The pastor who killed the men was convicted. He was however, not given a heavy sentence. The people had expected that he would be put in jail for the rest of his life. This was not to be. He was given the minimum sentencing. This did not go down well with the public who had implicit confidence in the judge. They had started to talk openly about betrayal by the judge. It was obvious that the judge had in a way favoured the association of pastors. People were speculating why such an erudite judge should betray the confidence reposed on him by the public. The judge however had his own opinion on the issue of sentencing. To him what mattered most was the conviction of a felon. Sentencing was more or less discreet though it depended on the degree of offence. But it was given as a deterrent to others as well as to punish the offender. The law usually was lenient in sentencing when the accused was a first offender.

No matter what anybody's legal opinion may be; the truth was that the judge who was in his mid sixties was also a member of a certain church that was now a member of the association of pastors. He was not however, a member of the association but his close friend and associate was one of the pastors spearheading the association. The judge wanted to keep his membership to that spiritual church a secret, and would not like to be drawn into the limelight. He had sympathy for the association but certainly he was not one of them. He would not allow his membership of a church to cloud his sense of justice, and had decided the case in accordance to the law, and to what he believed to be fair and firm. His friend, the pastor had however, exerted some influence on him to mitigate the sentencing which he had done. This was difficult to admit.

The judge had shared the secrets of his personal life with the pastor. He had a long standing feud with his wife. It was the pastor who had been reconciling them.

The judge's hands were thus tied by the pastor who he considered an important knot keeping his family together. Although the people were disappointed and grumbled about the sentencing, they still had faith in the judge.

This case was a very big eye opener for Efo, and members of her church. They had hitherto lived with trust in God and man. They were not out to ruin anybody or to steal anybody's property. They did not expect that anybody would be out to ruin them. They were now witnessing the reverse side of human beings. They would henceforth take extra measures to protect themselves. Efo's rejection of the invitation to join the association of pastors was not designed to snub anybody. She merely wanted to be on her own and pursue her pastoral career the way she felt the Lord wanted her to do without interference from anybody. She did not see how her innocent refusal would elicit vengeance from people she had not known before. She had therefore decided that henceforth she would be extra vigilant. The starting point would be the security system in her church. She fervently believed that those who carried corpses into her compound were not invisible. They were human beings and must have entered the compound from somewhere. Why did somebody not see them and stop them? She believed that they succeeded because the security system was lax. She must therefore beef up that area as a first measure. She did. She terminated the contract with the security organisation and decided to train her own security outfit. This she hoped would give her direct control of the security network.

Her trials and tribulations did not disunite her church as the association had hoped. It had rather strengthened it. The members of her church were resolute in carrying on the battle. They felt that they were being persecuted. It was normal. All soldiers of Christ including the Lord himself had from time immemorial been persecuted. It was written in the Bible. If the work of the Lord must continue on earth, members should not fear death. It was better to die while fighting for the Lord and receive everlasting life than be a coward and be condemned to hell and get consumed by the un-quenchable fire.

As a result of the victory won by Efo, more members were being admitted daily into her church. The judgement in the court had convinced others that this is the true church of God. They are honest. They do not kill. All others who have ganged up against them have been shown to be murderers. The people were wondering how murderers were qualified to preach the word of

God. “Not to me, not to me” and they started deserting the other churches in their thousands.

Efo received all those who came to her church with open arms. She charged them to be of good behaviour and have faith in the Lord. “The battle has just begun, be ye a soldier of God,” she told them.

Chapter Fifteen

The association of pastors had lost a case which was very important to them. They had been confident that Efo would be roped in. They had hoped to use the remote connection to the trial judge as a master stroke. It did not quite work out as they had planned. The after effect had become more biting for them as their members were deserting and trooping into Efo's church. They had not however, given up their fight. They had only lost the first battle. They believed it was a war. They hoped to win the war. That war was to destroy Efo and all she stood for. She was not good for their business. They hatched another plan against her.

This time around, they had used the opportunity of exodus into Efo's church to infiltrate into her church. They had selected a good number of their people who were well versed in church matters to join Efo's church. That however, did not mean that they would give up their own faith in their own churches. They had been selected because they knew the tricks of the business and were good public speakers. They would easily rise to the top of any church no matter how guarded. These people had been instructed to cause dissension in the woman's church and help to break it up. They knew it would take some time before they could rise to the top but were confident of the outcome. Efo had become aware of the battle she was facing but she did not know in what form it would take.

She was used to administering her church through committees. These new converts to her church soon found themselves in various committees. Some even became chairmen of these committees. It was like sleeping with an enemy without realizing it. It did not take long before quarrels and conflicts erupted within committees. It was like wildfire which was spreading. There would be a quarrel in one committee which she would settle. As soon as she finished settling that, another would spring up in another committee. She was now spending a greater percentage of her time settling quarrels among various committees. This was affecting her effectively preaching the gospel. In order to stem these quarrels she decided to open more branches of her churches in other towns and cities. She wanted to send away some of the more troublesome members of the church to go and head the new branches. She had thought of abolishing the committees and rule directly, but she rescinded that, because it would make the work more tedious. She went ahead and opened the branches.

Nobody rejected their new positing. They knew they could not. It was the work of the Lord that they were being asked to go and do. No true servant of God would refuse to serve the Lord. Her decision was a very good one. Immediately these troublesome members left to go to the branches, the tension at the headquarters cooled down. Things seemed to have returned to normal. She was happy that she had solved an explosive problem. She did it inadvertently. It was perhaps the Lord that was directing her. The association of pastors was however not happy at having its members who were holding important positions being posted out. They still had others remaining but these had not yet gained any status within the church.

The next move of the association was to launch assaults on Efo's church from the branches. That was where they knew that loopholes existed. They asked the branch pastors who were indirectly under their command but who reported directly to Efo to stop remitting stipends to the headquarters. They should in fact break away and declare themselves independent churches. They would however not do it simultaneously. They should do it one after the other so that it would look like one person's success influenced the other. One of the most senior pastors of Efo's church was the first to do it. He was trusted and liked by Efo herself. The man was a knowledgeable and powerful speaker. He was attracting a lot of people to the church of the Lord. He changed the name of the church and stopped all communication with Efo. Initially Efo did not take the man seriously because she knew she had invested a lot of her personal money in that church. The building was erected with her money. The land was acquired with her money. All the properties belong to her. She wondered what the man was up to. She issued an ultimatum to the man to rescind his decision and return to the Lord. She knew that the devil had set in the way of the pastor; but believed that God would always triumph over the devil. She invited the man to a meeting. She also called all her branch pastors, senior pastors and elders. The dissenting pastor scoffed the meeting. The elder's committee advised her to first of all appoint a pastor that would replace the man, and where that failed she should report to the police to recover the property of the church. She did.

She appointed another man she thought to be a loyalist to go and replace the man. The dissenting pastor fired back. He asked the new pastor not to step into the town or he would be dead. This was however, a ruse. The newly appointed man was a staunch member of the association of pastors. He belonged to the same camp as the other pastor. Both of them knew it. The new man defied the threat of the other pastor. He collected a huge sum of money, vehicles and other properties that will enable him to continue the work of the Lord in his new station. But immediately he stepped down in the new town he declared his support for the dissenting pastor. Efo and his loyalists were flabbergasted. They had started to think that something was wrong with their organisation. They have not determined exactly what was wrong. It was however, complicated. They did not know who to question any longer. They came up with the idea that before they could effectively deal with the problem posed by the dissenting pastors, they must do some house cleaning. They did. They decided that all members must swear an oath of secrecy and allegiance.

The police was informed to arrest the pastors and recover the churches' properties in their possession. The rebel pastors replied and warned the police to steer clear of the matter. "It is a private and civil affair. No policeman should interfere. Any policeman that sets foot on our church premises will be a dead man," they said. The police were not very much willing to interfere in the matter. They too believed that Efo should take a civil action to recover her properties; and leave police out of it. They however, knew that there was no way they could fold their arms and watch a potentially explosive situation cause a civil strife. They therefore arranged a meeting to reconcile Efo with her dissenting members. Both parties attended the meeting. The meeting was held under a peaceful atmosphere. There was no outward showing of what each others feeling was. They all agreed that the pastors should release all Efo's properties in their possession. Efo would on her part pay them a large sum of money that would enable them to rehabilitate themselves at another location.

The pastors had agreed to the deal merely to assuage feelings and satisfy the police. They wanted the police to keep their hands off the matter. They had masters they reported to. As soon as they got back home they reported to the association. They were asked not to honour the deal. They then sent word to Efo that she should not send people to come and take over the premises. They still regarded the church and premises as belonging to them. Efo did not believe them. She believed that the matter had been settled. She subsequently sent about four of her senior pastors to go and recover the property of the church. It was the last journey those emissaries made.

They were waylaid on the outskirts of the town by unknown persons and killed. They were burnt to ashes, beyond recognition. This was to obliterate any evidence that might show that they were the ones killed. The vehicle in which they travelled was also burnt beyond recognition. The news spread like wild fire. The citizens of the town carried placards to protest at the cold blooded murder of innocent people in the name of the church. They called on the government to seek out the culprits and punish them adequately. The dissenting pastors denied any involvement in the matter. But this was a lie.

They were clearly taken aback by the reaction of the public. It would definitely put an end to their career as pastors and make nonsense of the confrontation with Efo. Nobody supports a murderer. They would soon realise that; when their members abandon the church for them. The police were called in once again. Immediately they sensed the presence of police the two pastors disappeared. A special manhunt was mounted for them. Before their disappearance, unknown persons had set the church on fire. The fire destroyed every property on the premises. The search for the two men continued without trace of their whereabouts. The police did not relent in the search for the pastors. It sometimes takes several years before unravelling a crime or capturing culprits.

It did not take long in this case. The police got a tip off about shallow graves around the church premises. The police decided to check the graves. They were dug and two decomposing bodies exhumed. They were taken to a forensic laboratory where it was confirmed that they were those of the pastors. Their death gave rise to fresh rumours and speculation; and even questions about spiritual churches. Who are these church owners? What are they up to? The answers to these questions were known for years by the discerning members of the public who distanced themselves from these churches. There are others who knew that some of these churches are out to grab money by all means just like crime organisations. They are ready to kill in order to achieve their objective. There is no place in the Bible where God sanctioned murder. But the Bible is being used only as a facade, while the real motives of those churches are hidden from the public.

Efo had come of age. She did not allow her tribulations so far to affect her or the profession she had been called into. She had come to trust in the name of the Lord. She knew that the Lord giveth and the same Lord taketh away. She mourned her departed members. For over a month members of her church wore black clothes to the service. Special services were held in all the branches of her church for the repose of the souls of those gentlemen who died for the Lord. Her church continued to wax stronger after she had carried out a thorough reorganisation. She has become aware that the battle to remain intact must be fought from within too. She was aware of the presence of her enemies within the fold. But like a true believer, she believed that God would fight her battle for her. She would never seek revenge in any form.

Chapter Sixteen

Eka, the precious daughter of Efo had been living in the same house with her mother since she was removed from her foster parents. The girl had become an ardent Christian. She had been greatly involved in her mother's church. She was the next target of the association of pastors after the rebellion. The association had sponsored four handsome young men to ensure that Eka was pregnant.

They wanted to use that as a basis for bringing Efo to her knees. These boys who were in their mid-twenties were carefully selected. They were given anything money could buy. The boys thus became members of Efo's church. They were quite devoted but never made their identity clear. They never behaved as if they knew one another and always avoided occasions that would bring them together. They were however, meeting secretly in the city where they rented separate apartments. It did not take long before one of them started to date Eka. They professed love for each other. Things were going on well for two of them until the temptation of Eka. The next boy approached her and she fell for him. She thought she was being smart enough to keep two boyfriends at the same time. She professed love for this second boy and they started to date each other. The boys were acting in the true spirit of their mandate. They allowed some time to elapse before the third boy struck. He too was overwhelmed at his success. Eka in her stupidity also fell for him and they were professing their love for each other. The fourth boy struck not very long after and was very successful. He knew he would succeed. They had found out the weakness of Eka. She was happy having four boyfriends. She was playing them against each other. She was writing them love letters telling each that he was the only one in her life and that she loved him dearly. She did not reckon that the boys would one day meet each other. But they did. They were on a mission. They used to compare notes. They used to read Eka's letters to each other. They would normally laugh it off.

Eka was with one of her boyfriends one day and they were shopping at the supermarket. They accidentally ran into another of her boyfriends. She quickly introduced two of them and called one her cousin. The boys in expertly tutored guise agreed with her. The other boy soon left, and the one who came to the market with her did not bother to raise questions. He never batted an eyelid. He rather teased her for having a handsome cousin.

Eka continued with her cat and mouse game with the boys until one day she discovered that she had missed her period. There was one of the boys she liked particularly, so she decided he was the father. She approached him and calmly told him. She thought the boy would be happy at the news. She was wrong. He became hysterical and refused to accept he was responsible.

She was a bit confused. She did not want to compound things for herself. She thought of abortion before her mother should find out. She, however approached the second boy. He told her not to worry. She should keep the baby. It was God's gift. It is not everybody that can get pregnant. He reasoned that abortions are fraught with many dangers. The girl could die in the process; or, if she did not die, an important organ in her body could be destroyed. This would make it impossible to get pregnant again in life. Eka bought his argument and decided to keep the pregnancy. She thought that by the boy's argument he had accepted ownership of the pregnancy. She did not fear what her mother would say since she knew who the father of her baby was. She was wrong again in her assumption. It did not take long before the first boy she approached disappeared. He packed his belongings and left the town.

The pregnancy was growing and Efo had been observing the changes taking place in her daughter. She knew she was pregnant. She called her into her room and asked her if she was pregnant. Eka accepted being pregnant. Her mother asked her if she knew who was responsible. She said 'yes.' Efo then invited the boy to her house. She was happy he was a member of her church. Eka had brought the boy who told her to keep the pregnancy. She was hopeful that the boy would accept responsibility. However, when the boy was asked by Efo if he was responsible for the pregnancy, the answer she received was shocking to her and her daughter. The boy had said an emphatic no. He said he was not responsible. He produced letters Eka had been writing to another boy. Such love letters were revealing of the intimacy between Eka and another boy and wondered how he would be saddled with the pregnancy.

He wanted to make a scene and tell the world that he was being falsely accused. Efo did not want a scandal. She allowed the boy to go. She thought of aborting the pregnancy but it was too late. It could result in the death of Eka.

She asked Eka about the second boy. Eka called the third boy. He came. He was asked if he was responsible for the pregnancy. He too said no and brought out love letters, Eka had been writing to the fourth boy. Efo after reading the letters, placed her two hands on the table and placed her head on her arms. The hands were her pillow and she dozed off. She did not look up until after an hour. Before then the boy had scampered out of the door. Eka herself had gone back to her room. When Efo looked up, her eyes were heavy and red. All she did was to pick up her Bible.

She went to her study room. She stayed there for a very long time reading her Bible and praying. She went to bed very late. In the morning, the first thing she did was to go into Eka's room. She guided her in prayer and they read some passages from the Bible. This was to become a regular habit. She knew the implication of Eka being pregnant and delivering a child out of wedlock. Eka was her only daughter. She believed that her church would be ruined if the news ever got out. She decided that Eka would henceforth remain indoors. She employed a nanny to look after Eka and, all her antenatal examinations would be supervised by the church doctors. Nobody was allowed to visit Eka. Members of the church did not know how the daughter of their evangelist disappeared from public. All queries about it were rebuffed.

Eka eventually delivered. It was a baby girl. Her mother had not been happy since she became pregnant. She did not want the baby either. She thought it was a sin to be born without the parents being married. She was also thinking of the damage it would do to her reputation and the church. In order to avert adverse publicity, she told Eka to wrap the baby up and go and throw her into the river. She should not let anybody know what she was doing. The baby was carefully wrapped and given to Eka. It was only herself and her mother who decided to throw it away. She left at dusk with her baggage. That was the time they knew nobody would suspect anything. Eka got to the river bank. She brought out the baby still wrapped. She stood on the river bank with the baby for a very long time. She then took pity on the little thing she was carrying in her arms. Instead of throwing her into the river as directed by her mother, she opened the baby's cloth and saw her face. She smiled to the little thing. She took her mouth and put it at the nipple of her breast. After the baby had sucked Eka's breast, she decided not to throw her away. She came to the level ground. She did not know quite what to do. She was now thinking of how to keep the baby without letting her own mother know. She could not fathom any way this could be accomplished. She then decided to deposit the child in a narrow path which she knew was often used by people. She had hoped that somebody would pick the baby up and take care of her. She went to hide in another patch of the bush until the baby was picked up.

A certain woman was passing that path. She heard the cry of a baby. She was surprised and thought the cry must have been coming from a very far distance. She then continued on her journey. But the child cried again. This time repeatedly. The woman stopped and went to search from where the baby was crying. She saw the baby lying face up at the foot of a big tree. She lifted her up and tried to pacify her from crying. The baby however continued to cry. The woman took her and made an about turn from where she was going previously.

Meanwhile Eka had watched the whole episode from her hideout. She was exceedingly happy that the baby was picked up by a good samaritan. She allowed the woman to go very far with the baby before she could come out. She came out after about thirty minutes. She made a detour and took another road. She went straight to her home. When she got home, her mother had not come back from the office. She went straight to her room and slept.

The woman who picked up the baby went straight to the police station to lodge a formal report. She did not want to be accused of stealing a child. She would therefore act in accordance with the advice given by the police. The police thanked her and advised her to take the baby to a certain orphanage. The baby was taken to an orphanage while a search was mounted to locate the mother of the baby. Nobody had a clue as to who the mother was. The baby was being shown on the local TV station and people were being asked to make donations towards its upkeep. Donations flowed freely.

When Efo came back from the office, she went straight to Eka's room. She woke her up and asked how she discharged the assignment. Eka assured her that the baby was thrown into the river as planned. Efo was relieved. She asked Eka to continue to remain indoors until she recovered from the effect of delivery. When she recovered fully, she could come out and resume her normal activities.

The truth is that Efo was the only evangelist recognised within the area as the child of God. People had always believed whatever she said because they thought her to be clean and above board. The other preachers and pastors had always been regarded as murderers. By ordering the killing of an innocent baby, because it was sinful to have borne her out of wedlock was ironic. Murder is a sin in itself, so, it is a sin to use sin, to avert another sin. Also to order the killing of an innocent child to avert shame or because it would ruin her reputation is also not good. It shows that a crack had appeared in Efo's soul. If the people ever knew that she ordered that an innocent child should be thrown into the river, they would lose confidence in her and her church. Her belief that nobody would ever find out what happened was misplaced.

Eka had not told all the truth about how she carried out the assignment. Everyday, the child would be shown on the television as abandoned. Eka had timed the periods it would be shown. She used to sit down disconsolately watching the child. She knew the child was her baby. She wanted to reach out and snatch her back. She could not however do that. Her mother had occasionally observed her reaction when the baby was being shown but she never attached much importance to it. She thought that having delivered a baby herself, Eka would now love babies and sympathise with their plight.

One day Eka reminded her mother that it was long time that they had attended their charity work to orphanages. She told her that she did not like the way she threw her baby away. They should therefore visit orphanages and make donations. This would compensate for the child she threw away. Her mother agreed with her. Giving to charity was a part of her calling to serve humanity. She therefore instructed that the charity wing of her church should visit orphanages and make donations. Eka should be among those that would go. Eka rejoiced at the news. She had hoped to use that opportunity to hold and cuddle her baby. She was feeling guilty and unfulfilled. She planned to give a special present to her baby.

On the day of the visit Eka was feeling very buoyant. Nobody noticed her mood. They visited about five other orphanages in the town. The last one they visited was where her daughter was. She had been giving presents to all the babies where they visited. When it got to the turn of her baby, she could not hide her feelings. She lifted the baby up and planted a kiss on her lips. People around were surprised at her behaviour to this particular child. Yet they did not attach much importance to her actions. They thought she was charmed by the beauty of the baby. She later presented her with a special present. When they were leaving she turned several times to look in the direction of the baby. Eka's mind had not gone off the little baby even after they got home. She had been thinking what to do to recover the baby from the orphanage. People used to go to orphanages to adopt babies. She had heard of it but she dare not suggest that to her mother. She was too young to do that on her own. Everyday she would make sure she was near the television to see the baby when announcement would be made about her. She had also been praying that nobody should adopt her child until she was in a position to do so herself.

Meanwhile the police were still searching for a mother who had dumped her child by the riverside. They had not succeeded but they had not given up. The association had been busy underground. They knew that Eka was pregnant. That was a scandal by itself, but they hoped that the rout would be completed when she delivered. They had not followed what happened after the boys left. The boys left prematurely. They should have stayed to ensure that Eka delivered before abandoning her.

Efo had hidden her daughter from public view and nobody else except her and the doctor knew that Eka delivered a baby. The association was frantic to know what happened but there was nobody to tell them. They had sponsored a certain newspaper to speculate that, Eka, the daughter of evangelist Efo was pregnant. Efo did not waste time in refuting this allegation. She went to the TV station and showed her daughter to the world to disprove the malicious allegation the newspaper and its sponsors were making against her. She wanted them to desist from further maligning her person or else she would drag them to court. The next day one of the boys who impregnated Eka appeared in the same television. He was appealing to Eka through this medium to bring out their baby for him to see. He said that he was sorry to have disowned the pregnancy but would make up for everything if only Eka would allow him to see his child. He also said that he knew that the child was delivered because it was too late to carry out an abortion at the time he left them.

One of the nurses at the orphanage was a friend of one of the pastors. She had sympathy for their cause and was willing to work for them. Immediately she saw the boy make an appeal on the television, she made enquiries and got in touch with him. "I saw you on the television the other day," she told the boy.

He replied, "Yes."

She said further. "Are you sure you are the father of the child."

The boy still replied in the affirmative. "OK"

She began. "There was a child brought to our orphanage. This child fits the description of what you said on television. But there is a young girl who takes special interest in this child. She is the daughter of the evangelist. All of us in the orphanage are suspecting she owned the child but does not want to show it. She frequents the orphanage and buys special gifts for the child. She cuddles her more than she does the other children. Any time she comes around to see the child, we all snoop on her and start laughing. She has not been able to detect our presence. If you know it is your child and you are really interested in finding out the truth, you should come around the orphanage and lay an ambush. I am sure it will not be long before you'll catch her coming to see the child. She hardly goes a week without seeing the child. But under no circumstances should you betray me. If my bosses find out that I have told you this, I will lose my job. So, be careful the way you go about it. Good luck!"

The boy thanked the nurse immensely and promised there was no way a third ear would hear about it. He then started going to the orphanage everyday to lay ambush. The boy's decision to stay around the orphanage paid off. Within the week, Eka came as usual to visit the baby. She entered the house and greeted the nurses. They did not chat. She made straight for the child. She came with some presents wrapped in ordinary paper. The nurses knew her mission. They grinned. The boy who laid ambush quickly came near the building. He hid his frame behind the outer door while looking through the hinge of the door, to see where Eka had gone. Eka got to the baby and lifted her up. She kissed her. She was still admiring the baby when a voice yelled "Eka." The sound came from a close range. She was shocked to hear her name in that way. She turned with the baby in her arms. It was the boy who appeared on the television to make a claim. He was standing right there about an inch from Eka. "Eka, is this our baby?" he asked. Eka did not utter a word. She quickly dropped the baby in its cot and left. She made a quick dash towards the door. The boy followed in pursuit. The nurses gathered near the exit and were intrigued by the events.

Eka continued moving in quick steps with a set face and without looking back. She soon got to the main road. She flagged down a taxi and left. She had forgotten the present wrapped in a paper.

She could not give it to the baby as she intended. She wanted to give it to one of the nurses after she had played with the baby. It was impossible to do that under the present circumstances.

The boy could not catch up with Eka. He had been shouting "Eka, Eka, it's me," without word coming from her in reply. After Eka had left, he went back to the building and chatted with the nurses. He went and lifted the baby up before leaving the orphanage. He was satisfied that he had seen his child. He was not even very sure he was the father of the baby. He knew he was a co-father or not even a part of the baby. He was being sponsored to make the claim. He reported back to the association of pastors who took him to the police to lodge a complaint about Eka and the baby.

The association later took him back to the TV Station to debunk the denial of Efo and her daughter about her pregnancy. He announced that the abandoned baby was his child with Eka. The baby therefore was the granddaughter of Efo.

Efo could not believe what she heard on the television. She was all the time scratching her head as the announcement was being made. "Are they serious? Do they know what they are saying?" she intoned to herself. After the announcement, she invited Eka into her private room. She questioned her seriously quoting what was said on the television. She insisted that Eka must tell her the truth about what had happened to the child. Eka started to cry. She eventually told her mother the truth. She confessed that when she got to the riverbank, she had developed a faint heart. She was pitying the little child and subsequently left her where a woman picked her up. She had watched the whole drama from a hidden place. She later saw the same child on the television. She knew it was her child. That was why she went to see her at the orphanage. She begged her mother to forgive her. She knew she had committed a serious offence. She asked her mother to remember that Jesus used his blood to wash our sins. God had always forgiven our sins. We should all learn to emulate God by forgiving ourselves our sins. Her mother could not believe her ears. So her daughter knew as much of the scriptures too.

However, her concern now was not her daughter's sermon. Her main problem was the shame and effect of the disclosure of what had happened would have on her as a person and her church. She was confused. She asked Eka "Why have you not told me this all the time. See what problems you have brought to me. You have ruined my life." After scolding and preaching to Eka, she entered her study to pray. She stayed there for a very long time. She knew that the worst had happened to her. She knew that she would be called a murderer just like those pastors. She knew that the association of pastors had defeated her. She was still strong in spirit. She believed that what had happened was not sufficient to make her lose faith in the Lord. She begged God for forgiveness.

She assured herself that she would come out openly and claim back the child. She decided that the best way to handle the problem was to disclose everything that happened to the congregation and ask for their forgiveness. We are all human. They should not allow what happened to dampen their spirit or shake their faith in the Lord. The Lord is all knowing, all understanding and all forgiving. The next day she called a meeting of the elders' committee. She told them everything. She asked for forgiveness for herself and her daughter. She told them to help extract forgiveness from the congregation. The elders' committee took pity on her. They concluded that no human being is perfect. That was why we are all struggling to reach perfection. It is not easy either, to achieve that status which is reserved for masters like Jesus. They accepted there was a mistake. What matters now is how to rectify the mistake. They therefore resolved to set aside a day and call it "A dark day of the soul". They decided that on this day all the members would be asked to assemble in the open fields of the church to keep a vigil. They would bring candles and wear dark clothes. They would remain silent and seated. They would be guided in prayer and singing praises to the Lord. At the appropriate moment they would be told how the daughter of the evangelist had derailed. This was a special occasion to tell them the truth and ask them to remain faithful to God and the church. The church does not belong to the evangelist. It belongs to all of them. Nobody is above the church. The church would always deal with any of its members. They should not use a mistake on the part of the leader as an excuse to cause disaffection.

On the day of the vigil, a large number of the congregation turned up to honour the invitation. Efo was there with her daughter. Both of them dressed in black like everyone else. There was no stage. Everybody was regarded as equal. All would however sit facing the same direction and the senior members of the church would sit in the front row. It was some of them that would guide the congregation. As members arrived they would light their candles and place them on the small hand stool in front of their chairs. Women who came with their children were asked to control them and ensure that they did not cry, since absolute silence was required. The entire ground was illuminated by the light of the candles and the tiny electric bulbs used to make a fence of the entire field. Everybody remained silent but after an interval of thirty minutes a voice of one of those in front would ring out "May the Lord be praised." This was echoed by the congregation in response. After an interval of an hour a popular song of the church would be sung and the entire congregation joined in the singing.

Things continued this way until about 1.00am when the chairman of the elders committee stood up to address the congregation. He said, "My dear people. It may surprise you why we have gathered here tonight. It may also surprise you why I am addressing you for the first time in the history of our beloved church and not our Leader. She is right here with us and has given full approval for me to address you. I have also been mandated by the elders to talk to you. Today has been declared, "The Dark Day of the Soul". You may wonder what that means. It means a lot to me, to you, to all of us and to our dear church. Our church has been undergoing serious temptation recently. You are all aware of a group of young men who go by the name of the association of pastors. These young people had approached our leader to join their group but they were turned down. Since then, they have vowed to bring down our church and eliminate our leader. This must never be allowed to happen. These people are money hustlers. They want money. They are too young to appreciate the gravity of their action. They were never trained in pastoral duties and therefore are not capable of comprehending and disseminating the word of God as contained in the Bible. My dear people, it is this set of gangsters that carried corpses of human beings and deposited them on our church premises. They were responsible for the deaths of these people but they wanted it to look like it was done by members of this church. However, they failed as they will continue to fail. The next thing they did was to organise the gang rape of the beloved daughter of our Leader. Again their aim was to destroy our leader and pull down our church. They had gone to court. They had gone on television and radio in an effort to discredit our leader but they have failed.

It was after the raping of the daughter of our leader that the innocent little girl became pregnant. It is only natural that when a young girl is pregnant, she should know who the father of the child is. But where an innocent girl is raped by rogues, armed robbers or people of dubious character, it is necessary that something be done about that pregnancy. It is under this frame of mind that our leader thought it necessary that since the father of the unborn baby could not be ascertained, an abortion must be carried out to remove the fetus. However, the doctors thought it unsafe for the daughter of our leader. They believed that she could die in the process because the pregnancy was advanced. It was with heavy heart that our leader and her daughter allowed the pregnancy to stay. The child was subsequently delivered by Eka. My dear brethren, the birth of a child should normally elicit joy and jubilation; but, not always and not in all cases. Certainly not in this particular case. This is a church founded and run by a highly reputable evangelist. She knew and thought that her reputation was at stake. She was right. If you had spent so many years sacrificing everything to be where you are, then, you deserve to remain there as you want. You should not be corrupted by the sins of other people. What I am telling you this night is that our leader had achieved a high reputation and did not want anything to pull her down.

The association of pastors had been doing everything to tarnish this high reputation but our leader had resisted them. It had come to a stage where every evil placed in the way of this our church must be seen as a design by that evil association to pull us down. That was how our leader saw everything. We are all human. There is no rule for human jettison, as declared by a notable judge, and our leader erred by advising her daughter to do away with the child. It was a sin to do that. She had realized it and she is prepared to take back the child and atone for that sin. As I said we are all human and therefore very imperfect in our ways. Perfection is only reserved for such masters like Jesus for whom we praise his name every day here. We are all striving to be like him and we hope to reach that stage at our transition.

We are gathered here today to ask you to listen to the story and forgive our leader. We do not want you to go out and start hearing rumours of what was happening and what would have been. You must decide for yourself - here and now. Our leader has sinned. She knew it was a sin against God but, she has ever since been praying to God and asking for forgiveness. She also wants you to join in praying to God; and, be ever more ready to defend yourself, your leader, and your church. The church belongs to us all. It does not belong to any one individual, and we must be ready to fight and defend the church at all times. That defence of our church starts this day. That is why we have declared today 'dark day of the Soul". It is a momentous day in the history of our church. It is a day we must recognise as the day a great temptation visited our dear church. It is a day we must recognise as the day our leader erred but has set aside this day for repentance. It is a day we must recognise as a day of penitence and ask for the remission of our sins. It is a day we must observe every year and forever. May God almighty be with you all."

Most members accepted in good faith the explanations given to them about what happened. They resolved to stand firmly with their leader and defend their church. They accepted it was a mistake which could happen to anybody.

The police on their part swung into action. The arrested Eka for questioning. During her interrogation she admitted everything as it happened. She begged to be forgiven. The police wanted to caution and discharge her but the association of pastors mounted a different type of pressure. Her mother was also invited for questioning by the police. The two were charged together. During the trial the prosecution asked for conviction and maximum sentencing. This would provide a deterrent to all those young girls out there who are thinking of bringing innocent children into the world and throwing them into the river. The defence counsel countered and demanded that his clients be discharged and acquitted. He cited cases to buttress his arguments. He said that a mere intention to do a thing does not amount to commission of the act. "There was a man," he said, who made up his mind to kill another man. He secured a gun and got ready. When he got to the man's house, he observed that the man had been killed by another person. He left without carrying out his intention." He then asked the court. "Is it right, just and fair to convict this man for murder for the mere fact that he had the intention?" he answered "No."

He further drew analogy to the case he had cited to the one before the court and concluded that it was an intention which was not executed because of its impossibility. "In the present case" he said, "that the society and the baby will stand to benefit if her natural mother was discharged to go and take care of her." If the mother of the baby is incarcerated the little thing will suffer. The society as a whole will lose because she may turn out to be delinquent." The trial judge agreed with the defence. He discharged and acquitted Eka and her mother. The verdict of the judge did not end the matter. The boy who had come forward to claim the child on television sued for the custody of the child. He was being backed by the association of pastors. The judge still dismissed his claim saying that he found it difficult to believe that a man would disown a pregnancy and turn round to claim the child after it had been born. He told the young man "You cannot be the rightful owner of the child. You cannot even be a putative father of the fruit of a womb you denied." The baby was thus handed to Eka and her mother to bring up. There was rejoicing and jubilation at the church premises. A special day was declared for the dedication of the child. The entire membership of the church were there that day. In fact it was like a carnival.

Chapter Seventeen

Efo had gone to court twice and twice she had defeated the association of pastors. She had come to accept that her battle against the forces of evil was a life-long affair. She knew that they would come again but she did not know in what form they would strike. In whatever way, she was prepared. As a soldier of God she would not run away. The association on its part wanted nothing short of destruction of Efo and her church. They had approached the land owner who sold the land to Efo where she erected her church and bought him over. They had paid him a very large sum of money to revoke the sale of the land. The man had initially refused to acquiesce to their request but they threatened to deal with him if he refused. The man later agreed. He did not want to revoke the sale outright. He sold the land for the second time to a member of the association without informing Efo the original purchaser.

It was with shock that Efo and members of her church saw some buildings springing up in one extreme part of their land. The concrete fence at that end was bulldozed down. About three houses had already been built. They rushed to the scene to confirm what they were seeing. They were correct. They asked the workmen on the site what they were doing and who sent them. "Did they not see that the land had been demarcated with pillars and beams." The men denied any knowledge of anything. They were ordinary professional builders whose services had been hired. They gave the names of the people who contracted their services. They were ordered to leave immediately. They left.

The structures on the ground were demolished, and new fences put up. It was a lightning operation by the members of the church. They decided to keep security men permanently on that part of the compound. They did not want it to end that way, or, else the people would come back. They went to the land owner to find out why he had behaved that way. He had sold the same land twice to two different people. They threatened not only to take him to court but to expose his evil deed. He was the son of the devil. The landowner was nowhere to be found. The association had already sponsored a trip overseas for him. They had arranged that he should go to a private resort overseas and have a rest for a month. They had hoped that by the time he came back, tempers might have cooled down. It did not cool down. The members of the church were angered. "Where had he gone to, where has he gone to?" they repeated. Members of the church reached a decision to sit-in, on the man's premises. They resolved that they would converge on the man's house and keep a twenty-four vigil until the man came back. They also resolved that members especially women should bring chairs from their houses, and the clothes should be all black including the head-gear. They would also bring candles which they would burn throughout the night. It would not be a carnival but rather a mourning period reminiscent of the day called "the dark day of the soul". The members had grouped themselves in a manner that would ensure that sufficient numbers remain on the ground.

It would be like shift duty where some relieve others. The women came with their children. It was a twenty-four hour non-stop service going on in the man's compound.

Onlookers used to come and observe what was going on especially during the night when they must have closed for the day's business. It was a spectacle to behold and people were enjoying it. However, it was not all fun for the neighbourhood who had started to feel the pinch of the noisy atmosphere. It was also hell for the family of the landowner who were miffed at how the members of the church had taken over their house and compound. Life had become near impossible since they could not move freely nor have any secret in their lives again. It was in exasperation that the wife of the man sent a wireless message to him to come home immediately. She had told the man that his house had been razed by fire and that his youngest child had died in the inferno. All this was however, a ruse to bring the man back home, to handle the situation himself. It was not surprising that the man decided to return home immediately. He was fidgeting when he received the message. He sent back a message and informed his wife of the day of his arrival. The wife went to the airport to meet him. It was there that she told the man the truth of what was happening. At that stage it was not possible for the man to go back and continue his holiday. He made up his mind that he would go back to his house but not immediately. He would stay at the airport hotel for that day while his wife would go and buy a black dress for him. He would disguise himself as a woman. His wife bought everything as directed. She brought them to the hotel, and that same night the man dressed like a woman in a black dress. He had his candle and chair. He quietly sneaked to one extreme end of the ground of his house. He mixed in with the church members. Nobody noticed his presence since they were praying when he came. When they finished with their prayer and singing, they just saw a new member who had just come. They did not know who it was but nodded their heads positively towards him. He reciprocated their nods. This was their manner of greeting and welcoming new arrivals when they are in service.

The landowner had quietly joined in their activities. He was a good actor and behaved as if he was an old member. His plans were working perfectly well. He intended to enter his house which was at the centre of the human barricade late in the night. He thought that would be a suitable time since most members would likely succumb to nature by dozing off. He did as he planned. In the early hours of the night he sneaked through the maze of sleeping women and children and entered his house. There were a few who were not sleeping. They had noticed his going up but they thought it was one of them since he dressed like a woman. When he climbed up he went straight to bed.

It was while inside the house that he contacted the law enforcement agents. He instructed them to clear his premises of the nuisance. The police enquired how he hoped they would do it but he claimed he did not know. The police arrived at the scene, anyway. They appealed to the women but were scoffed by them. The police then went to their evangelist. They promised her that justice would be done in the matter. It was Efo who arrived at the place and ordered his members to disperse. He told the women that the landowner was back from his leave and the matter would be taken to court immediately. The women subsequently left the place.

The landowner was charged in court for double dealing, stealing and corrupt practices. The association of pastors hired a notable lawyer to defend him. The man was an inherently honest man. He knew he had been used. He was awful sorry to have undertaken an assignment that was against his natural beliefs. He knew the society was corrupt. He had been in the forefront of those fighting against corruption. Now look at the mess he had put himself into. He shed tears. This is how innocent people are dragged by the rot in the society to fall into behaviour they do not believe. There are a few honest men but these are tainted by the majority who are corrupt.

Although the prosecution had adduced overwhelming facts against him, he had made up his mind to confess what happened.

He believed that he would be able to atone for his sins by confessing so that others might take a cue. The society could still be salvaged if all corrupt people would renounce their evil practices by confessing and adjusting their ways. He made a confession to the court. He said that he was an old man. He continued by saying that at his age he was not the type of person anybody could use to achieve an end that would cause commotion in the society. It was wrong and immoral for anyone to sell land twice to two different people. It is a corrupt practice that should never be condoned. He expressed surprise that the people who were behind all these were pastors. "Pastors are supposed to be men of God. They should help in cleansing the society instead of corrupting it. If those who profess the will of God are themselves corrupt then this society is finished. If pastors can stoop so low to condone evil, then where are we heading to? His statement was very moving.

While he was speaking the court was very silent. The judge was staring at him after he had finished. Nobody knew what was in his mind but he was also moved by the man's speech. The man's lawyer was speechless. He wondered why his client made a confessional statement without prior discussion with him. He kept quiet but as a professional, he knew he would not give up. He knew he had a bad case which he could not have handled if he knew it would go this way. However, he was hired by another body and not this man. He stood up and pleaded with the judge to mitigate the sentencing. The judge did. He convicted the man but allowed him to go home after cautioning him. He concluded by saying that he agreed with all he said about the corruption in the society. "But all of us must put our hands together and clean the society." The judge then turned to the faceless association of pastors and noted that this was about the third case that had been sponsored by the association to his court. They had lost in all the cases. They should desist from further, hiding under the facade of the Bible, to perpetuate evil in the society. He promised to unmask and disrobe them unless they truly go back to God. He said that as at now, he only sees devils in their midst. "If you have taken an oath to serve God, you serve that God." They swore to serve God and preach his gospels to the people but they have been dissipating energy pursuing selfish ends. He further told them that if they wanted money, they should go into business; that is where to find money. They should not think that they can deceive the people all the time. God is watching them and only He can make them pay for their sins.

After his speech, he was thanked by those present at the court. Members of the church went back with jubilation because they had won another victory. "God triumphs over evil. The pastors are evil and will continue to lose," they said. They have so far survived all the tribulations, and after each ordeal, their church is strengthened and more members flocked in. They gave praises to God.

The landowner had found it difficult to believe that he gave in to such ungodly people as the association of pastors. He thought they were honest people. He later went to Efo's church to tender an apology. He came to one of their special services where he confessed all that happened, before the entire congregation. He told the congregation that he was sorry for what happened and the suffering they had undertaken to come to his house to keep vigil. He was used, he said, but promised to stand firmly behind them. "I want you to regard me like the biblical Saul who was converted after he had sinned against the people. I have sinned against you, and against the people, but I want you to regard your sacrifice as a cleanser. It has cleansed my sins. From today on, I have taken a new name. I shall be called Paul. This is in recognition of the similarity of what happened to Paul and myself. I have also decided to be one of you and a member of the church. It is only in this church that you can still find the vestiges of honesty among its members." His declaration for their church brought jubilation among the people. "Praise the Lord, Hallelujah" was heard everywhere inside the church. They proclaimed, "It is the work of God, it is the work of God." Some said, "It is a miracle."

There is no doubt that this is one of the things spiritual churches call "miracle". If a man survives an adverse situation in life, it is a miracle or if he overcomes self-inflicted problems, it is called a miracle. Miracles are rare occurrences and applies to only those things that cannot be explained. There is no doubt therefore that these churches abuse the word.

Chapter Eighteen

So far, Efo had not been able to know the type of attack, or when and how the association of pastors would attack her and her church. But she had been able to survive it all, in what they called miraculous ways. They believed that God would always fight for them.

There were still a large number of members of her church who were being sponsored by the association. They could be found in all strata of the church hierarchy. Inspite of the oath of allegiance administered to members, these dissidents were ever ready to work for their outside masters. This is why there was a stiff opposition about a recommendation of the committee of elders to promote Efo. The committee which is the highest decision making body in the church had recommended that Efo be consecrated an archbishop. This is in line with what is obtaining in all the spiritual churches at the moment. The founders of such churches had always assumed the role of Chief executive officers. They manage and run the church as their private estates. In order words these churches are a one-man show. Any attempt by any other fellow to aspire to its leadership is ruthlessly dealt with. The aspirant may even lose his life in the process. These church owners are forever seeking new ways that will always keep them on top of affairs of the church. Every church owner is now either a bishop or an archbishop. These are the highest accolades in any church hierarchy. This, however is unlike the Catholic or the established churches. In the Catholic church, for example, the leader and the spiritual head is called 'the pope". He is regarded as the 'holy see' and oversees the affairs of the church throughout the world. He did not found the church and could be appointed from any of the numerous cardinals, who qualify to fill the post, if the incumbent dies. A pope is normally elected for life but could be removed from office if he is deficient or found wanting in any way. The pope, as all other officers of the church, are treated as the property of the church and not they treating the church as their property. They are sustained by the church and are not allowed to own property. This is unlike the spiritual churches who acquire wealth by all means. They kill in order to acquire this wealth and they used the wealth for themselves to the exclusion of their impoverished and suffering congregation.

On the other hand the church of England is structured after the Catholic church. Its head is the king of England but it has a spiritual leader who administers the day to day affairs of the church. The spiritual churches are not prepared to adopt the structure of the church of England. This is understandable because the king, even though, the head of the church, is insulated from the affairs of the church. The wonder churches cannot afford to stand aloof, and be mere on-lookers in what they regard as personal properties. They even find it difficult to allow their subordinates to preach during their service. They must be seen as the alpha and omega, and without them there will be no church. That is why they now want to go by the highest name available in the church. The only name they have not found enough courage to adopt is the pope. This may be because the protestant churches who they form their offshoots from do not use the word either.

Efo had been recommended to take on the title of archbishop which is the highest rank available in their church. This was in recognition of her services and sacrifices in ensuring that the church has a firm foothold. This recommendation did not go down well with some members who had been looking for loopholes to plug down the leader and the church. They opposed the idea and argued that what they were operating was not a recognised church. Nobody should therefore be ordained an archbishop which is a name reserved for established churches. "It will be a mockery to go ahead with the plan," they said. They further said that they were mere believers who assembled together to solve spiritual needs. "Anybody who has ambition to be a bishop or archbishop should go to a proper church and have the necessary training that will lead to her ordination."

Their line of argument surprised a lot of people including the leader of the church. Their eyes were now being opened to the low level their church had sunk.

They questioned themselves. "How can we have this sort of people in this church without knowing it. Something must be wrong with us." They began to think of what to do. They knew that there must be a total clean up and reorganization of the church. They knew that these dubious characters must be fished out and dealt with once and for all. The elders were worried as much as their leader was. They knew they must act fast before these people would pull down the church.

With their argument the dissidents had won an initial victory. They struck with a vital element of surprise which wins wars. People were carried away and by their argument believed them. That initial success enabled them to stretch their argument further. After all, it was a war. Those who got carried away did not realise that these dissidents were members of the association of pastors who had infiltrated into their church. They had been operating clandestinely. They would use any opportunity to disrupt the church. They issued a bulletin and accused Efo of several wrong doings. They accused her of being overambitious. They traced her life history right from the time she got married to Joda and concluded that she was not qualified to be a pastor, much more an archbishop.

"This woman was formerly married to an armed robber. Her daughter is a freak who bears children out of wedlock. How can such a person be called an archbishop?" they queried. Above all they accused the evangelist of misappropriating the funds of the church and converting it to her personal use. They demanded that Efo render account to all the funds accruing to the church since it was started. "It is when she proves her piety as a child of the living God that she can claim higher honours and put the prefix archbishop before her name," they said.

The elders committee met to consider the allegations against the leader. They found them to be baseless.

They also discovered that those who levelled the accusations had a bad history about their past. They recommended that they be excommunicated as unworthy of being members of the church.

The elders committee made an error in assuming that the people they investigated were acting alone. They were sponsored people. They still had some top ranking members of the church waiting on the sideline. Petitions were flying all over the place. More accusations were being made against the leader. They called on her to tender her resignation and quit the church. The people who were excommunicated refused to leave. They queried "How can you sack a man because he is asking for his right."

Meanwhile Efo had kept quiet. She had refused to make any statement. But her character was being smeared and her church being torn apart. The dissidents embarked on recruiting more members for their cause within the church. There were demonstrations and more calls on the leader to resign. Efo was being called embezzler and devil, while church properties were being destroyed and stolen. The demonstrations were disrupting the activities of the church. A new person was put forward by the dissidents to be consecrated as archbishop of the church.

Efo guessed correctly that this was the work of her enemies. She was therefore forced to break her silence. She invited members to a special service. She had learnt to tackle her problems through the congregation. She would lay her cards bare at the table of the congregation and ask them to decide for themselves. She had successfully used it on previous occasions to defeat the association. She would do it again. At the meeting she produced statements and records of all receipts of the church from inception to date and asked the members to judge for themselves. She further told them that she was born with a silver spoon in her mouth. She had not known poverty before. She inherited wealth. It was with her personal wealth that she built the church. She wondered if the church had enough to settle its indebtedness to her. She told them why she went into church ministry. "You should know that my spiritual journey transcends material wealth. I have not come to make money. I am here to serve God and preach his words." She capped her speech by donating a sum equal to the total receipts of the church from inception to date. She said further that she was declining the offer to be archbishop because according to her "God's work cannot be measured in nomenclature."

Members present were stunned by this remarkable woman. Her speech and donation had struck a devastating blow to the dissidents and their masters. Efo had won back the loyalty of those members who were deceived into joining in dissent against her. Those who had said anything bad against her were ashamed of themselves. They realized they had been misled. They resolved to continue to stand by their leader as they had always done. They joined in calling for the excommunication of the dissidents. This was done.

This was another loss to the association of pastors who stirred the dissent. Who knows what their next plan would be. The offer to become an archbishop was once again made to Efo. She was persuaded to accept the honour because it would not only enhance her personal image but that of the church. She agreed and accepted to be archbishop. She was subsequently consecrated. The day of her consecration was like a carnival. It was attended by many important people in society.

The dissidents may have lost out but the problems of the spiritual churches still remain. If they can democratize their churches, there will not be enough room to point accusing fingers. In a situation where the founder is everything and treats the property of the church as personal ones, there will always be doubts in the minds of the followers.

Chapter Nineteen

Efo did not reckon with the willpower, and determination of the association of pastors. She had on several occasions attempted to flush out those who infiltrated her organisation but that attempt had remained a half measure. More of the sponsored members of the association were still holding important offices in her church. She was not aware of this. She thought she had dealt finally with them, after she had administered the oath of allegiance before her consecration as an archbishop. She was mistaken.

A well trusted member of the church had advised Efo about a deal of assistance to the church during his recent trip overseas. He had told her that an affiliate church overseas, looking for a way to promote the interest of the local church had agreed to give to their church a cash gift of $2 million. But this would be possible if the local church would raise an equivalent sum, and appoint a management committee to manage the funds. This looked a wonderful proposition to the leader. She bought the idea but first, she must consult with the elders committee which was the conscience of the church. She subsequently tabled the offer to the committee. The committee was satisfied. They therefore gave a go-ahead. A funds-management committee was subsequently appointed. They were reputable men and women. The only way to start to raise the fund was by launching; and inviting wealthy members and outsiders to contribute money.

It was not by mistake that the member who brought the idea

found himself on the management committee. He insisted that he must be there as a condition for the overseas affiliate to honour their own side of the bargain. He argued that they trusted him and only his membership of the committee can satisfy them. He was thus appointed a member. He in fact, was the first to release a sum of half a million dollars to the church as his own contribution. This was to show both his honesty and sincerity of purpose. This money was given before the official launching day. He was hailed and praised as a man of God whose good deeds shall multiply threefold. Again this is where people are over-trusting, and do not reckon with the diabolical nature of other people. After donating half a million dollars, the trust placed on him rose higher than, even he himself anticipated. He was now fully in control; and dictating the tune. He told the church of a special account into which the fund collected would be paid. His own donation was paid into this account. Nobody doubted his motives. The official launching day came and people out-donated each other. Everybody was struggling to become the highest donor. At the end of the day, about the equivalent of $4 million dollars was raised. Members rejoiced over the success of their effort. "It was God's hand work," they said. The intermediary between the local church and the overseas affiliate once again advised that every cent should be paid into the special account while the leader and few other senior people of the church should travel overseas to go and inform the affiliate of their success and thank them for their idea and assistance to the church. Efo believed him.

After Efo had survived the last ordeal and had become an archbishop, she travelled abroad. She had gone on what they called a working visit to an affiliate church overseas. But in reality, the elders knew what she had gone abroad to do. They were expecting her back with good news. "Their church activities would be expanded by the time she came back," they thought, rejoicing in their hearts. But, unfortunately they started to hear rumours while she was still over there. It was not a rumour of "good news". It was a disturbing news which was rocking the church to its foundation. The rumour had it that cocaine was found in the luggage of their leader. Nobody knew how it started but members dismissed it as one of the latest ploy of the association of pastors. "This can't be true. It can't be true," they said to one another.

It was not a ploy. It was true. The true version had trickled in. A call was made overseas and confirmation obtained. It was real that substance suspected to be a hard drug was discovered in the luggage of one of the members of her entourage. But it was not in the luggage of the leader. The hard drug was planted there by the association of pastors who had been trailing her movements. They had put the drugs in the wrong luggage, believing it belonged to the evangelist herself. They were mistaken and she was lucky to escape their mischievous intention. If the drug had been in her personal luggage there was no way she could escape the repercussions. No amount of denial would do.

However, the fact that it was discovered at all had tainted her image. The owner of the luggage was arrested and charged in court. Efo had to wait to see the conclusion of the case before coming home. It was not an easy case considering the harsh penalty that is attached to drug cases. This particular case was made worse by the fact that they profess the word of God while they commit heinous crimes. But like Efo's personal philosophy "Let the will of the Lord be done. If God says it will not happen, it will not happen." This means she had resigned herself to fate.

She was able to prove in the court that they carry the Bible and preach the word of God. They are not cocaine pushers. She used the opportunity to tell the court about her tribulations at the hands of a faceless organisation. These people pretend they preach the gospels whereas they specialize in crimes. She begged the court to forgive and temper justice with mercy. She promised that she would never allow this sort of thing to happen again.

Efo's latest ordeal disturbed her greatly. She was terribly

confused. She went to the affiliate church to inform them of what happened; and tell them, why she had not reached their organisation since her arrival in the country. When she got there, she told them the purpose of her visit. "We have raised the funds you asked us to collect," she told them. "You should try to fulfil your side of the bargain. We raised double the amount you asked us to raise. Praise God. My only problem is this cocaine story which is brought about by our enemies. We shall overcome it.

I hope to be going back as soon as the case is over. Please prepare for us so that we can go back with the money."

While she was speaking, the people kept quiet. They listened attentively. When she finished their leader asked her, "What actually are you talking about? We did not quite follow your statements."

Efo blushed and said, "Oh, I am sorry. I mean the money you promised my church."

The man replied, "Which money? We never promised you any money. We did not ask you to raise any money either. Who must have told you that."

Efo was stupefied. She was as surprised and shocked as the people themselves. In her stupor she was still arguing about the launching of funds they had asked her church to organise. The people insisted there was nothing like that. At a brief moment during the discussion she asked herself whether she was dreaming or whether she was at the right place. The thought nagged her that her mood changed. The people noticed it and pitied her. They knew she must have been deceived into all this. They regarded her as a responsible woman; who could not have been acting foolishly without an underlying cause. They wanted to rally round to see what they could do to help her.

Efo kept quiet for some time before she realized that she was not dreaming and, in fact she was in the right place. She decided not to stretch her argument further because something must be wrong. Meanwhile, back at home the intermediary had disappeared. He had feigned illness and had continued to absent himself from church activities and even from church services. People did not attach much meaning to his absence. He was an ordinary member after all, they thought. They were even wishing him a quick recovery from his sickness before their leader would be back because he had created a special role for himself in the affairs of the church.

While the church members were sympathizing with him, the man had gone and secretly cleared the money that was realized from the launching. He had tricked the church to lodge the money into his personal account. Of course, nobody doubted his advice because the original idea was his and he had donated half a million dollars.

Efo had been immersed in the cocaine case, that she did not have time to contact home to disclose the disturbing news about her mission. She had hoped to do that when she returned home. But the thought that she had embarked on a fruitless mission continued to nag her. "Can this be true?" she intoned to herself. Can it be true that the young man was not told to raise funds. Then why did he donate half a million dollars. What is the purpose for that. Something must be wrong," she concluded. She absolved the young man of any wrong doing and thought he must have met with dupes.

She believed that all was not lost. After all, the church was richer by $4 million dollars. That is a pretty sum which could be used to expand church activities. She heaved a sigh of relief that such a large sum was available to the church. Efo was still unaware that the money collected during their launching of the church fund, had been cleaned off by the man who brought the idea. She was abroad to know what was happening, and the cocaine case did not allow her to contact home. Even those members at home were not aware too, that their money had vanished. But there was a time Efo had a hunch, and she soliloquized. "Is it possible that somebody will steal the money? She replied to herself. "No, it is not possible but, well, if that happens it is the wish of the almighty. Nothing happens without his wish. May his name be praised." With those overused words she abandoned the thought, and faced immediate pressing problems about the court case.

The court had discharged and acquitted Efo and her group in the case. The judge had sympathized with their plight. He told them that he had applied his best judgment to discharge them but they should note that the law is not a respecter of anybody. He advised them to be extra careful so that others would not use them for evil purposes.

Efo rushed back home to her country after the case. She knew that her *raison d'etre* for going abroad was a flop. The failure might have a root in her country. When she got home, she quickly called a meeting of the elders and told them about her mission and the embarrassment it had brought to the church. Somebody suggested that the young man who brought the idea should be brought at once to come and throw more light into the matter. An emissary was sent to his house but he was not there. Neighbours confirmed that he had packed without leaving any forwarding address. When the emissary reported back to the committee, they knew something was wrong. They went to the bank to check on the safety of their money. They were informed that the "owner" of the account had closed the account after withdrawing all the lodgements. It was then that their eyes cleared and they realized that they had been dealing with a crook. A manhunt was organised but the young man was nowhere to be found. Efo lamented her fate and noted that, of all the tribulations that had come her way, this was the first time that the association of pastors had succeeded in reaping the reward of their crime. She prayed for them and asked God to forgive them for they did not know what they were doing.

Chapter Twenty

Dreams, visions, premonitions, hunches, clairvoyance are some of the phenomena the spiritual churches rely on. Whenever they or any of their members experience these, they claim that God has put a word in their mouth for their congregation, or, that God has anointed them with a special message. But, the phenomena are not reserved for these pastors alone. They are natural and can occur to anybody at all; for everybody is, indeed, a spiritual being. These churches have gone very far in their claims about dreams and other phenomena. They induce these dreams to occur to them. They also encourage their members to bring forward their dreams which they interpret to be visions. They interpret the dreams the same way they interpret the Bible. This is the way that will suit their purpose. All they care for, is what will make them have more powers; or, claims; to have powers. Some pastors are known to use talismans or consult oracles. All in the quest for powers. There is no doubt that some of these pastors are out to deceive their congregation. That is why some good ones have not found favour with them and have refused to join them. That is why they have set a lot of tribulations on the way of Efo. But, she had come to understand and appreciate life better since the tribulations were set on her way by the association of pastors. She now believes that for anybody to grow, he must conquer obstacles or face challenges. Growth will be achieved either here, now, or hereafter.

She swore never to give up. She has been having some dreams of late. She believed in dreams as an important tool for her trade. It is not a dream that is the problem, it is the interpretation one gives to it. She has been careful about the interpretation she gives to her dreams. She has been concerned about her recent dreams. They came to her in stages and were clear in the message they brought.

First was that she fell into a trance. She was sitting in her office, and doing her normal duties when suddenly she was blanked out. She had her eyes open but could not see anything. Her head seemed swollen and larger than its normal size. She saw herself walking through a narrow path. She was in the middle of the pathway, when a huge spherical rock blocked her way. Both sides of the way were not passable. She could not climb or scale the rock in anyway. She halted; and, stood frozen for a while, not knowing what to do. She was still standing, when the rock gave way and the road became clear again. She continued on her journey. However, she was going to no place in particular; when she woke up from her trance.

When she regained consciousness, she could not ascribe any meaning to what had happened. But she saw it as a warning that her enemies were about to wage another of their battles against her. It was nothing new and she resolved to deal with the situation when the time came. She went about her duties without disclosing what happened to anybody.

It was not long after this experience that Efo had a dream. It was a dream that shook her and kept her worried for some time before she recovered from it. In the dream she had seen her two dead husbands. The day seemed normal and she finished her assignment for the day before going to bed as usual. In the middle of the night she dreamt about her first husband called Joda. She had a child with this man. They were separated for a very long time before the man was killed. She had nothing to do with the man since then except their daughter.

Joda approached her in the dream and appealed to her that

they should get married. She rejected his request and turned to go. He still came after her; and was pleading that she forget the past and accept to marry him. She insisted on not marrying him. She told him that she does not have anything to do with a poor man again. Just as Joda disappeared, her second husband who died overseas appeared. He was calling to her "Efo, Efo, it's me." He raised his hand to draw her attention. Efo turned in the man's direction but continued on her walk. The man started to run and soon caught up with her. He asked Efo if she was denying him. Efo did not talk but continued to look at the man. The man asked once more "Efo, it's me. What's wrong with you, have you forgotten your husband? Come, let's go home." Just as the man was finishing these words, Efo woke up from her sleep. She wondered what was happening. "Where am I?" she said, and sat up quickly on the bed as if she had been pricked. She had seen her two former husbands just now. She remembered they were dead and realized that she must have been dreaming. She wondered what type of dangerous dream she had. Since the two men died, she had not been thinking about them. She had adjusted her life; and, she knew that for the rest of her life on earth, she will never marry again. Her present pastoral duty had ensured that. However, she had her personal opinion about the men who had appeared in her dream. She believed that they were not actually the right men she could have married, were it not for circumstances. The first man was completely out of the question. Their love expired before the man died. They were betrothed because of custom she did not approve. "How then can this man come back and say that he wants to marry me. I cannot marry him. He should flow to his level," she soliloquized to herself. She was still lying on the bed and had not understood why she had the dream, in the first place. "Why the dream?" she thought. She thought about her second husband and believed that they married out of necessity. Their life together was not fulfilling. The man died when she needed him most. However, he was a nice person but their marriage was a child of circumstance. She thought that if she lived her life all over again, he would not be her first choice and probably would never be her husband again. "Why then should he come after me," she queried.

After thinking about the dream, she got up and went about her normal duty. She did not tell anybody about the dream. She did not consider it necessary. Dreams, however, are part of her church ministry where members narrate their dreams as visions.

Efo had not quite recovered from the effect of her last dream before she had another one. She was stunned by what she saw in this dream. She had seen herself in a coffin. There was a large number of mourners. A church service was being held. She saw her daughter draped in black.

After the church service the normal funeral rites were performed. People eventually gathered at her residence. She was still in a dream state when an apparition appeared to her. It was a woman. She was robed in black and very beautiful. Efo seemed to have recognised her. It was the same apparition that appeared to her before she started her ministry. She told Efo that her time was up. She should therefore get ready to join her Lord in heaven. She had done good work on earth but her services were needed more in heaven. As soon as the apparition finished those words she disappeared.

Immediately she left Efo woke up. She was dazed. She knew she'd had a dream. "It was a bad dream, she thought. She also thought that this was the second bad dream in less than two months. All the dreams have portended a bad omen before her. She lay on her bed unable to know what to do. She decided to get up. She stood but slumped into the bedroom cushion. She needed a glass of very cold water. This was not her habit. She used to prefer a cup of hot tea whenever she woke up. This was the first time that she needed an opposite drink. She pressed a bell in the bedroom.

A house keeper came in. "Please get me a glass of cold water," her feeble voice quivered. The housekeeper left but in less than five minutes brought the glass of water. She wanted to stay and collect back the glass after Efo had finished. Efo thought differently. She gestured to her to go. The housekeeper left. Efo then sipped the water. She picked up her Bible. It had become part of her life. It was also her habit to first open any page and read the passage on the page. Such a passage would form part of her thoughts for the day. Such passages also gave her strength in moments of despair. It was obvious to her that tonight's dream needed no interpretation. The message was clear. She therefore needed all the strength she could afford to carry on her assignment for the day. In fact, she even needed greater strength to carry on the work of God. It is not everybody that hears that he will die and still move about. To make matters worse, she was never told when death would come.

Efo read the passage. Immediately after reading it she seemed to have found the courage she needed to continue the work for the day. She got up and got ready. She left for her office. She did not disclose what happened to anybody. But she prepared the sermon she would preach the next service day. It was just two days away. She decided that she would deliver the sermon as if it were the last one. After all, she did not know when she would die. It could even be before that date.

The service day eventually came and Efo delivered her sermon. It was an unusually long sermon in two parts. The first was titled "The reality of Life". The second was titled "Beware of Impostors". In the first sermon, she traced her life history. How and, why she came to the ministry. Her tribulations. She talked about life and death and observed that one day everybody must die. Nobody should be afraid of death and the best way to prepare for it is to do the will of God. Those who do the will of God will be welcomed to his bosom where they will reap eternal life. She told her audience that she would soon embark on a very long journey. Although, she believed in life after life; and reincarnation, it would not be necessary to expect her to come back in the same form from her journey. She therefore said that during her absence the most senior pastor would run the affairs of the church.

In the second part of the sermon, she dwelt on the danger posed to the church ministry by imposters and those fake prophets who carry the Bible. She lambasted the association of pastors and declared them criminals who were out to deceive the people. She said that a comparison could be made between an armed robber and a false prophet, and predicted that an armed robber poses less danger to the society than a false prophet. She said, "An armed robber can kill only one person or maybe two during the course of robbery. It is not so with a false prophet. A false prophet can ruin millions of souls." She told her audience to beware of such people. She said that she hoped that her church would continue unhampered. She did not foresee any more problems from those fake pastors.

Efo cleared her throat. Then she led the congregation in prayer. After the prayer, she said, "The sermon I will preach today is entitled *'The Reality of Life'*. It is the first part of today's preaching, thereafter we take on the second part."

"My Life and my Ministry." She started with her early life and her ministry. She began, "Brethren, I started my church ministry about fifteen years ago. I went into the ministry as a result of direct calling from the Lord. Before then, I was an ordinary believer and was working in a business organisation after my graduation from school. I came from a small town situated about a hundred kilometres south of the capital. My family members are all Catholics and I was brought up in the Catholic church. I got married quite early in life. The marriage was betrothed when I was very young, in accordance with the custom of my people. The marriage did not quite work out and we separated. There was an issue. After some time I got married to another man. I had hoped that the

second marriage would work. But God knows better. The man died while attending a course overseas. There was no issue.

After the death of my second husband, I made up my mind not to marry again. By then, I had stopped attending the Catholic church. I had embraced the spiritual church and became a believer. I left the Catholic church because I was not having enough fulfilment. My spiritual needs were not being met. I thought that I needed a change. I found that change in the spiritual church. I was involved in what was going on. I started reading and interpreting the Bible. Something that was thought improbable in the Catholic church. In short, I was a part of everything and that appeared to have satisfied my need and hunger for spiritual uplift. However, it did not take long before I discovered that some of these spiritual churches are not what they profess to be. Some of them are devilish organisations. They are interested only in making money and not to serve God. They kill, maim, and steal other people's properties. They run their churches as if they are private estates. There is nowhere in the Bible where you will find these vices as part of the work of God. Brethren, believe you me, if you sow evil, you will reap evil in return. But if you sow good, you will be rewarded by the Lord who is in heaven. These pastors have been sowing evil. They have not thought of what will happen to their soul when they die. They have not thought of what will become of their churches when they are gone.

My dear people, I did not become an evangelist out of necessity; or, to make money. Before I was called into the church ministry, I had never given it a thought, that I would become a pastor or own a church. Even though, I was attending a church I was still immersed in the material world. Enough wealth was at my disposal and I could do anything I wanted. I could go to any place I wanted to go. My dear brethren, my pastoral calling was a directive from God. It was a surprise to me. As I said earlier, I had not thought of becoming an evangelist in my life. It happened suddenly. It was a dream. It was the type of dream I had not experienced before. In the dream, I had seen an apparition. It was a woman. She looked very angelic. She told me that the Lord wanted me to join in spreading his word. That I should renounce all wealth and material things, and pick up the Bible and follow God.

When I woke up, I did not know what the dream meant. I told some close friends. They advised that I seek an expert opinion for an interpretation. There was an elderly pastor who was experienced in the interpretation of dreams. I was advised to consult him. I did. When I went to the man, he listened intently. After I had finished narrating my dream, he told me that the meaning of my dream was that God needed my services. That I should go and renounce all worldly things and come forth and serve God. That there were a lot of souls wandering in the wilderness. That God wanted me to help in harvesting those souls.

I did not believe in what he was saying. He noticed my doubt but urged me on. He prayed for me and told me to free my mind of negative thoughts. I left him without accepting to serve God before him. Things started to move in rapid succession and, subsequent events in my life made me believe that I was actually called to serve God. I therefore went to the pastoral college where I obtained my training. Subsequently, I set up this church. My dear brethren, the going had not been easy. You are all living witnesses of our journey so far. No sooner did we set up this church, than a group of young men approached me. They told me that they wanted to form an association of pastors. That, it was being done elsewhere. I was shocked beyond belief to hear these words from people who parade themselves as men of God. How can somebody regulate religion? It was the worst thing that can come out from the mouth of man. I told them to count me out of it. I told them that every individual should be at liberty to practice religion the way he sees fit without being pushed into a straight jacket. I had a mission to preach and teach the word of God to those who are prepared for it. I did not come into the church ministry to make money.

The young men left. They did not say much but it appeared that their pride had been wounded. I was therefore not surprised at what followed. They had lined themselves against our church for vengeance. But if I may ask vengeance against what? It was difficult to know the grounds of their vengeance. How can pastors be seeking vengeance for a wrong that never existed? My dear brethren, you can judge for yourselves the subsequent events that followed.

Tribulations: These misguided young men unleashed an assault unknown in the history of churches against us. They started by killing innocent souls and depositing the corpses in our church premises. Their aim was to make it look like those people were killed by members of this church. But God does not sleep. Their evil intention was discovered and exposed. Is there anywhere in the Bible where it is written that people should kill and tell lies? The judgement is yours. Thereafter, you all know what happened to my daughter. You are, also witnesses to the double dealing in the land masterminded by these young men. Numerous ordeals and tribulations have been placed on the way of our beloved church. I thank God for His mercies. It is through His will that we have survived all these assaults. It is God Almighty that has been fighting the battle for us. We have survived it all; and, are still prepared to survive; and, overcome future assaults. God says "Seek ye not revenge, for revenge is mine". We shall not seek any revenge; after all, we have survived not by our own will but by the will of God. This church was established by God, and he has been defending His church. May His name be raised. Amen.

Life and Death:- Life and death are the realities of life. You must accept death as you accept life. It is written in the Bible that God created man and breathed into his nostrils the breath of life and man became a living soul (Genesis 2:7). Without the breath of life there is no man. It is the breath of life that makes man what he is. We can liken man to a container. If you have an empty drum or container and you put something inside it, the container encases what you have put in there. If you take back what you put there, then the container becomes empty again. This is what happens to us. Our physical bodies are but containers which contain the breath of life. This breath of life was put in there by God. When God takes away the breath of life, the soul leaves our body and returns to the creator. What remains of it is the body which remains lifeless. We can dispose of this body. God keeps the breath of life which he can breathe into another body.

My dear people, the breath of life or the soul which has returned to God does not know any suffering. It is no longer part of this sinful world. It resides in an advanced state where everything is perfect. My people, I do not want you to be deceived. The problem of this world is caused by our sins. Man suffers because he cannot do the will of God. He suffers because he has turned his back on God. Our Lord Jesus, came to this world and washed our sins with his blood. But inspite of that, man continues to live in sin. Unless there is repentance on the part of man, we shall continue to suffer.

From what we have said so far, it is established that man dies only a biological death. It is his body that dies. His soul does not die. It goes to heaven where it rests on the bosom of the Lord. But, is it all souls that go to heaven? The answer is no. It is only the souls of those who have lived in accordance with the will of God that will go to heaven. All sinners will quench in the bottomless pit where nobody will save them. Only those who are ready to be received in the bosom of the Lord will go to heaven. You must therefore prepare yourself for it; so that, you will be one of those to be received by the Lord. You must prepare yourself by doing the will of God. You must prepare yourself by preaching the gospel and propagating the word of God, to all corners of the earth. It is by doing this that you can prepare yourself for the last day. Those who do the will of God and preach his gospel will inherit eternal life. They will be received by the Lord in his kingdom where there is abundance of life. My dear brethren, we should not cry and mourn when somebody dies, because there is life after this life and I believe in it. Also, a man comes back to this earth after he has spent his time in the spirit realm. He is bound to come back to continue his work on earth. When a man departs this world, he has only changed form; and will surely come back one day. May the spirit of God fill your hearts, your souls and your entire being.

Long Journey:- There are two men who embarked on a long journey. The first knew in advance that he would go on the journey. He made adequate preparation for it. He put his house in order and appointed a caretaker who would take care of his estate while he was away. When he left, the caretaker took over from where he stopped. He had been told what to do, so that he had no problem in running and managing the estate the way the original owner would have done if he was there. He received maximum cooperation because everybody recognised his authority. The estate flourished and prospered. Everybody was happy. It looked as if the owner was still around.

There was yet another man who embarked on a long journey. He did not know that he would go on the journey. It came to him suddenly. He left and did not have enough time to put his house in order. He did not appoint a successor or a caretaker. When he left, nobody took over the running of the estate. The estate became nobody's property. It floundered and was scattered.

Things disintegrated. Those who knew the estate when the owner was there lamented the woes that befell the estate. They wished the owner was around.

My dear brethren, this church belongs to us all. I shall soon embark on a very long journey. It is a journey every living soul must one day undertake. When I shall be away the most senior pastor shall be the leader of this church. People should not struggle for power. They should not struggle for leadership. This is a church and there is need for a continuity in the church. I do not want our church to be likened to the second man. I do not want our church to flounder and disintegrate because I am away. I want this church to be like the first man. I want this church to flourish and grow so that everybody will be happy. There must be peace to enable the word of God to reach those souls that need to be saved. Do not fear death. You should rather prepare yourself for it. The only way to prepare for death is by doing the will of God. We were created to help spread the will of God. Jesus came to this world after the fall of man. He suffered in order to wash off our sins. We must emulate Jesus. He saved us. We must save others. We must get ready for the last day by doing the will of God. The kingdom of God belongs to those who do the will of God. They shall inherit the kingdom of God. May the good Lord in his infinite mercies bless you all. Amen."

Beware of Impostors:- She read some passages aloud from the Bible. She was reading from 1 John 4 and Matthew chapter 24 about false prophets towards the end. When she closed the Bible, she closed her eyes and prayed. After her prayers she began her sermon. "It is written in the Bible that in the last days there will be many false prophets. You are all witnesses to what has been happening to our dear church. Believe you me, it is not all those who shout the name of the Lord that actually do God's will. These days a lot of people are in the church ministry as a means to an end. They are hungry and they need food. They know they cannot find employment because they do not have the qualifications nor do they have any special skills. They know that they cannot do other businesses because they are lazy and would not be able to find their feet in the highly competitive business environment. They have erroneous belief that the easiest way out is to carry the Bible and parade as pastors. All they need to do to become pastors these days is to go to the market and buy a Bible, a bell and a cassock or white robe. Once you buy these items you are in business. You do not even need a house to start. You can start in an open ground or any shanty house, and apply your half-baked knowledge to deceive millions of innocent souls. This sort of people are what is referred to as false prophets. They have neither any education nor any formal training. They imitate what they see others doing and make endless claims. They claim they perform miracles every day. A miracle is something that does not happen often yet these charlatans go about deceiving people about how they perform miracles every day. For every word they speak they claim God had put the word in their mouth. That they have been anointed by God to deliver the words. They are seers and clairvoyants at the same time. I must admonish you, brethren to watch out in order not be deceived. These false prophets manifest in various ways. You can always observe them dancing on the pulpit or doing different acrobatic displays. They promise to do anything under the sun thereby arrogating to themselves the power of God. If every pastor is God how many gods shall we have? The little power they claim to have is actually of the devil, and not from God. The devil can give people power in order to destroy them. The problem with this sort of people is that they are more dangerous than armed robbers. An armed robber may kill only his victim, or he may kill few people during a robbery but, a false prophet with a Bible can destroy millions of souls at the same time.

There was a man who became a pastor out of necessity. He had regular employment but, would go preaching during his spare time. This is a way of supplementing his income. He was asking people to donate a certain percentage of their income as tithe. He was using this tithe to run a private business. He was living very well while his flock was dying in abject poverty and penury. One day armed robbers struck simultaneously in his church and residence. They made away with properties worth millions of dollars. These properties were acquired from the money he made from the church. When he reported what he lost during the robbery, sympathy turned into jeering murmurs. People who came to sympathise with him wondered how he came about the money with which he bought those properties.

My dear brethren, it was the robbery that opened the people's eyes about what he was doing. That too was the beginning of the end of that man and his church.

There was yet another man. He too was a part time pastor. He was working in a large Company. He was holding a very important position where he was dealing with outsiders. He became notorious because he was duping the people who came to do business with the Company. If they gave him money to give to other people, he would misappropriate the money and convert it to his personal use. He owned a church. When he closed from work or at his free period, he would go and preach there. What he was doing amounted to heresy. The people who were coming to do business with the Company knew what he was doing and would always sneer and make jest of him. Some of them were planning what to do to pull him down as a revenge.

They decided to set up a trap for him. They conspired and positioned one of them on the route through which he was known to pass. On this fateful day, he drove past that route. It was a dangerous area known for its bad spots. He saw a man standing in a place he thought was unsafe. He knew the man very well. He was their customer. He decided to help the man. He stopped and picked him up. He did not know that he had entered a trap. The young man thanked him sincerely for rescuing him. He told the pastor false stories about what brought him to that place at that time. He said that were it not for the pastor he feared he was finished. The area was known to harbour criminals who would have robbed him of his possessions. The pastor assured him that praise should go to the Lord. It was the Lord that was using him to rescue him. He was merely an agent of the Lord.

Later, as they drove on, a conversation developed between the two. The young man told the pastor of a business deal. He knew he would be interested. He was well known to be greedy about business. This deal involved millions of dollars; and it is from a reputable Company. It was also simple to execute if the finance is there. He told the pastor that he decided to tell him about the deal because he had just saved his life. It was only proper that he reciprocated his kind gesture. All these were just phoney. However, the pastor did not recognise it was all false. He was excited at the deal. He was interested and told the young man so. They now drove straight to the pastor's residence where they mapped out their strategies. They agreed to contribute money to execute the project. The share of proceeds would be in proportion to their contributions. The young man, did not waste any time. He rushed home and brought his own contribution which he gave to the pastor to keep. This was to convince the pastor about his sincerity.

He did not need to convince him that way. He was already convinced soon after hearing about the deal. Later, the next day, both of them went to the Company. There was a caravan on the premises. They went to meet the people at the caravan, and not to the main building. It did not occur to the pastor at that time to question why they went to the caravan instead of the main building. Such a big Company should be able to conduct its business in its own house. However, in the caravan, they met people that can be said to be gentlemen. They were welcomed. Original documents were brought out. A local purchase order was issued on the notable Company's letter head. Everything was done to look genuine. The pastor and the young man collected the purchase order and left. The pastor was now convinced beyond doubt that the deal was genuine.

He did not have all the money that he was required to contribute.

He excused himself and asked the young man to come back and meet him in his house. He then went and started to borrow money from other people at outrageous rates. In some cases he agreed to pay double of what he borrowed. He eventually raised close to a million dollars which he used to finance the business. They travelled to a distant market where they knew they would buy the materials at a cheaper price.

They brought the goods and, it was still delivered to the caravan. Again it did not occur to the pastor to ask why this was not delivered to the warehouse since they were dealing with a reputable Company. However, they were given a date to come and collect their cheque. When they came back the next day, they were told that the cheque was not ready. The first signatory had signed but the second signatory travelled. He would come back that same evening and probably sign the cheque for collection the next day. The pastor did not realize that at that time the people were merely playing for time. They wanted enough time to evacuate the materials and leave the place. The next day he waited for the young man to come to him so that they would go together to collect the cheque. But this day, the young man did not turn up. He decided to go alone and check if the cheque was ready. What did he see? He saw nothing. He did not see the caravan. He did not see anybody near the spot. He thought it was a dream. It was not. He stood still for more than ten minutes lost in his thoughts. He later gathered himself and cleared his eyes. He did not know what to do. He decided to go to the main building. He asked about the caravan and told the story of the materials supplied. The people did not understand what he was talking about. They told him that the caravan belonged to some workmen who came to do some work for the Company. They had finished their assignment and had left. The story jolted the pastor. He staggered out. When he got back he was ashamed to tell anybody what happened. But he could not hide it from the people forever, because he borrowed the money from the people. These people needed their money back and he had no money to pay back.

I have told you this story first as a good illustration of greed among pastors and second to show how God's miracle works. What you sow, you reap, the bad shall not go unpunished. My brethren, these pastors are not out to serve God. They are abusing the name of God and hiding behind the bible to commit atrocities. You can compare these stories to the ordeal this our church had suffered in the hands of the association of pastors. You will recall the murder of our beloved pastors at the branch. You will also recall how the association organised the rape of my daughter. God is not evil. He is all pervading and just. Those acts of the association of pastors were acts of the devil and false prophets. God does not sanction such acts. It is written in the Bible that if any man wants to truly serve God, he should renounce all wealth and evil and serve God with all his mind and all his soul. But people who kill others because they want to make money are not of God. People who steal from the poor and add to their pockets are not of God. People who do nothing but think only of evil are devils. Beware of such people. Such false prophets are now on the increase. That shows that we are near the end time. You have nothing to fear, my brethren, so long as you do the will of the Lord. Those who do the will of God will be received in his bosom where they will inherit his kingdom."

After the service, some senior members of her church went to ask her what was wrong. If she foresaw anything, she should let them know so that they would prepare their minds for it. But, Efo was not ready to discuss the matter beyond what she had said during the sermon. She told them to go and preach the word of God as it is written in the scriptures. They should not indulge in the type of acrimony and vengeful activities for which the association of pastors was known.

Efo had become a changed person after her sermon. She could

be observed tidying up things about her and writing a lot. The church members were becoming increasingly worried. They had been guessing correctly, that their leader had foreseen her death, but had refused to tell them. She was right not to tell them. If they knew they would be fighting for succession even before she died.

Some international observers had been watching the tribulations and sufferings of Efo and her church at the hands of the association of pastors. They had been preparing to hold a solidarity outstretch in Efo's country to encourage and support her in her fight against the association. They wanted her to keep up the work of God, no matter the difficulties. The rally was fixed. During the rally, preacher after preacher, talked about the need for unity among the churches. They said that they believed that all of them no matter by which name they called themselves have the same purpose which was to preach and teach the word of God. There was no need for them to turn against themselves and prove to the people that the word of God can be intermingled with crime. They called on the association of pastors to come forward and renounce their evil ways, so that the work of God can be continued. They thanked Efo for her courage and sacrifices; and urged her not to give up.. "The kingdom of God belongs to people like you," they said.

Efo talked during the outstretch. She did not say anything about her problems with the association. She rather talked on the topic "Abundance of life". She believed that the life we live after death is as important as the life we live here on earth. The way we live now will determine where and how we shall live hereafter. She asked those who strayed from the path to get back. God is ever willing to forgive.

Everything went on normally at the rally. After the rally, Efo went to her car. She entered the back and headed for her home. She did not reach her house. At the gate a volley of bullets were emptied at her and she died on the spot. It was an unexpected event. In fact, a tortuous day for her church. Nobody knew who did it. The news spread like wild fire. Some of those who attended the rally had not even got home and so were not aware of what happened. The foreign visitors also were not aware. It was later in the evening that the news of Efo's death came up on the air. Every accusing finger was pointed in the direction of the association of pastors.

The association knew it would be accused of killing Efo. They were quick in going on the air to clear themselves. They issued a statement and denied knowledge of anything that might have killed the evangelist. They praised her life and her work; but, absolved themselves of causing her death. People did not believe the denial of the faceless association. They still held them responsible.

The death of Efo nearly caused civil strife in the city. Her church was nearly torn apart, but they were consoled by one of their notable preachers who told them to remember that "God giveth and the Lord taketh." He said that he believed that it was the Lord who called Efo home. They should remember that Efo had predicted her death which meant that those who carried out the assassination were agents of the Lord. They should be forgiven "For they knew not what they were doing."

Chapter Twenty One

After the burial of Efo, the most senior pastor nominated by her assumed the leadership of the church. This was however, opposed by some of the people.

The feud that was generated gave rise to fractious groups who owed allegiance to different people. Some people thought that Eka should have been made the leader. "She should be given the chance to continue the good work of her mother," they said. Another group argued that church matters were not an inheritance issue. Eka was too young to be in control of such a big church as their own. They would be playing into the hands of the association if such a small girl should be allowed to take over from her mother.

Eka was an ambitious girl. She was quite willing to follow her mother's footsteps and take up the leadership of the church. The other group stood its ground. The power tussle that followed resulted in the faction led by Eka pulling out of the church and forming their own church with a similar name. They had thought that with the influence and good work of her mother, Eka would pull a lot of members of the church to go with her. This was not to be. Most members stayed back and continued with the old church since it retained the very premises used by their dead leader. Eka and her group had gone to another place to erect another church altogether. Eka's church was getting new members but not as such as the old one. Some of her members had suggested a reconciliation with the other faction but Eka refused. The others were also not ready to accept her back unless she should just return quietly and become an ordinary member.

Eka had the courage of her mother. However, she did not have any formal pastoral training. Her knowledge of what she was doing was, bits and pieces picked up while she was with her mother. She did not have the experience of life to carry her through. She had born a child out of wedlock. She did not even know the father of her child. The child was still a toddler and was disrupting her church activities.

Her courage was not enough because that meant that if she ever faced the type of problem her mother had, she would simply give up. The temptation actually came. Eka had fallen in love with a young member of her church. The love was very strong and like her child could be a major factor that could destroy her church. The elders of the church were worried that an amorous stance of their leader could be used not only to disrupt the church but, in fact be a set-up by detractors to even up things. They called a meeting in which they invited Eka and her lover. They appealed to them to get married. They accepted the advice of the elders and a wedding was fixed.

It was characteristic of churches to ask those who opposed any marriage proposition to make representations to it; and, state why they felt that the couple should not marry. The members of Eka's church were confident that no objections would be raised against their leader. They were mistaken. Before the expiry date for receiving objections, a young man appeared on the television to state why he opposed the marriage. It was the same young man who had earlier claimed to be the father of Eka's child. He claimed that Eka had his child and therefore he was the rightful husband of Eka, and, not the present person who wanted to wed her. This was not the type of objection the church was looking for. It had no merit and therefore was not capable of stopping the couple from wedding.

The wedding took place and Eka and her husband started to live together. Her husband was still an ordinary member of the church. He retained his former work before marrying Eka, who is a full time pastor and leader. The husband was thinking of resigning from his work and taking up full time ministry. That decision was yet to be carried out.

One bright morning, he had gone to work. Eka was alone in the house. She used to go to her office later in the morning after taking care of her baby and the house. Suddenly there was a knock at the door. She was surprised that somebody would come directly to the door and knock. The man should have been stopped at the gate. It was after the gatemen got clearance to allow the visitor in, that he would be asked to proceed to the building. Even though Eka was surprised she opened the door. It was the young man who had been claiming her child who was at the door. Eka wanted to slam the door in the man's face, but he used his weight to block the door. He pushed the door open and entered the house. He was very sure that Eka was alone in the house with the child. He had timed his visit when the husband would be away. Immediately he entered the house he pulled out a tiger type of knife used in hunting. He had tied the knife to his femur and covered it with his white robe.

He pointed the knife at Eka's face and blurted out. "Where is our child? give her to me or I will kill you. If you do not give her to me I will kill you and still take the child. So it is better to give me the child and save your life."

Eka knew that there was nothing she could do. She asked the man to give her some minutes to produce the child. She went into the inner room. She was closely followed by the young man. The young man took the child by the hand and warned Eka not to report the matter to the police or he would kill her. He also told her to ask her husband to stay away from the matter since it did not concern him. If she ever told her husband and he took any action towards the recovery of the child, he would come back and kill both of them. He told Eka that he considered the child to be his; but warned that he was not acting alone. He was sent by his members to come and collect the child, he said.

After the young man had closed the door behind him, Eka started to cry. She did not take any steps to prevent the young man from passing through the gate nor did she tell the police. She kept it to herself. She was thinking what to do but could not decide on anything in particular. However, when her husband came back from work, she told him everything. She told him not to take any action. The only problem she had in deciding whether the young man was actually the father of the child was because he denied paternity of the child at the crucial moment. All she cared for now was, not to engage the man in physical fights or legal battles because these could lead to death as the man had threatened. She wanted an arrangement that would make it possible for her to visit the child from time to time.

Her husband agreed to abide by his wife's wish, but he could not understand how a man like himself could make such an affront on his house and go scot free. He asked his wife to allow him to deal with the man but the wife refused.

Eka continued with her normal duties. But, the thought of what happened was affecting her and her work. She did not want members of her church to know what had happened. She wanted to keep it to herself. It was, however, difficult to have such a heavy object on her conscience, and at the same time discharge her pastoral duties. The church members had started to notice changes in their leader. They observed that she was growing thin and she was not boisterous as she used to be. The elders decided to hold a meeting with her to find out what was wrong. At the meeting Eka could not hold herself. When she was asked to confide in the elders, she burst out crying. She cried for nearly thirty minutes on her husband's shoulders before letting the cat out of the bag.

The elders concluded and advised her not to allow such a thing to bother her. It was a mistake they said not to have told the church members earlier. They told her that as a leader of their church, she was their property and therefore any assault on her was an assault on them; and, ultimately on their beloved church. They reminded her of how her mother used to solve her problems by bringing it before the congregation. She should adopt the same strategies. They were bound to work for her. They promised her that all legal avenues would be explored to bring the child back to her mother's house.

The first thing the church elders did was to report a case of forceful kidnapping of a child to the police. They then went to the court and sued the young man. The young man had acted alone. He had liked Eka and was genuinely interested in marrying her. But the problem he had when he was named the father of the unborn child was that he was sponsored by the association of pastors to behave in the way he did. He knew in his inner heart that he wanted Eka but, feared that the association would kill him if he failed to act in accordance to the terms of their agreement. He had been making fruitless efforts since then to get closer to Eka.

At the court hearing, the judge declared that there was no substance to the case. He noted that he had already decided the case previously. The action of the young man to ignore his earlier pronouncements on the matter was a contempt of his court. He was lenient to him then, because he felt that he was being used and was too young to know the implication of his action. But, now the setup was different. He therefore jailed the man for five years without any option of a fine. Eka's child was handed back to her. Eka was overjoyed at receiving back her child. She recalled that this was the second time she was recovering the child. She cuddled her and decided a special service must be held in the church to thank God and the elders who had fought this battle for her.

Eka continued with her pastoral duties the way she could.

She was not a trained pastor but was closely associated with her mother from whom she learnt what she was doing. She was doing her best and the membership of her church was growing. The association of pastors was not against her but one young man was. That was the young man that had just been jailed.

He was really obsessed at having Eka as his wife. He had been dreaming of the day himself, Eka, and, their baby would live together as a family. Even while in jail, he had not given up hope. He had assured himself that when he came out of jail, he would still try to talk to Eka. If she refused he would deal with her.

The young man had served a considerable length of time in jail before he was paroled. He was adjudged a good prisoner. Indeed, he was. Apart from the obsession to get married to Eka, he had no other criminal tendency. Immediately he came out of jail, he purchased a white robe and a cassock. He was determined to put the evil thoughts in his mind into effect. He then took his tiger brand of knife and a gun fitted with a silencer and made straight for Eka's church. Eka used to minister to souls every day at certain periods. This formed the major part of her daily duty; even on days when there were church services. She had an out-house adjoining the church building where those with problems, both spiritual and otherwise came to complain to her. She used to attend to them as doctors do to their patients. She used to stay in one of the inner rooms while those who had come to see her would sit in an open hall and go to her in a clockwise movement. Benches were placed by the walls while there was a large space in the centre. Her aides controlled the crowd as nurses did in a clinic. These aides ensure that those who came first were attended to first. Patients knew that here was a church where the highest discipline was expected. They therefore behaved in orderly manner and waited for their turns. As soon as the person inside came out, the next person would be asked to go in. It was under this atmosphere that the young man with evil intention came to see Eka. He was dressed in a white robe like a pastor and therefore caused a stir when he entered. All eyes turned towards his direction. Some were wondering in their minds what he had come to do. If he was a pastor as his dress suggested, why would he come to meet another pastor? However, it seemed that they quickly realized that it was not in all cases that a physician would heal himself. Maybe he needed another pastor's ears to unburden a load. Everybody soon minded his own business. The pastor sat down quietly in the seat he was offered and waited patiently like others. He had his Bible. He opened it and was reading some verses. As he read he would occasionally look up as if in prayer, as if he wanted to absorb something, or cram the passage. Most people in the room never cared about his ways. They reasoned most pastors do the same. They cram the Bible in order to be quoting the chapters and verses off head for their congregation. This would normally portray them as being well versed in the scriptures. There were others in the room however, who were excited by the man's extraordinary ways. They considered him as being queer. If he wanted to learn the Bible that was not the right place, they said. They reasoned that it was a private matter. However, there was nothing anybody would do about the man. He had ignored all the thoughts flying in his direction and waited patiently. Soon it was his turn to enter to see the evangelist. He did not seem to know until one of the church aides touched him saying. "Master, you can go in." He said, "Oh." He stood up. He walked with a little difficulty to the central door but, nonetheless, opened the door. He closed the door behind him. He was soon face to face with Eka. It was not the habit of Eka to look up and see the face of those who had come to see her, but in this case, she did. The man's outfit had flashed through her eyes and attracted her attention. She looked up and offered the man a seat. The man sat down calmly beside the table. Eka did not recognise who he was. He had put on an artificial face and false beard. Eka was the first to speak. She said. "May the Lord be with you." The man did not respond. Other church members would normally say "Amen" since this is a form of prayer and good wish. Eka then asked in a very soft tone. "What can we do for you."

It was at this juncture that the man pulled out a gun and, while holding the trigger with his right hand, he tore away his artificial face and beard and ordered Eka "Do not shout or I will kill you." Eka was petrified. She did not know what to do. She had recognised the man. She was alone with him in the room and there was no way she could call for help. She asked in a hushed tone. "Do you want the child? Let me go and bring her for you."

The man said. "No, I want your life, because you will reverse any deal we make here. Remember I told you when I collected my child that you should not let anybody know about it, not even your husband but you ignored my warning. You subsequently put me in jail. Well, I am out of jail, and since I cannot have you as my wife, both of us must die." Eka had started to cry but the young man warned her to stop. He placed the nozzle of the gun on the left side of Eka's chest over the heart. He pulled the trigger and Eka fell to the ground. The silencer had prevented the sound of the gun from being heard by those in the adjoining rooms. The man got up from his seat and went and rolled Eka over to ensure she was dead. He shot her in the mouth and put his gun back under his robe. He came out. He held the door handle after closing it while facing those who were waiting anxiously for their turn. They had been thinking he had been unusually long. Anyway, some people do stay much longer especially if they have complicated problems and the leader needed to pray with them.

The young man did not leave. He still held the door and started to address them. He told them that the leader had asked him to give the testimony of what miracle the Lord had done for him just now. "She is inside praying and does not want anybody to come in for an hour. Everybody should therefore listen and hear how the miracle of God works. Everybody was excited and eager to hear the latest miracle. They believed him as they always did whenever anybody came forward to give testimony. He began "Hallelujah, I want to give a special praise and thanks to the Lord today. I have been dumb right from the age of eight when I fell from the first floor. My parents had taken me to different hospitals and my case had been handled by the best doctors in the world, but nobody could cure me or get me to talk. I have equally attended so many spiritual churches but could not hear.

It was on the recommendation of one of the churches that I gave my life to serving God. That was how I became a pastor, devouring the scriptures in the hope that one day God would answer my prayers. My church activities had been limited but today, however, here I am talking to you. This means that today marks the beginning of my preaching and teaching the gospels as it should be done. This had been done through the handiwork of the leader of this church. Praise the Lord." Everybody shouted "Hallelujah." Some people were jumping in excitement. Workers in the inner rooms and other adjoining buildings had started to gather to hear the man's testimony.

They did not know that their leader was lying inside in a pool of her own blood. The man further exploited their hysteria to order them to follow him outside the room to dance in a circle and clap hands so that more people would come and hear the miracle of God. They all followed him and there was dancing and clapping and shouting. More people had started to gather. Up to now nobody had raised an eyebrow about the whereabouts of their leader. Anyway, they had been convinced that she was praying inside the room and it was not yet an hour. When the young man found it safe, he sneaked behind one of the buildings where he was hidden from the mob. He pulled off his white robe and cassock and left them on the ground there with the gun. He brought out a small bottle. He emptied the contents into his mouth. It was poison.

He had prepared the poison which he would take after killing Eka. It was his intention that if they could not be husband and wife here on earth, they should be in heaven. After taking the poison, he dropped the empty bottle on the ground where he left his robe and took some quick measured steps through the gate. The crowd was not even aware that he had left. They were too much preoccupied with hysteria about the miracle the Lord had done.

Immediately the man went through the gate and out of view of the security men he ran. The poison was biting very hard in his stomach. He did not understand why he had taken the poison. He did not want to die again. He ran up to a small store and told the owner that he had taken poison. He asked to be taken to the nearest hospital. The owner, showing indifference to his plight, merely pointed to a direction for him. He started running again towards that direction. He met another man. He asked about the hospital. The man took pity on him and drove him to the hospital. When they got to the hospital he was asked to tell everything as it happened before he could be given treatment. He narrated everything as it happened and concluded by saying that he did not want to die again. Some of the nurses there snubbed him. The doctor however gave him an injection. He never woke up from the subsequent sleep.

It was the hospital authorities that alerted the police as to what happened. The police drove straight to the church compound. They met the people still rejoicing, dancing and shouting the name of the Lord. The police ordered them to stop, and asked. "Where is your leader?" They replied in unison that she was inside. The head of the police replied. "I am sorry. It is difficult to say, but, your leader is dead. She was murdered by the very person who had given you testimony." The people were surprised. They thought the police were there to crack a joke. They surged towards the house. But the house could not take all of them at the same time. The police ordered them to go back. The police then selected two people to follow them inside the house. When they got inside they saw Eka stone dead. With the help of the police, her body was collected and put in a body bag. When they brought her outside, and the crowd noticed that she was truly dead their earlier rejoicing was turned into wailing. They started throwing themselves on the ground and crying at the top of their voices. Some made out to go and look for the man but they were stopped by the police who told them that the man was dead too. He had taken poison.

The death of Eka created confusion in the church. The church was still in its infancy and things had not taken shape. It was not like the church established by her mother where everything was well organised. She did not equally have time to prepare for her death since it was not expected at this time. She had therefore not appointed a successor. Her death was a big blow to her church. Members could be seen shedding tears openly.

One man stood akimbo and lamented her death aloud. "What type of life is this," he said. "I knew her. She was the daughter of Joda and Efo. Her father was gunned down, her mother was killed by assassins' bullets; now she has been murdered for no fault of her own." He had not finished talking when another man who had been listening raptly interjected. "No, you do not know them. Come and let me tell you." He drew the first man who spoke aside. He wanted his ears only to hear what he wanted to say. He began, "I am from the same place as Joda. What killed this family you are talking about is fast life brought about by modern ways of living. The man left his town in the countryside and embraced the new found life of the city. He turned his back on his people. He got enmeshed in city life to the detriment of the life as lived by his ancestors. It is only natural that he was consumed by the new life he loved."

The first man with eyes wide open replied. "Eh! how cruel can nature be. How can one family perish by bullets at different times and locations, yet in a similar manner. This is unbelievable. My God forgive evil doers."

The man actually felt that the violent death of Joda and his family had something to do with evil that existed in their family. They were merely paying the price. He hurriedly left the scene and swore not to attend spiritual churches again. Arrangements were made to bury Eka. She was the last of the family that perished by the gun. Her death was not given any prominence. This was partly in accordance with the tradition of her people and partly because of the circumstances of her birth by Joda. In her area when a person dies so young without much achievement in life, he is buried without fanfare. This is because the people believe that the young should bury the old and not the old to bury the young. Again, Eka was the daughter of Joda who refused to abide by the custom of his people. Her father was not considered fit to be the son of the soil unless he renounced his city life and alien cultures and return home and carry the staff of his ancestors. Joda refused to do this. That was why he was not accorded the rightful place in his town. He was not mourned by his people when he died. When his wife died, the same fate befell her. She too was buried in the city. Eka is now dead and the same fate awaited her and she was buried in the city too.